EASTON

SILVER TEAM
BOOK 2

RILEY EDWARDS

EASTON
SILVER TEAM 2

Cover design: Lori Jackson Designs

Written by: Riley Edwards

Published by: Riley Edwards/Rebels Romance

Edited by: Kendall Black

Proofreader: Julie Deaton

Book Name: Easton

Paperback ISBN: 978-1-951567-59-0

First edition: July 1, 2024

To my family - my team – my tribe.
Always.

This book is for Liz, thank you for raising a daughter who
uses the word "fudgeycakes".
Megan and Johnna thank you for making me laugh and
laugh and laugh until my belly hurts. When the three of you
hit a signing I know it's going to be a good time.

PROLOGUE

"I hear you, Maddon, and you know him better than I do, but I don't see this playing out in your favor."

Understatement.

After I finished my warning, I went back to doodling on the legal pad I'd found on my father's black leather desk blotter. Any time I was on the phone, I jotted down notes, parts of the conversation I didn't want to forget, names I needed to research. But when I was scheming I doodled. It helped me think, helped me strategize my next move, helped me plot my next maneuver.

In my world, it paid to be three steps ahead.

So I made sure I always had the next five moves planned.

"It's the only way you're getting a sit down with Viper," Maddon mostly repeated.

Yes, Viper.

The one and only man I knew better than to go up against. The one man I'd done everything I could to steer clear of. Zane Lewis was not a man anyone outmaneuvered.

But the time was ripe.

Maddon was desperate. He *needed* me to meet with Zane.

I scratched a line across the pad connecting a heart and a star and waited. As good as an operative as Maddon was, he was impatient.

Desperate and impatient—a deadly combination.

I heard Maddon let out an irritated sigh and I smiled.

Come on, jackhole, push harder.

"Nebraska, we have no choice. Charlie has an in. Use it to your advantage; it's the only way to get Viper to play—"

"Zane isn't a man you play," I told him something he very well knew. "You play him, he fucks you. And no offense to you or him or your mission but the last person I want to get fucked by is Zane Lewis. I'll find another way, I always do. Charlie can take the meet, tell Zane's men he's no threat to Bridget Keller, and send them on their way. This is a suicide mission, you know it and I know it."

"Nebraska—"

"If it's not, you go in and tell Zane the truth. Tell him Charlie was never a threat, the whole Raven project was a carefully crafted setup that was working brilliantly until some overzealous woman killed an employee over an OSHA violation that would've cost the company a couple hundred thousand dollars in fines. Instead, she fucked your mission. Tell him that everything was in place until that idiot Mark Shillings thought it was a good idea to blackmail Kathy Cobb and from there the web you cast disintegrated. If this is such a great plan, you take the meet. You tell him you need his help. You explain the situation. If after the sit-down you're still breathing, I'll go in and negotiate the deal."

"You're a far sight prettier than me, Nebraska. You've got a better chance coming out of that meeting breathing."

Dick.

"This isn't a honeytrap."

"You know your father would never send you in if he thought you were in danger," Maddon carefully said in an attempt to win me over.

His point was debatable. Charlie Michaels's first love was CIA. Not that I actually thought my father would put me in harm's way on purpose but he wouldn't blink an eye sending me into the Viper's den if he thought I could charm the snake into helping him. Which was exactly what Maddon was banking on.

"You do remember I don't actually work for you, right? I only agreed to listen to the plan, which I did. I'm telling you it's shit. I'll find another way to get what I need."

"And in the meantime what do I tell my team?"

"To stand down," I suggested.

"You know I can't do that."

Yes, I knew he couldn't tell his team their mission was off. That would ruin Maddon's plan.

Again, desperate.

"Well, Maddon, then you and Charlie need a new plan. There's no way I'm going to sit in front of Zane and pull wool. His hate for the CIA is legendary. There's no way I can spin this, no lie I can tell that will get him to agree to help you."

"You underestimate your skills."

No, I didn't underestimate my skills, but Maddon did.

I took the backhanded compliment for what it was. Praise for my ability to lie and scheme. Not something I was particularly proud of but true, nonetheless.

It was time to throw him a bone and remind him of our connection.

"You're only saying that so you can take credit for teaching me those skills."

"They've made you a very rich woman, *Dove*."

Leave it to a morally bankrupt man with no wife, no children, no family, no true loyalty to anyone but himself to think I did what I did for the money. I learned a long time ago, men like Maddon who'd pledged their allegiance to their country then spouted off crap like "I do what I do so no one else has to do it" are the biggest liars of all. They do it for the power, for the control, because they like playing God. Old Agency men who couldn't or wouldn't leave the job because they get off knowing they pulled all the strings.

Men who thought they were invincible.

Men who underestimated women.

Men who were so blinded by their perceived power they missed the real threat.

Today I was that threat.

"They have," I sweetly agreed. "I'll take the meeting with Zane. But I want it on record—he's going to kick me out of his office within the first ten minutes. I can lie through my teeth and he'll still sniff Agency on me. And that's if I'm lucky. I've heard he has moods, if he's in a bad one, I expect white lilies and pink stargazers on my casket."

"Your request is noted."

Maddon disconnected before I could say more.

"You did well," Charlie said from the doorway of his study.

I slipped my phone into my RF blocking Faraday bag, rendering my cell useless before I voiced my biggest fear, "You're positive he doesn't suspect anything?"

"All he's focused on is his payday. Blinded by it. Too damn stupid to see you coming."

God, that made me sick to my stomach for a variety of reasons. One being Maddon was selling out his country for a payday. Two—Maddon was one of Charlie's oldest buddies. Three—I knew it was killing Charlie to do what needed to be done.

Maddon's treason couldn't stand.

He had to be dealt with.

"I'm sorry, Father," I murmured.

I'd long ago been taught never to react to other people's emotions, but seeing my father's flinch cut me to the bone.

"All I ask is when the time comes you make it quick."

I nodded my understanding.

"And Zane? How do I handle him?"

"You were correct in your assessment. You don't *handle* Viper. He'll either help or he won't."

I had a bad feeling Zane wouldn't be helping. He hated spy games. The moment I laid out the web of lies I'd be out on my ass.

I had a backup plan. I always did.

The problem was, Plan B was messy. It meant I got my hands dirty and I really hated blood stains—they were a bitch to wash clean.

"When will his men be here?"

"Less than an hour."

I glanced at my old worn messenger bag already packed and situated by the door.

"Then we have time for lunch before I leave."

I pushed my father's well-worn big leather chair away from his desk and stood when a memory assaulted me. I'd been with my father a week when he caught me at his desk drawing. He was standing in the doorway watching me just as he was right that moment. He'd looked reflective then, too. The difference was twenty years ago I was an orphaned twelve-year-old little girl scared out of her mind, not knowing if I was going to be in trouble. Now I understood Charlie. But that memory of him watching me draw had never left me.

Then and now he looked like he wanted to tell me something.

Then and now he simply smiled at me before he turned and left me at his desk.

I knew one day he'd tell me his secret. But like with everything else with Charlie, it would be on his time.

ONE

I was uncharacteristically nervous. Uncharacteristic in the sense I didn't get nervous—not ever. Showing fear or uncertainty got someone like me dead.

This was not the first time I was being escorted into a meeting with powerful men. Nor was this the first time I was going into an unknown situation.

Yet none of those men were as dangerous or unpredictable as Zane Lewis.

Perhaps it was the hours of silence. No, I was used to that; criminals didn't tend to chitchat before a sit-down.

Maybe it was because I'd opted for casual. That had to be it; my jeans and flip-flops were throwing me off my game. The normal clicking of my heels on the tile was absent—weirdly, sound centered me before I faced down the filth I normally sat across from.

Theo Jackson stopped to place his hand on a fingerprint scanner. As I waited I looked around the empty reception area. The space was oddly bland—a typical receptionist's desk that, from my view, didn't look like it had anything on it but a phone. A boring two-seater leather couch, two chairs, and two end tables. No signage above the desk. No magazines to read while you waited. There wasn't even a plant to liven up the room.

Nothing in the room gave away this was the Z Corps office.

But what struck me as odd was the lack of an elevator. We'd come in from the garage by way of stairs and there was no elevator in there either.

A car honking drew my attention to the street. Large, framed plates of thick glass on either side of a glass door gave an unobstructed view outside.

"Polycarbonate ballistic windows," Easton Spears weirdly stated.

"I'm sorry?"

"They're bulletproof."

Of course they are.

I didn't get to respond—not that I had anything to say about bulletproof windows—before Theo opened the door. Easton wordlessly gestured for me to enter the hallway. For the first time since Zane's men had picked me up, real apprehension curled in my belly. I was well aware I was unarmed and entering a windowless hallway with two very big men. For some reason being in a plane with them hadn't felt this concerning, neither had the silent car rides we'd taken to and from the airport.

But here, in this tight space, there was no escape. No one to help me. No weapon on my person to defend myself with.

I tried to remember my father's earnest expression and the relief I heard in his voice when he explained his plan.

He'd said Zane's call to him had been serendipitous and was the in we'd needed. That might've been true, but I wasn't feeling the same relief my father was feeling. There was too much at stake. Too much that could go wrong. If I didn't maneuver this *just* right everything would implode and I would be the cause of it. One wrong move and I could be the Yoko Ono of Z Corps.

My last call with Maddon had been subterfuge except the part about Zane. Fudging the truth with a man like Zane wasn't the right way to go about this. Keeping secrets from him from afar was one thing—up close and sitting across from him was entirely different.

This was not a good idea.

We stopped in front of an elevator. Theo turned and pointed to the scanner on the wall.

"Place your hand on the screen."

The guy obviously didn't like me, not that I could blame him. He thought my father posed a threat to his fiancée Bridget Keller. That was the flaw in my father's plan. We should've come clean. I should've requested a meeting with Zane so I could come clean and tell him the truth. Keeping up appearances would do me no favors.

"Why?" I asked.

"New protocol." He pinned me with his dark gaze. "No one enters the office without their fingerprints on file."

I held his stare and asked, "And if I say no?"

"Then we take you back to the airport and send you home," he said like it was all the same to him.

That sounded like a much better idea and if Maddon wasn't selling information to the Chinese I would've told Theo to take me back to the airport.

Reluctantly I placed my hand on the scanner.

A moment later a green light flashed.

"You're good."

That wasn't surprising. My fingerprints wouldn't give them anything I didn't want them to know.

I removed my hand. Theo touched the same screen. Moved to another scanner higher up on the wall and leaned forward.

"Retina scanner," Easton unnecessarily explained.

The elevator door slid open and again Easton waved me on to precede him. And again I was bracketed in by two men who didn't like me or my father.

Wasn't the first time and I was positive it wouldn't be the last.

Thankfully the stifling ride was short.

The door opened and much to my surprise the top floor was nothing like the bland downstairs reception area. The cavernous space had an industrial vibe with a bent for chrome accents. But what caught my attention was the large enclosure in the middle. The smoked glass made it impossible to see in. The obstruction seemed out of place in the center of the large room.

"This way," Theo directed before I finished my perusal.

The next room we entered was different from both the reception area and what I assumed was the main office. The conference room was a mix of high tech and luxury. A large flat-screen hung on the far wall. A long credenza with crystal decanters, a silver ice bucket, and other accessories took up the wall to my right. I recognized the hand-carved doors of the cabinet and knew it cost a mint. The wall to my left housed a well-appointed coffee station. But it was the monstrous table in the middle of the room that held my attention. I quickly counted eighteen chairs. Though only six were currently occupied.

Patheon.

So the rumors were true. All of Patheon was now working with Z Corps. It struck me then how much I didn't know about the man who paid my salary.

Interesting but not surprising seeing as Zane's intel specialist Garrett Davis had been on a CIA Ground Branch team with Jonas Lang, Smith Everette, Cash Phillips, and Easton Spears. Though sometime in the last ten years since they'd left, the Central Intelligence Agency had renamed GB to Ground Division.

To complete the Patheon team sitting at the table was former CIA case officer Layla Monroe, although when she'd worked at the Agency she was Layla Cunnings. This actually gave me hope. Seeing former Agency at the table meant Zane might be open to my cause. Next to Layla sat Kira Cain, formerly Kira Winters.

And finally, sitting at the head of the table was none other than the man himself. Zane Lewis.

The moment Zane's piercing gaze landed on me, my heart rate ticked up until it was rabbiting in my chest. I realized I'd been wrong.

The time was not ripe. I should've gone with my gut and kept my distance.

Damn my father for putting me in this situation.

"Miss Michaels," Layla started. "Please have a seat."

I felt a hand touch my lower back. The touch was unexpected. My reaction unfortunate. I jolted, giving away more than I wanted. I knew better than to show weakness in a room full of predators.

Regrettably Zane didn't miss my tremble.

"Nervous?" he drawled from his place at the head of the table.

The viper king sitting on his throne waiting to command his snakes to bite.

Powerful men can smell weakness, Nebraska. You have to own every room you walk into.

I straightened my shoulders, plastered my well-practiced fake smile on my face, moved to the nearest empty chair, and ignored his question.

"Thank you for seeing me."

"Your father didn't give me much of a choice," he returned as he picked up a tablet from the desk.

That was a stretch.

"Forgive me for saying so, but that's not exactly the truth, is it? You don't strike me as a man who makes a deal because you were forced into it."

He waited until I sat and adjusted my bag to rest in my lap before he dealt his death blow.

"You're correct. I could've saved us all the trouble and the expense of sending my jet and simply had your father taken out. And make no mistake, Nebraska, that option is still on the table."

That was not the first threat against my father's life I'd heard. Though it might've been the most credible. I'd long ago learned to lock the fear those intimidations caused away in a box I only opened when I was alone. Those were the only times when I admitted to myself how truly scared I was. The rest of the time, I played my part. I did what my father needed me to do.

Charlie Michaels deserved my loyalty.

I remained silent as Theo handed the thumb drive my father had given him over to Kira before he sat to Zane's right. The woman was the brains behind the facial recognition software called Patheon—not to be confused with the team of men who had operated in the shadows under the same name. She plugged the thumb drive into her laptop.

Easton pulled out a chair, leaving one empty between us. But instead of sitting closer to his team he stayed near the door.

There would be no quick escape from the room.

The large screen behind Zane flickered to life. Neatly arranged file folders from the thumb drive appeared on the monitor. Everyone's gaze except Zane's went to the screen. He kept his on his tablet.

Until his blue eyes tipped up and narrowed on me.

"I think it's time you explain why you're really here, Nebraska."

Indeed, it was time.

Too bad I couldn't tell the whole truth without exposing a secret Zane would rather keep buried.

I just prayed my father hadn't made a mistake.

TWO

In the months I'd worked at Z Corps I learned to read my boss. Or rather, I'd learned to read what he purposely showed. If Zane Lewis didn't want you to know what he was thinking, he closed down in a way that was impenetrable.

His mood had shifted from annoyed but curious to DEFCON 1 in the blink of an eye.

I studied the file folders on the screen. Other than the one marked Raven none of them registered as dangerous.

Raven was the company that Bridget had worked for. She'd turned her boss in for selling the plans for a microdrone the company was developing under contract with the CIA to some unsavory characters. We already knew that Charlie Michaels had invested millions into the UAV company and had lost that money when Raven went bankrupt. That was the whole reason Nebraska was here. To ensure that Charlie wasn't looking for payback.

"I take it you know who Maddon Judd is?" Nebraska Michaels asked.

I had to hand it to the woman. She hadn't cowered under Zane's obvious unwelcoming attitude.

"Who the fuck are you?" Zane growled, taking the current DEFCON rating to nuclear.

"It's not who I am that matters. It's who my father—"

Zane didn't let her finish her explanation. "Are you referring to the man who adopted you or your biological father?"

What the fuck?

My gaze swung to Nebraska in time to see her eyes narrowing on Zane.

"Am I supposed to be impressed you know Charlie's not my birth father?"

I glanced around the table. All eyes were on Nebraska.

Jonas, Smith, Cash, and Layla were all studying her. Kira stared at her screen, her lips twitching.

"Are we starting with the Raven file or Maddon Judd or..." Kira paused and blinked at her laptop screen. "The Candy Apples file."

I heard Cash snicker, then he muttered, "Vintage."

Kira's brows pulled together and she shook her head. "I don't get it."

"Candy Apples versus King Dong," Cash educated her. When Kira didn't register understanding, he went on. "In the late nineties, Candy Apples held the gangbang world record—"

"Candy Apples is a porn star?"

"I can't take credit for that one," Zane started with a grin.

"That one?" Kira pushed.

"A good friend of mine taught me that trick. There's

something satisfying knowing the stick-up-their-asses suits are reading briefs with their lips curled in disgust."

"Are you saying you name your operations after porn stars?" Kira said through a laugh.

"Unofficially."

"How did I not know that?" Kira went on smiling huge. "That's brilliant. I wanna choose a name."

Of course she did. Kira was Zane's mini-me. Though it'd shock the shit out of me if sweet Kira could rattle off adult film star names without the help of the internet.

I glanced over at Nebraska. Her expression was bland but those gorgeous eyes of hers looked like they were dancing with amusement. She wanted to smile like the rest of the people in the room but she wouldn't allow herself. Since we'd left her father's house she'd been all business, careful words, fake rehearsed smiles, no hint of a personality. She was watchful, guarded, alert in a way that stated plain it was habit.

But there was an underlying wariness. She almost looked tired, and fuck if I didn't understand that. Ten years being on constant guard, years before that always being on high alert, never knowing when or from where a threat would strike. It was the kind of tiredness that seeped into your bones until you forgot it wasn't normal to be strung so tight there was a real possibility you'd snap.

Nebraska's gaze shifted around the table, cataloging each person in the room. I'd bet my cushy new job the woman knew exactly who we were. Further, I'd put my townhouse, truck, and bike up that she'd done her homework and had a full dossier on each of us. Her glances weren't curious, they were knowing. And when her gaze stopped on me, I knew I was right.

Time to test my theory.

"Not sure your man would be best pleased you perusin' PornHub, Seven," I joined, using Kira's callsign.

Nebraska's eyes went straight to Kira before they dropped to the table.

Too late.

Zane caught her fuckup, too. I knew it when his study of Nebraska became acute.

"Time to start talking, Miss Michaels."

"Where would you like me to start, *Mr.* Lewis?" Nebraska returned snidely.

Christ.

The woman must have a death wish.

"You can start by remembering you're here because I was curious what Charlie Michaels needed help with. That curiosity was more amusement than actual interest. I don't make a habit of helping criminals out of tight spots. I certainly don't entertain men who make threats against women who are under my protection. But now that we've established you're an Agency lackey, spit it out so I can tell you no and you can get on your way."

Smith's fingers drummed on the table across from me. This was so unlike him I gave him my full attention. He was the quietest, always watching, listening. Then when the planning was over he was the one to point out any flaws or oversights. Not only was Smith the best tracker we had, he was also scary brilliant when it came to strategy.

"You look familiar," he murmured. "I can't place it, but I know I've seen you before."

Without hesitation or prevacation Nebraska returned, "Brazil."

Smith nodded.

"Fortaleza?"

"Bahia," she corrected. "Vitória da Conquista during the riot."

What the actual fuck? Brazil was Smith's last assignment for Patheon before we wrapped up and handed everything we had to Layla's CIA contact.

"Jesus. Fuck me running," Zane cursed low and slow. "No need to explain why you're here. The answer isn't no, it's a fuck no. Go home, tell Charlie to keep his business out of mine and we'll forget he pulled this bullshit. He so much as whispers Bridget Keller's name I'll unleash Theo. If that's not incentive enough, which it should be, explain to your father Theo won't be alone and the last time I had to take time out of my day to go out into the field, it got messy."

Kira leaned close to Layla. "Is that what he calls breaking his tooth off biting someone's throat?"

One could say my first in-person encounter with Zane Lewis was something straight out of a horror flick. Through the years, I'd heard whispered stories, tall tales that sounded more like myths than truth. Finding Zane in the basement of a house during a rescue operation proved those tales were indeed myths—the man was far, far more dangerous than any story I'd ever heard about him.

My introduction to Zane Lewis was one of the most grotesque of my life, and that was saying something after spending ten years in the most impoverished, crime-ridden cities in the world. The man had been covered in blood, and yes, he'd been missing a tooth. His captor lay dead at his feet, looking like he'd been mauled by a lion. I'd never asked straight out if he'd torn the dead man's throat out with his teeth. Partly because I didn't want to know, mostly because I respected Zane and a man had to do what a man had to do to get himself out of a hostile situation. Thus, it made no difference to me how he'd freed himself.

But it had been gory and brutal.

And it would seem Zane had passed this particular trait down to his nephews. Linc's sons, Robbie and Asher, had a bad habit of sneaking into the conference room and hiding under the table to eavesdrop. Their mother, Jasmin, called this recon training—I guess that's what you got when two top-shelf operators bred. Another example of that would be the random and frequent Nerf gun wars.

However, Jasmin wasn't happy with her boys when they'd snuck in before an important meeting with the Marshals assigned to protecting Bridget. The meeting went south when one of those Marshals proved to be on the take and pulled a gun and took Kira hostage. The man holding Kira at gunpoint had stepped too close to the table. One of the boys took this as his opportunity to play hero and savagely bit the man's calf. The pain and shock took his attention, giving us the opening we needed to take him down without him shooting Kira in the head in the process.

Since neither boy ratted out the other, that proved biting wasn't the only thing they got from their uncle but also his unwavering loyalty. Zane had christened them Cujo and Chewy.

Nebraska brought the conversation back to why she

was there. "If you'll look at the Raven file, you'll understand Charlie is no threat—"

"Don't need to look at a file to know Charlie Michaels is not now nor will he ever be a threat," Zane cut her off. "You can leave now."

Nebraska nodded and pushed back from the table.

That was it?

She came all this way and was giving up?

For reasons I didn't want to explore, that disappointed me.

When she took to her feet she glanced around the table one more time, stopping on Layla to warn, "You can't trust Ashcroft with this."

It was then an already tense situation turned twitchy. The air in the room went stagnant and the temperature fell by a few degrees at Nebraska's outrageous claim.

Inspector General Ashcroft had been the man behind Patheon, or at least the man who had given Layla approval for building the team. As soon as Ashcroft and Layla approached Cash, Smith, Jonas, and myself we quit the CIA and went rogue under Layla's leadership. Implying Ashcroft couldn't be trusted wasn't offensive, it was a disrespect no one in the room would stand for.

"I suggest you use the door before you can't," Zane growled.

Nebraska didn't heed Zane's warning. Maybe she had a backbone after all.

"Maddon has a lot of friends. He's been with the Agency a long time. Well beyond when he should've retired. However, his global contacts make him invaluable. I'm not suggesting Ashcroft isn't trustworthy, I'm saying

Maddon's network is such that you shouldn't trust anyone outside this building with what's on that drive."

All eyes were on Nebraska, but Smith's stare was different. If I didn't know any better I'd say it was laced with a tinge of respect.

Zane, being Zane, didn't miss this either.

"Do you have something to add, Smith?"

My teammate glanced at our boss before he went back to Nebraska.

"Why were you at the prison?" Smith inquired.

I wasn't tracking his question, but obviously, Nebraska understood.

Again, without hesitation, she answered.

"I needed to see Paulo Alves. I got word that two members of the PCC were planning to escape before they were transferred. That escape plan included a riot. Chaos is the greatest distraction. I slipped in, did my business, and slipped back out."

"You mean you slit his throat," Smith returned.

Nebraska held Smith's stare as she answered, "Like I said, business."

"Do you want to know why I was there?"

"I don't waste time asking questions I know the answers to," Nebraska quickly replied, hitching the strap of her bag higher on her shoulder. "Now, I'll see myself out."

"Easton will walk you down," Zane countered.

With a dip of her chin, Nebraska wasted no time making her way to the door.

"That's it?" Zane's voice boomed.

Slowly and fully composed, Nebraska turned back to face the room but stayed where she was.

"I don't know what you're used to, Mr. Lewis, but I don't beg. Not anyone. Not for anything."

Nebraska's pretty blue eyes flashed through my mind. The next thought came on the heels of the first—only, those eyes were now staring at me, hazed over with desire, and those perfect lips begging.

"Not even when your father's life is on the line?" Zane pushed.

That garnered a reaction, though it was nothing more than a slight movement in her shoulders.

"I'm my father's daughter," she evenly stated, giving nothing away. "One of the many lessons he taught me—know when to cut your losses and never, but never, give someone the upper hand. Pleading with you would give you just that. Begging you to do the right thing would only serve your ego. I'm not interested in feeding you a line of bullshit just as you have no interest in eating it. So, yes, that's it. Also, yes, even if my father's life is on the line. But if you think you're the only man who has threatened his life straight to my face? I hate to break it to you, Viper; you're not the first, and you most certainly won't be the last."

With that she turned and left the room with her shoulders back and her head held high.

I wasn't sure if I was impressed or if I thought she was insane.

What I did know was, I was fascinated.

THREE

Welp.

That went exactly like I thought it would go.

By the time I was at the elevator I had my burner phone out, preparing to give my father the update I knew I'd be giving before I boarded Zane's jet to fly to Maryland, wasting an entire day when I should've been fleshing out plan B. I also needed him to arrange a flight to Egypt. If Zane Lewis wouldn't help—and I knew he wouldn't—I'd call in every favor I had and take Maddon down myself.

But at least I wasn't walking out of the office with a limp—or worse, oozing blood—so there was that. And he didn't seem to know who I was, so that was good. I hadn't completely ruined everything. Now I could work the plan I wanted to work without Charlie breathing down my neck to involve Zane.

My concentration on my phone was such I didn't hear Easton come up behind me, but boy did I feel him when he reached around me and pressed the button to call up the elevator. I felt him in a way my senses couldn't ignore

—not his heat at my back, not the scent of his soap that was on the right side of manly without being overpowering, but it was the way his arm brushed mine that had me stiffening.

I wasn't out of the Viper's Den yet. I needed to pay closer attention to my surroundings instead of being in a rush to escape and focused on my phone.

"Do you have plans?"

The flutter in my belly was not my style. I wasn't a woman who was prone to flutters or butterflies. But at Easton's question butterflies took flight. At the feel of them I wished I was a different kind of woman and he was asking under different circumstances.

That was new, too. I was who I was and I'd long ago accepted my place in this world—the morally gray fringe. A place where, when a man asked me if I had plans he wasn't asking in the hopes he could take me out on a date where there'd be dinner and drinks, possibly candles and romantic lighting at some fancy restaurant. Whereas on this date I could wear a sexy dress and sexier shoes, small talk and flirting would commence, we'd feel each other out, discover if we were jiving in a way that would lead to us finding ourselves sharing a bed for the evening.

Nope.

That was not my life.

Never had been.

Never would be.

I didn't bother pretending to misunderstand when I answered, "I always have a plan."

He didn't lean away when he murmured, "That tracks."

Easton's gravelly voice turned the belly flutters into a shiver.

The elevator door slid open. I hustled in, not caring it was obvious I was trying to flee the warmth at my back, the scent of his soap, the way his slight touch stirred a riot of unwanted sensations not only in my belly but other parts besides.

It wasn't my proudest moment, but necessary.

Once the door slid closed I shoved my reaction to Easton aside and went back to planning the rest of my day. I'd call an Uber, get to the airport, then head to Florida. I had enough contacts down there I could get anything I needed within hours of landing. I needed to get to Egypt, sit down with Amani Carver, and warn him Maddon was tying up loose ends. Not that I labored under any notion Amani didn't know the state of play, but the man was about loyalty and trust. A sit-down would be viewed as a show of respect and I needed all the allies I could get.

My father had taught me that, as had Maddon before the bastard turned and got greedy. They drilled into me never to miss an opportunity to turn a foe into a friend. That advice had served me well, as it had Maddon, and therein lay the bigger problem—Maddon's network was such it would take a miracle to breach. I had to outsmart the man who had taught me everything I knew. I had to figure out a way to outmaneuver the man who had spent more years than I'd been alive building his web.

Now that Zane wasn't an option—not that I ever believed he would be—I had no choice except to go at this alone. Not that I wasn't used to that. I was the Mediator, the Dove, the woman who was called in to solve problems however those problems needed to be resolved. I'd earned respect, I'd proven I went above and beyond to get the job done—whatever that job may be.

The elevator came to a stop, the door opened, and without a word I hastily exited. The sooner I got away from Easton the better.

With the exit to the lobby fast approaching Easton broke the silence.

"You know who I am."

Again, I didn't waste precious time demurring.

"Yes, I knew you were Patheon before you and Theo retrieved me from my father's house. For the last five years I knew Patheon was in play, but I didn't know where until I showed up in the same region. Then I did my best not to let my business interfere with yours. Unless, of course it was unavoidable like with Smith and the prison. But still, I stayed clear of him and got out without interrupting his mission. And I'd heard the rumors you all had joined Zane's team but I didn't have confirmation until I entered the conference room."

I paused when I got to the door and made the grave mistake of looking at Easton's handsome face. The rest of my explanation died in my throat when I caught sight of those sapphire eyes now full of suspicion.

I was used to that look, the one that stated plain the giver of that look was sussing out the truthfulness of my words. But for some reason Easton staring at me like he didn't believe me, cut to the bone.

I was immune to lying; I did it often and I did it well. However, I had yet to tell him an untruth.

"Charlie Michaels is CIA," he stated.

"Semi-retired, CIA." I corrected.

"How does that work?"

"The Agency still calls on him from time to time, but he is no longer in the field or active. He's more of a contractor. When they need his contacts, they call. Other than that, he's out of the game."

Easton nodded then asked, "And you? You're Agency?"

There had been a time I'd flirted with the idea of following my father's footsteps, but he'd quickly shot down the idea. And not because there was more money to be made in the private sector. Charlie had been clear he didn't want that life for me. Though the one I'd forged came with its own moral dilemmas.

"No."

Naturally my answer was met with heavy skepticism. To drive his point home, Easton lifted a brow in disbelief. The brow lift was unnecessary, his gaze said it all.

"PMC?"

Private military contractor.

One could argue that Z Corps was a paramilitary unit. If not that, an NGO who benefited greatly going into places and doing the things the government had no interest in being tied to. So it was ironic how he spat those letters out like that wasn't exactly what he was.

But I wasn't a PMC as such.

"Something like that," I returned.

"That's—"

"All you're going to get," I cut him off to put an end to a conversation that could've taken place in the conference room but now wasn't going to happen at all.

I had places to go and people to see and a traitor to kill.

"Thanks for walking me down. I think I can find my way from here."

With that, I opened the door and saw myself out.

Each step I took away from Easton the knot in my stomach tightened. By the time I made it outside the building and heard the heavy glass door lock behind me I had a feeling I'd made a mistake.

Perhaps I should've begged for Zane's help.

Perhaps I should've pleaded my case.

Perhaps I was in over my head.

I blew out a breath, gazed up at the clear blue cloudless sky, and hoped I hadn't just made the biggest mistake of my life.

The sky offered no answer.

So I went back to my phone and made the necessary arrangements to get to Florida before I texted my father an update.

His reply: *Be safe.*

Not *come home.* Not *I'll handle this.* Not *I love you.*

Just, *be safe.*

Modus operandi.

Zero emotions.

I was indeed my father's daughter. The daughter he'd trained to be a mercenary.

The Mediator.

The Dove.

And the time had come.

The student would become the teacher.

And Maddon Judd would learn my lesson with his last breath.

FOUR

Zane "Viper" Lewis

"WHAT THE FUCK JUST HAPPENED?" Cash asked the room at large.

But it was Zane who spoke. "This is what's called the gift that keeps on giving. Like a case of anal warts—once you have them, good luck trying to stop the itch."

Yeah, that was the CIA, the bad fart that lingered. The boil that festered. Zane thought he'd lanced that bitch open and purged the poison from his life.

It would seem he was very wrong.

He felt his team—no not his, Layla's, but his all the same—shift their eyes to him. And not for the first time his throat filled with the putrid remnants of war. The vestiges that neither time nor distance could ever erase. The feeling in his gut that shit was about to go sideways gnawed at him.

A feeling he never ignored.

An instinct he'd honed over the years. One that had served him well.

So he knew, not only was shit going to go sideways but it was going to corkscrew out of control faster than his last drop into a warzone.

Candy Apples.

Fuck. Nebraska Michaels should not know that name. Though it wasn't surprising since Maddon Judd, the fuck, had been the base chief during that operation.

Zane had locked that clusterfuck of a mission into one of the many boxes he never opened.

The past and present colliding was never good, but this could be catastrophic if Zane didn't get a handle on the situation and fast.

This could be the one thing, the one secret, the one *lie* his team might not forgive him for.

And Kira would find it. There was a reason her team called her Kid Genius. If there was something to be found, her spidey senses would tingle and she wouldn't sleep until she uncovered the missing piece. And this was one piece Zane didn't want dug up.

It was only fitting it would be his own team who uncovered the truth he'd managed to keep hidden for a decade.

Zane ignored the weight of the stares and looked back to his tablet.

The file was right there. He knew what the after-action review said because he'd written it. He knew what the mission brief outlined because he'd given the brief. He'd been young and cocky, full of ego before he understood the difference between arrogance and confidence was life or death. He'd yet to learn when to throttle up and when to pull back. The importance of finesse. The true meaning of being a leader among leaders. He'd thought he knew. He'd thought he understood. Until he learned he didn't.

And Candy Apples was a pivotal turning point.

It was that mission and what came after that moved him to sink further into the gray. It wasn't his massive fuckup that had pushed him there. It was witnessing the lengths the Agency would go to get what they wanted. It was also the mission that led him to cutting ties with the CIA. It would take years and a lot of them before he could disentangle himself from the Agency but it was from that mission Z Corps was born.

The original team was formed.

Not Red but Black.

The team he'd managed to keep in the shadows.

The lie.

Not an outright lie. But an omission of the truth between brothers and sisters was still a lie.

Zane leaned back in his chair, nabbed his phone off the table, and called his brother.

As soon as Linc picked up the call Zane didn't give him a chance to speak.

"Where are you?"

"Where do you need me?"

That was Lincoln.

Always alert. Always ready to take his back.

Strong. Solid. Dependable.

"Conference room."

When he was done, he chucked the phone on the table and looked at his protégé.

"Is she gone?"

"At the curb getting into a silver Toyota." Zane wasn't surprised at Kira's ready answer. He knew she'd be watching the security cameras. "Registered to Seth Greenbrier," Kira went on as her fingers clicked on her keyboard. "He's on file at both Lyft and Uber. As well as Ride-Connect."

"Any idea where she's headed?" Jonas asked.

Kira lifted her eyes to narrow them on her teammate. "I was getting to that. She bought a ticket out of BWI to MIA. Flight leaves in two hours."

Smith let out a low whistle. "Cutting it close."

Zane didn't have to look at his brother to feel the waves of hostility overtake the room when Linc saw what was on the screen.

"So is it true?" Linc spat.

"Is what true?" Easton asked as he reentered the room behind Linc.

There was no missing Easton's biting tone. He wasn't happy Zane had sent Nebraska Michaels away without hearing her out. Nor had he missed Easton's reaction to the woman. Not that Zane could blame him. Even the most committed man—and Zane was committed—couldn't miss Nebraska's extreme beauty. But he knew that wasn't what Easton had been drawn to, at least not fully. The woman was ballsy and confident but she couldn't hide her underlying fear, not from any of the men in the room and especially not from Easton. Yet she hadn't backed down, turning that fear into bravery. A trait every person in the room respected.

This was not going to end well.

Not for the future of Z Corps.

Not for Zane personally.

"Seems so," Zane answered his brother.

Linc blew out a breath and took a seat at the end of the table.

"Will one of you please clue us the fuck in on whatever you're talking about?" Theo grumbled.

Zane felt that all too familiar clench in his gut.

The one that told him a mission was going tits up.

"Pull up the Candy Apples files." A moment later more folders appeared. "Open the mission brief."

Then with his eyes locked with his brother's, Zane Lewis did something he never thought he'd have to do.

Explain how he was out-played, out-maneuvered, and outsmarted by Nebraska's mother.

FIVE

The room braced.

There was no other way to describe the atmosphere other than tense.

Zane was giving off cataclysmic vibes. Lincoln's energy was only a notch down from that.

"Candy Apples or OPLAN 3033 was an intelligence gathering operation. Find a man who claimed he had information on a coup and if need be, relocate him and his family," Zane launched in.

"When was this?" Cash asked, even though the brief was on the screen.

"Haiti, after the earthquake. Right before the elections."

Without looking at the brief Zane went on by rote, "Earthquake, mismanagement of relief funds, fraud, cholera outbreak. Once again the country that had never been stable was more unstable. The elections were coming up and it was becoming clear Martelly was going to win. Word was there was going to be a revolt. The concern was there would be a replay of the 1991 coup. Intel was making its way back to Washington that this threat was viable. My assignment was to escort a base chief and a CO into Sun City, find the brother-in-law of a gang leader and get him and his family to safety in exchange for information on the coup."

"Who was the base chief?" Jonas asked.

I had a sick feeling we all knew the answer to this question.

"Maddon Judd," Zane confirmed.

"And we just let Nebraska walk out of here when she has confidential material on your op and intel on a BC?" My observation was unnecessary seeing as we'd done just that not even ten minutes ago.

I watched the vessel running up the side of Zane's neck pulse before his eyes cut to Theo.

"Once upon a time I was a lot like you were before you left the CIA. Guided by principle, blinded by ideology, and the knowledge I was on the right side of wrong. It took you less time than it did me to realize there is no such thing as black and white." Zane pulled his gaze from Theo and locked eyes with his brother, looking like he was about to admit a mortal sin. "I was riding the high of mission success, the adrenaline that fuels the next battle, and all the bullshit that comes with being told you're the best. I ate that shit up, rode it all high and mighty. I thought I knew best, I thought I was the best, then I was taught differently. And the person who delivered that lesson was a woman called Ann Robinson. She went by the pseudo, Pigeon."

"Honey trap?" Cash asked.

A scary smile formed until both Zane's dimples came

out. That was never a good sign. But I didn't understand why that smile was directed at me.

"Even drenched in sweat, covered in dust and grime, fully kitted out, combat ready, the woman was gorgeous. She had some years on me, and not a few of them, but still she turned every man's eye, including mine. It was the pool-blue eyes that held a man captive."

Pool-blue eyes.

Suddenly the sick that had gathered in my stomach started to churn.

"Are you saying..." I trailed off, not knowing exactly what Zane was implying, just that I didn't like where I thought he was going.

"That Ann Robinson is Nebraska Michaels' mother, yeah that's what I'm saying. Though I wasn't sure until Nebraska walked into the room. There's nothing in Ann Robinson's file that indicates she had a child and Nebraska's birth certificate lists a Jane Smith as her mother. But Nebraska's a spitting image of Pidge, all the way down to how she carries herself. It was like going back in time watching Ann walk into the TOC."

Oh yeah, that sick was churning and all those dirty thoughts I had about Nebraska suddenly felt wrong. Very, *very* wrong knowing my boss had fucked her mother.

"You said Charlie adopted her. Who's her biological father?"

Zane's dimples depressed deeper and his hands came out of his lap, palms facing the table in a stop gesture.

"Not me."

Well, thank fuck for that or me throwing up would be

the least of our worries. Zane's wife Ivy would likely dismember him.

"So she fucked you for information?" Theo inquired.

"The woman fucked me, alright, but I never touched her."

Why was that such a relief?

"I don't get it then," Kira put in.

"There are many ways to fuck a man without having to bed down. The greatest lie ever told was that women are the weaker sex. Men perpetuated the lie. But women, see, they're smart enough to allow the propaganda to be persevered. Generation after generation the lie is told and women are underestimated. When the truth is women are far more cunning than men. Sly in all the ways they fuck with a man's head. It's not about physical strength; it's a power dynamic that men have very little chance of winning. Pidge was the last woman I underestimated. I would've seen a honey trap a mile away. I would've been prepared for that. Pidge was smart. She observed me, got to know me, asked questions, then she used my weakness against me. I handed her everything she needed to know in less than a week kicking back at night around a fire, tossin' back a few beers. Stroking my ego, making me feel needed, placing me in the one role she knew I couldn't turn away from. One night in some great admission she told me she was scared. This was her first time out in the field with a team. She was nervous. Sun City was mostly a shanty town. The residents lived in extreme poverty, run by gangs. It was hella dangerous but for a woman it was worse. But she didn't want to be viewed as fragile or a strap so she did her part even if she was scared to death. She told me in a way that made me believe she trusted me to keep her safe. I became her protector. And once that happened, and she cemented that bond, I trusted her with more than I should've."

Holy fuck.

Kira's fingers were flying across her keyboard.

I didn't wait for her to find what she was looking for before I asked, "Ann was the case officer?"

"That's what we were told."

"But she wasn't?"

"Nope. She wasn't a blue badge, she was a contractor."

"What'd she get out of you?" Cash asked.

"Not *what*. It's *where* she landed me and Dutch."

That was all he said but he spat it out like he couldn't get the words out unless he expelled them from his throat.

Kira pushed her laptop toward Layla. Her eyes immediately dropped to the computer, and I watched them move over the screen.

"Where?" Theo asked, like he hadn't noticed Kira and Layla leaning close, looking at KK's screen. But the frown on Layla's face had me concentrating on her as she continued to scan whatever Kira pushed in front of her.

"We'd found the man we were looking for, collected the evidence he had, cabled it back to Washington, and were waiting for it to be authenticated. The plan was to move as soon as we got approval. Dutch was the TL. He was briefing the team on the evac route. It was going to be a quick snatch and grab made to look like a kidnapping. We finished our brief when Ann came in looking distraught. No, she looked completely terrorized. Dutch went on alert, I went on high alert—I'd promised to protect her and she looked devastated. The story she told us was she'd gotten word a gang had rounded up teenage girls, kidnapped them, and were in the process of transporting them. Dutch and I loaded up and moved out. No questions asked. I trusted her. We get to the location she gave us, found five girls in a rundown warehouse but no guards. We loaded them up and were back on our way when we were stopped by Haitian police. We explained we worked for the US Government, blah, blah, blah. We'd received intel on a kidnapping, blah, blah, and we'd rescued the girls. The police officer spoke to one of the sobbing girls. She lied and said we'd taken them from their homes. That *we'd* kidnapped them. Dutch and I were hauled in and spent three days in custody until someone from the embassy came and got us."

"Holy fuck," Theo mumbled.

He got that right.

"What happened to your target?" Smith asked.

"Mission was halted while we were in custody. Maddon was pissed as fuck. When Dutch and I returned to the safehouse Ann was gone and so was our target."

"She set you up."

Even though my statement was just that, Zane still verified.

"She set us up. I spoke to Maddon, explained what had happened. He didn't believe me or Dutch and since Ann had been pulled she wasn't there to be questioned."

Throughout Zane's brief, Layla's attention hadn't moved from the screen. Her frown had deepened and the two lines between her brows were so pronounced they formed a perfect eleven.

"What are you two looking at?" I asked.

Layla didn't glance up when she answered, "Nebraska went to live with Charlie Michaels after her mother was murdered when she was twelve. According to old medical records Kira found her mother's name is Anna Bauer or at least that's whose name in on the intake form. No father mentioned."

Anna Bauer's driver's license photo flashed up on the screen.

Holy hell.

Nebraska was a younger version of her mother. She wore her hair longer and her nose was straighter but other than that, there was no denying Anna was her mother.

"That's Ann Robinson and she was very much alive when I was with her in Sun City. She was very alive years later when I saw her in Germany and she winked at me as she left a bar I was entering with some of my teammates. And she was also as beautiful as ever when I saw her in D.C. about five years ago."

Zane's response was met with silence.

Until Kira broke it. "Do you think Nebraska knows her mother's alive?"

"With all the bullshit fuckery that comes with the Agency..."

Zane let that hang and shrugged.

The shrug and vague answer was very un-Zane-like.

"What aren't you saying?" I asked.

"A lot," he admitted.

"Where do Charlie Michaels and Maddon Judd fit into this?" Smith joined.

"Maddon Judd is still active CIA," Kira answered.

"The reports Nebraska gave us are going to take some time to sort through. They go back twenty years. The file on Charlie Michaels isn't as comprehensive."

"Not surprising," Theo mumbled.

"But," Kira continued. "It looks like Charlie officially retired a little over four years ago, but he still freelances. The Raven project was a contract. His life as an art forger is his cover."

"Not unusual," Layla added.

She would know. She and Theo both were CIA case officers. Thankfully my time in the CIA had nothing to do with spy shit. I was a trigger puller—less bullshit, more adventure.

As uninterested as I was in Maddon Judd and Charlie Michaels now that we knew he was of no risk to Theo's woman, I was very much interested in what we were going to do about Nebraska Michaels.

"What are we doing about Nebraska?"

"Nothin'."

Zane's answer was like a sucker punch I didn't understand.

"Nothing?"

Zane's gaze focused.

"Don't let those pretty blue eyes and all that soft you think you see under her hard exterior fool you. She's a fixer, same as her mother. She'll sell her services to the highest bidder. Women like that have no loyalty. And right now, she holds more power than I'm comfortable with. Until we understand what she wants and what she's willing to do to accomplish her mission, she's on her own."

"Kira, can you get me the files on the prison riot and Paulo Alves?" Smith asked.

"While you're at it," Jonas started. "Send me the Maddon file."

"I'll take the Charlie Michaels file," Theo requested.

"Well, I'd say send me what you have on Nebraska but I'm not feeling like getting into hand-to-hand combat with Easton while I'm wearing my favorite tee, so I'll take the Candy Apples file."

Cash was a smart man. I might've loved him like a brother but I had zero issue punching him in his ugly mug to get my hands on Nebraska—or her file.

"Tomorrow morning, eight o'clock, we'll brief." Layla okayed our self-appointed assignments. Part of what made her such an effective leader was she didn't micromanage. We were grown-ass men, used to doing big boy things with little to no direction. Now that we weren't out in the wild working our cases how we saw fit but instead working within the parameters of Z Corps she treated us no differently—same big boy rules. As long as the work got done, she didn't care how.

"I'll track her movements and dig into her mother."

I wanted to ask Kira to keep me updated on Nebraska's location but refrained.

For a reason I wasn't willing to dissect, I hoped she hadn't been sent in to reenact her mother's play.

It would seriously suck if she turned out to be the enemy.

SIX

"Please tell me you didn't do the one thing I always warned you not to do," Stella, my friend-slash-part-time-enemy, said in my ear as I made my way outside of Miami terminal.

Why did it always have to be hotter than Satan's breath in Florida? No, it was Arizona that was hotter than Satan's breath. Florida was stickier than a working girl after an eight-hour shift in the red-light district. Any RLD, country be damned.

"I have no idea what you're talking about," I lied.

"Hmm," Stella hummed. "Want to catch up and have dinner tonight?"

"I can't. I'm hoping to meet up with Walter, grab my cover, and jam."

There was a beat of silence which was good since I wouldn't have heard her over the blaring horn of a truck trying to wedge its way to the curb while a Kia wasn't looking where it was going and almost backed into the pickup.

Why were people so damn impatient?

And rude.

No one liked to be stuck in airport traffic.

"Promise when you get back you'll make time for me."

This was highly unusual. Stella had never asked me to promise her anything. The same way I'd never asked her to make me a promise. Like me, Stella wasn't prone to keeping her word. Not unless you were someone she'd pledged her allegiance to—then I could see her making vows and keeping them. But as far as I knew, Stella's only loyalty was to herself. Not that I blamed her; she'd been burned and hung out to dry by the very organization she'd once committed her loyalty to.

"What's happening right now?" I asked suspiciously.

"Always so distrusting," she murmured.

"I'm sorry, are you not the woman who got me drunk on my favorite pinot and waited until I was three sheets past shit-faced before you asked me about a certain prince, then used what I told you to seduce him and share a weekend in Monaco?"

Yes. Friend-sometimes-underhanded-enemy.

Frenemy.

"Ah, yes, Prince Chester the kitty killer. Too bad he was such an asshole. The man had skills in the bedroom that were mind-bending."

I wouldn't know anything about mind-bending bedroom skills. The only thing I used my bedroom for was sleeping. And the few times I'd used it for other things the sex was total crap. I couldn't understand what the big deal was about.

I guess sex was like chocolate-covered cherries—the appeal was subjective.

"If I wasn't happy to see his demise I would've been pissed."

"Listen, I did you a favor. I knew you wanted to tell me about the twat but couldn't. And don't bullshit me and tell me you didn't want to see him put down. So I bought you your favorite wine and gave you something to blame your loose lips on. It was a win-win. You're welcome. Now promise me you'll make time for me."

It had been a win-win; again, that's why I wasn't angry at her. She'd used what I told her to stop Prince Chester from poaching large cats. The asshole had twenty-five mounts of different varieties of cats, most of them on the verge of extinction, in his monstrosity of a home that was too small to be called a castle, too big to be called a mansion, and nowhere near just the right size.

There was something off in Stella's tone. Either that or my ears were still clogged from the flight and now filling with sweat from the soupy air.

"What's wrong?"

"Nothing."

"I feel like you're lying."

"Seeing as I lie seventy-five percent of the time I understand that. But you're not a job, and I try my very best not to lie to my friends."

"So we're friends today."

"I'm wounded."

That was a lie.

It would take more than a few words to offend or wound Stella.

Where the hell was my Uber? I hadn't been outside for

more than five minutes and already my bra was saturated in sweat.

"Cut the crap, Stel, and tell me the truth. Are you in trouble?" I paused before I changed my question. "Let me rephrase, since trouble is relative. Are you in danger?"

"Nope. Just want some face time so I can slap some sense into you until your head is screwed back on straight."

My neck tightened at her threat of bodily harm. With Stella one never knew if she was joking or if she was serious.

"I have no idea what you're talking about." Another lie, I had a pretty good idea. "And if you think I'm going to promise to make time to be on the receiving end of a bitch slap, you think wrong."

"I don't bitch slap. That's for prissy girls. I slap-slap."

"Was that a Missy Elliot quote?" I asked as a white Honda Accord muscled its way to the curb. I checked my app and sure enough that was my Uber.

Perfect timing.

"What?"

"Never mind. My ride's here. I have to go."

"You need to be careful, Nebraska. You're playing with fire, and trust me, sister, once that fire is lit it will burn out of control."

"I don't—"

"Zane. Lewis," she enunciated slowly. "Everyone knows to stay away from him and you waltzed your happy ass into his office today. Not that I wouldn't have followed Easton Spears into an Afghan cave if he promised some happy-ending fun before we met certain death. But, Zane? No, boo, you fucked up with that. Now you have Kira

Winters or Cain or whatever her last name is now digging places you don't want her to dig."

Shit.

Shit.

Shit.

"Everything's fine and did you just call me '*boo*'?"

Big fat lie. Nothing was fine.

I knew going to Zane would be more trouble than it was worth. But I needed Maddon to believe I was willing to do anything he asked.

"I don't know how you think that when we're talking Kira here. Garrett, and I'm not throwing shade, he's got it going on, and can find ninety-nine percent of shit you don't want him to find. But Kira, that woman has a God-given talent to find that one percent Garrett can't. And that one percent is always what fucks you."

I knew this.

It was always the smallest detail you couldn't hide that screwed you in the end.

"Are they still watching me?"

"Yes."

Thought so.

The Uber driver had exited the Honda and was staring at me over the roof of the car.

"I don't have any bags," I told the gentleman. "Sorry, I'm speaking to my grandma, she's very ill. I'll be off the phone in just a second."

"Lies." I heard Stella mutter.

"I have to go but never call me boo again. You're closer to fifty than you are fifteen; it doesn't work for you."

"What about nob? Does that work? Or how about, flange?"

"If you were hot and British I'd say yes, but you're American and I don't have time for you to break out into your fake British accent to sell the lie you're from some small village in the West County of England. My Uber driver looks pissed and I have to go."

Stella being Stella—in other words completely ignoring my time restraint—continued to berate me. Also Stella being Stella—in other words, thinking she was hilariously entertaining (which was the truth most of the time, just not when I needed to get into an Uber idling at the curb at a busy airport or when she was getting me drunk to pry secrets out of me) —did this in a proper British accent.

"I warned you, never to get on Zane's radar. Whatever happened today, landed a red bullseye on your forehead."

Shit. This was really not good.

"Listen to you sounding all classy and cultured."

She switched back to irritated-American. "Nebraska—"

"I get it. Thank you for caring. We'll talk later and I'll fill you in, but right now I have to go."

Suddenly the line went dead.

This was Stella's typical send-off—she hung up instead of offering a farewell.

I got into the back seat of the Honda, muttered my apology, then confirmed for the driver the hotel I was staying at.

I had numerous calls to make checking on my plans for the evening. But those would have to wait. Paying attention to the route the unknown driver was taking was more important.

Always pay attention to your surroundings, Nebraska. Never allow yourself to get distracted. Always know where you are and know when your route is being diverted.

One of the many lessons Charlie had pressed upon me played in my mind. The Honda merged into the left lane exit headed to Miami Beach.

So far so good.

All I needed was to meet up with Walter then I'd be headed back to the airport to catch a flight out of the country.

That was if Walter felt like being on time. If not I'd sleep at the hotel and leave tomorrow.

Knowing Walter would likely be his normal hour behind schedule, I booked a suite with a kickass tub. Later I'd order a bottle of red wine and take a soak.

It would do nothing to ease my stress but it would be the last bath I'd have for the foreseeable future so I was determined to enjoy it.

THREE HOURS later I found I was correct when Walter moseyed into the bar forty-five minutes late—fifteen minutes shy of my estimation—looking like he'd been on a four-day bender.

"Miami looks like it's agreeing with you," I fibbed.

Walter's clear, bright eyes locked with mine belying his haggard appearance.

"Nice to see you, too, Dove."

I took in his appearance. The man looked more like a drunken beach bum—five months overdue for a haircut, same with a beard trim, clothes clean but well-worn—instead of the seasoned spy I knew him to be. Though he'd never worked for the CIA, he was still a spy in every sense of the meaning. If you didn't want people to know your business you took great pains to not know Walter. The problem was, Walter made it his business to know everyone. If you didn't want him selling what he knew about you to your enemies, you bought his silence. If you needed a cover and had the money, you went to Walter.

The guy was a master at blending in.

"Going native," I mumbled.

With a nonchalant shrug of confirmation he handed me the thick Manila envelope he'd brought with him.

"I heard you met with Viper earlier," he started with a frown. "Not smart, baby girl. You know better than to show yourself to the enemy."

I let the baby girl comment slide.

"The enemy of my enemy is my friend?" I queried as a brush-off to his censure.

"There is no enemy worth getting yourself tangled with Viper over unless you're ready for a rectal exam. Word is he's not gentle and has yet to discover that lube makes the process less painful."

I felt my mouth twist in disgust.

"Thanks for the imagery. What's next? Are you going to start humming *My Humps* and get that stuck in my head, too?"

Walter's confusion at my song choice stated plain he wasn't familiar with the Black Eyed Peas and it would take more time than I was willing to expend to explain who Fergie and will.i.am were.

(By the way, you're welcome... *My hump, my hump, my hump, my hump. My lovely lady lumps my lovely lady lumps.*)

"Never mind," I muttered and waved the envelope. "Thanks for coming through."

"I hope you know what you're doing."

That was the second time in the last few hours two people had essentially said the same thing. The truth was I knew exactly what I was doing, it just wasn't a very good idea. Sooner or later my meeting with Zane was going to catch up with me. My only hope was by the time that happened my mission would be complete. Then I could do the very thing I'd always said I'd never do—beg for forgiveness.

I was absolutely sure pleading with Zane Lewis for mercy would taste like shit.

But what was a girl to do? I needed Maddon to believe I was onboard with his idiocy even if it meant Zane Lewis performed an outpatient colonoscopy on me.

"Don't I always?" I replied with more bravado than confidence.

"Either you have the largest lady-balls I've ever seen or you've made what could be a fatal error in judgment. I guess time will tell." Walter dipped his scruffy chin in farewell but stopped and looked back at me. "What does the fox say?"

I scanned my memory banks for some coded message I was supposed to know but came up with nothing.

"Huh?"

"*Ring-ding-ding-ding-dingeringeding! Gering-ding-ding-ding-dingeringeding!*" he sang as he walked away.

Bastard.

Ten minutes later my head was bobbing to the beat of what was quite possibly the most annoying song ever released.

An hour later, sitting in a luxurious bath full of bubbles with a glass of red wine balancing on the edge of the tub, I was still humming. *Ring-ding-ding-dammit.*

Ass. Hole.

So much for relaxing when I couldn't stop the refrain of nonsensical sounds from invading my mind.

SEVEN

Pounding on my front door woke me up. With a quick look at my alarm clock, I snatched my Glock off my nightstand and rolled out of bed.

Nothing good comes in the form of a middle of the night visitor. I was almost to my bedroom door when my ringing phone had me retracing my steps.

Zane's name on my phone in the middle of the night was worse than an unexpected visitor.

"What's going on? Someone's at my door," I told him.

"That's me," he grunted.

Okay, I'd been wrong, the worst thing that could happen was Zane pounding on your door in the middle of the night. That meant whatever it was, was bad enough he dragged his ass out of bed leaving his wife in that bed. There were very few things that would pull Zane from Ivy. None of them would be good.

I disconnected the call, tossed the phone on my bed, kept the gun, and made my way through my townhouse.

I checked the peephole, saw Zane angrily staring at the door.

"I know you're looking at me, asshole. Open up."

Once I had the door open Zane wasted no time barreling through with none other than Charlie Michaels on his heels.

What the actual fuck?

"Smith's on his way over," Zane announced like it wasn't after three in the morning and my teammate was coming over for a beer.

"Why's he here?" I asked instead of asking what I really wanted to know—where was Nebraska and was she all right.

"He's concerned Nebraska's walking into a trap."

In true Zane fashion he walked to my couch, sat down uninvited, and left Charlie standing in the foyer.

"Have a seat," I begrudgingly offered. "I'll make coffee."

My condo had an open floor plan—at least that's what the real estate agent called it when she was giving me her sales pitch. I called it one big room with a bedroom and bathroom off the living room. The realtor used that as a selling point, too, a downstairs master. All that meant to me was I didn't have to drag my laundry down a flight of stairs. But it's biggest advantage at the moment was I could make coffee and still see Zane lounging and Charlie stiffly sitting on my couch since the kitchen was unobstructed.

"Wanna fill me in on what's going on?" I prompted as I pulled yesterday's grinds out of the basket.

"Ole Charlie here came bearing gifts," Zane started.

I didn't get the chance to ask why Charlie chose a

middle-of-the-night visit to deliver whatever he wanted to give Zane before there was another knock.

I watched Zane fold out of his sprawl to answer the door while I added a third scoop of grinds to the filter. It was going to be a long day; strong coffee was going to be my only coping device.

"Nice jammies," Smith snickered.

I glanced down at my gray lounge pants complete with bright yellow combat-ready rubber ducks—a Christmas gift from Kira. I was pretty sure she'd given a variation of mine to the whole team. My rude hand gesture to Smith was met with a chuckle.

Zane cut through the exchange to announce, "The two of you are on a flight to Cairo. It leaves in four hours."

I had yet to process the Cairo part before Zane went on, "Nebraska is meeting with Amani Carver. Her flight will land a few hours after yours."

"Amani Carver, the man who bought the microdrone tech from that dipshit, Mark Shillings?" Smith inquired.

"One and the same," Zane confirmed.

"Why is she meeting with him? The Raven project is dead. The Sparrow was scrapped in testing and the payload capabilities were never authenticated," Smith correctly pointed out.

"The Sparrow project was completed," Charlie contradicted. "Or the sale of the plans were completed. Amani has a talented team ready to reengineer any hiccups. The meeting isn't about the drone. Nebraska requested a sit-down as a show of loyalty to warn Amani Maddon is ready to execute his end game."

I didn't want to think about why Nebraska would be

loyal to the man who bought the schematics to a micro-drone that was so small it was basically undetectable with the plan to use the silence and maneuverability of the UAV to drop nerve agents to decimate throngs of people.

Amani Carver was a modern-day Chemical Ali.

"What's Maddon's endgame?" Smith asked Charlie though his eyes were glued to the percolating nectar of the gods slowly filling the coffee pot.

"Did you read the files Nebraska gave you?" Charlie asked impatiently.

"No. I was more interested in Paulo Alves and why Nebraska was there to kill him."

I was too far away to get a read on Charlie but I didn't miss the slight tic in his cheek. The prison riot wasn't in the files he sent.

"Paulo was personal."

"Personal how?" Smith pushed.

"He was a low-level criminal. Content to sell drugs, pimp women, do his part in his gang, but never made moves to move up. Could've been he was lazy or too strung out himself. Either way he was a street dealer. Not someone we would concern ourselves with. But Nebraska had an informant—husband and wife. She liked them, they were good people doing what they could to clean up their neighborhood. She was in Brazil getting intel on a large shipment of cocaine Primeiro Comando da Capital planned on moving out of the country. She went to see her informants. When she got there the neighborhood was in mourning. Her informants' daughter had been brutally raped and murdered. Everyone knew Paulo had done it but no one was talking. Before she could find Paulo he was picked up on drug charges. With overcrowding and the corruption, Paulo would spend a week in Conjunto then he'd be released. Nebraska made sure he didn't leave the prison."

How could one woman be such a contradiction? She'd mete out justice to a rapist who otherwise would walk free for his crimes while sitting with a man who was planning what would amount to mass murder.

The better question was, why was I contemplating the woman's actions?

I yanked four mugs out of the cupboard while I forced myself to listen to Nebraska's father and ignored the knot of apprehension quickly twisting at the thought of her alone in Egypt meeting with a very dangerous man.

"It's my understanding she knew you were in the prison and left your mission undisturbed," Charlie finished.

"She did," Smith confirmed, but offered nothing else. "What's Maddon's endgame?"

The stretch of silence had me turning back to the living room. Charlie's gaze was fixated on my TV. His face was stoic. His shoulders tense. It was a given the man wasn't happy to be in my living room in the middle of the night, but it was more. I'd venture to guess it even went beyond his daughter meeting with Amani Carver.

"I've known Maddon for the better part of forty years. When I met him, he was fresh to clandestine services. He was a cocky asshole like the rest of us when we started. Came in hot, thought he could make a difference and was ready to get out into the field. Back in the eighties we were ass-deep into the war of drugs. New tactics were in their infancy. Maddon excelled at gathering sources. He managed to build a network in Central America that didn't just help the cause; it propelled the operation into over-drive. So much intel was being sent back to Washington they had to scramble to bring in more analysts."

As interesting as that was, I wasn't sure why a history lesson was relevant. I jerked the half-full carafe from the machine and filled my mug.

"I'll take one of those, too," Smith called from the living room but was already making his way into the kitchen.

Zane had moved to a chair Layla had convinced me to buy to complete what she called the aesthetic of the room. She also called it a club chair, whatever the hell that meant. I called it uncomfortable and useless. But right then with Zane sitting in it staring at me I could add too small to uncomfortable.

"Is Maddon's time in Central America pertinent? My men have a flight to catch," he asked impatiently.

One could say my boss didn't like his time wasted. Taking that a step further he really didn't like it wasted in the middle of the night.

"Looking back, I think that's when it started," Charlie went on. "Not to say he was dirty back then, but that's when he learned how to play the game. He cultivated a network—not assets. He was smart, he made them beholden to him in a way that was generational. One of his informant's children needed medical attention, he paid for it. A relative needed out of the country, he secured documents. A brother needed help paying for his education, Maddon paid for that. With no wife, no children of his own, no permanent residence since he was in the field so often, he had the money to spend. The locals called him a savior. In the nineties when operations turned to the

Balkans he did the same thing. After 9-11 our focus changed again and he was assigned to Afghanistan to support OEF."

Smith stared at me over the rim of his mug as he slurped down the hot liquid as if it wasn't scalding his mouth, with a look that mirrored my wish Charlie would hurry the hell up and get to the point.

"Again, Charlie, my men have a flight to catch."

"I began to suspect something wasn't right when I was in France. My cover as an art forger had long been established. I hadn't been in an active war zone since Nicaragua. My business and Maddon's hadn't crossed for a long time. It was a coincidence I was in Paris the same time he was."

"You said business, but you remained personal friends over the years?" I asked for clarification.

"Correct. Maddon remained a close personal friend. With my cover, I didn't cultivate friendships. I lived that cover, I was an art forger, until we decided to broaden the scope, then I had an *accident* that left my right hand damaged. Instead of me being the forger I became the man to broker the deals. I had five of the best forgers in the world working for me."

"Back to France," Zane prompted.

"I was in Paris to oversee the delivery of a Gustav Klimt. Maddon flew to Paris to meet with an asset. There was word al Qaeda was planning an attack. I didn't know who his asset was, I just knew he was in the country and asked me to meet for a late dinner before he went back to Afghanistan. During that dinner he complained the asset didn't have what he needed so he was sticking around for a few days. The next morning I met with my client, Jules

Laurent, and delivered the Klimt. After the deal was complete, he invited me to stay for a drink. Not unusual but I sensed there was more than simply toasting a successful transaction. I was right. Jules tells me the night before, he's met with an American who's selling strategic movements of DCRI. Jules had the contacts to broker this deal, but he's reluctant to work with the American and asked me if I could look into the man."

"Maddon Judd was selling out the Central Directorate of Interior Intelligence," Zane growled his assertion of the situation.

Now we were getting somewhere.

"He was using the alias Peter Brady. As soon as Jules said the name, I knew. But I didn't want to believe Maddon was selling out our allies at DCRI. I thought it was a double-cross or a tactical maneuver to sell misinformation. I told Jules I would make some calls and get back to him. Before I left Paris that night, I called Jules, told him Peter Brady checked out. A week later a church blew up. Fifty-three men, women, and children died. Among them five were DCRI and three were national police. That was the first time I doubted my friend. But it was not the last. I started watching, using my connections to follow Peter Brady, collecting evidence. The problem is, Maddon's the golden boy of the CIA. With each administration change, retirement and replacements of the seventh floor he works hard to prove how invaluable he is. He has so many people in his back pocket there's nothing I can do with the evidence without tipping him off. So I sat on it, waited, watched, and that brings us to now—Maddon's end game. He's tying up loose ends before his finale. Amani is a loose end. He's met with him face-to-face. Amani can identify him."

"What about the others who have met with him?" Smith asked.

"Jules died of cancer a few years ago. The rest of the men and women are in the file along with their causes of death. Some natural, some not. When the Peter Brady name became trusted Maddon stopped face-to-face meetings until Amani Carver demanded a sit-down."

"I'm unclear why you sent your daughter to meet with us," I interjected.

Charlie's gaze swung to me before he looked back at Zane. His expression shifted, communicating something to my boss I couldn't read but clearly Zane did and whatever that was Zane didn't like.

"Nebraska was supposed to explain Maddon's plan. He has a GB team at his ready to take out Amani but Maddon doesn't have the sign-off to use deadly force until he can give the Agency more than the purchase of the drone. It's well known your team can retrieve information when others can't. It's also well known that during that pursuit you don't mind taking out a target. Either way, Maddon gets what he wants, Amani dead. By your hand or his team, he doesn't care. But he needs Amani dead before he can move on. We need Amani alive."

And since we didn't listen, Nebraska's on her way to Cairo to warn Amani.

Fuck.

"And now you want us to go to Cairo to what?" I continued. "Back her play?"

Seeing as Charlie had spent the majority of his life

living a deep cover I wasn't sure I believed his look of concern but he certainly tried his damnedest to sell it with his deep frown and pinched brows.

"I believe Maddon has caught on."

"Right," Zane murmured. "Don't tell me he's changed his behavior sometime in the last twelve hours."

There you go, Zane's not buying it either.

"Not toward me. But Badger's been in touch."

At the mention of Badger, Zane went on high alert.

"Why in the fuck is Badger contacting you?" Zane seethed.

"Nebraska tried to negotiate a deal for him several years back. The deal was unsuccessful yet still bore fruit."

Zane entirely shut down. Every emotion slammed closed, leaving him looking like he suddenly had no interest in any further discussion.

"Who's Badger?" Smith asked what I wanted to know.

"The last man you see before you meet your maker," Charlie answered.

I wasn't a fan of riddles in general. Most especially not when I was woken up after a few hours of sleep. In my exhaustion I tried to remember if the name Badger had come up in any of the files Kira had given me on Nebraska. I was coming up blank.

"He's an assassin?" Smith pressed.

"Assassin. Mercenary. Take your pick. Though he's not a killer for hire. He lives and works by a moral code that cannot be bought. And will only step in when all other forms of negotiations have failed."

"Are you saying your daughter negotiates deals for a merc?"

I couldn't be bothered to hide my disdain at the idea.

"No. What she negotiates is behavioral change. If she's successful and the party agrees to the sanctions or abandons their actions she doesn't call Badger or someone of the like."

Words. So many words floated around in my head begging to be shouted out of my mouth.

Words like: *are you fucking kidding me* all the way *to what kind of man allows his daughter to consort with the types of criminals whose crimes are so egregious the only way to stop them is death.*

"What's Badger's concern?" Zane rejoined.

"Maddon contacted him under the Peter Brady alias to tell him he had proof the Dove had turned."

Fury etched into Zane's features, his study of Charlie became razor sharp.

"Who's Dove?" I asked when it became obvious Zane didn't plan on sharing whatever had tweaked him.

"Nebraska's the Dove," Charlie answered

I felt my muscles seize as the bitter coffee in my stomach turned rancid.

I could hardly recognize my own voice when I asked, "Maddon's called in a hit?"

"*Attempted* to call in a hit." Charlie's variation did nothing to still the conflicting emotions warring in my head. "What Maddon doesn't know is, Badger's in the know about his alias. Not that Badger would ever believe Nebraska turned and Maddon has to know that. Yet still he reached out to deliver a warning."

"And that is?" Zane asked.

"Nebraska's going to warn Amani as a show of loyalty

in hopes he will return the favor and keep his eyes and ears open to Maddon's movements while Nebraska makes the moves she needs to take out Maddon."

No.

Fuck no.

Hell to the fucking no.

Again, how in the actual hell was this man okay with the danger his daughter was putting herself in?

Before I could stop the words they spewed from my mouth, giving away more than I would've liked. "That's not going to happen."

"It very much is, Mr. Spears. Nebraska is highly skilled. She will—"

"No, Charlie, you misunderstand. Her skill set is not what's in question, the insanity of the operation is. Your daughter is out there alone playing a game of cat and mouse. She thinks *she's* the cat. Maddon thinks *he's* the cat. In a game like this it's a crapshoot who's *actually* the fucking cat. The odds aren't in her favor. They're fifty-fifty at best."

Charlie nodded. "That's where you come in."

Yeah, this was exactly where I came in.

To put a stop to this recklessness.

To do that I needed to pack.

Which meant Charlie needed to leave so I could speak to Zane.

"Was this the gift, or did you have something more?" I asked.

Charlie shifted, opened his suit jacket, and pulled out a thumb drive.

Great.

"Maddon's safehouses, bank accounts, and most trusted associates," Charlie said and tossed the drive on the coffee table in front of him. "Also what I believe is his end game."

"Wanna cut the suspense and just tell us?" Zane sighed.

"Electrical grid," Charlie announced. "From what I've pieced together he's been working with the Chinese. Best way to attack the US is to take out our electrical grid. Once that's down, the chaos that will ensue will make us an easy target. Ports will be next. Think 9-11 but with ships. Take out the bridges near the major ports. Once that happens the United States will fall into panic. Step three would be a cyberattack. Then you have all the makings for war."

Jesus Christ.

"You know this—"

"I don't know anything as fact," Charlie interrupted Zane. "This is my gut. Me knowing him for over forty years, trusting him, working in the field with him, learning from him, confiding in him, him confiding in me. This is what I would do if the Chinese were paying me to plan a war with America. On that drive you'll find an account. Once Kira traces it she'll find the payments are direct from the CCP. It won't take but a few minutes for her to find it, seeing as it only took me a week."

Fucking, fuck.

"Find Nebraska. She'll lead you to Maddon. Quietly take him out, put someone in his place to continue talks with the Chinese, and you might be able to stop World War III." Charlie stood, straightened his jacket and moved toward the door but looked back at Zane. "As a failsafe, I've given Badger duplicates of what I've given you. In the event of my death Nebraska knows how to access all my personal files. As a backup, Badger now has access as well. He has my permission to hand everything over to you if something were to happen to myself and Nebraska. You'll have everything from the time I started my career to as recent as yesterday when I updated my files."

Charlie turned back to the door but slowly turned when Zane called his name.

"Does Nebraska know her mother's alive?"

The man didn't look surprised Zane knew.

"No."

"Come again?"

"As far as my daughter knows her mother was murdered when she was twelve. I'd ask you to keep Pidge's secret but I know you won't so all I can do is ask that when you tell her, you do it in a manner that will cause the least amount of harm."

"I'm sorry, are you seriously asking one of us to do your dirty work?" I asked through gritted teeth.

The nerve of this motherfucker.

"Yes. I should've told her years ago but I'm too much of a coward. Telling her Pidge is alive would be to betray an oath and shatter my daughter's heart. Neither of which I have the courage to do."

"Where's Pidge now?" Zane's voice was laced with disgust. He was a father who would under no circumstances leave his children.

"Off doing Pigeon things. Whatever they may be. She checks in once a year on Nebraska's birthday to ask after her. She never tells me where she is or what she's doing and I never ask. On Nebraska's eighteenth birthday was the last time she asked me for a photograph. And in the years since I have not offered. She is not of my blood but she is my daughter. Not Anna's and certainly not Dmitri Zenin's."

Zane came out of the chair he was lounging in, stood at his full height, and scowled at Charlie.

"You're shitting me. The Zenith is Nebraska's biological father?"

"Unfortunately."

"Jesus fuck. Anything else you need to tell us before you leave? Is her godfather Satan? Any relation to Harley Quinn?"

"I think as far as the parental lottery goes her father being a notorious Russian contract killer is shitty enough, don't you?"

My head was getting ready to explode.

Or my temper.

I wasn't sure which but something had to give to release the pressure that was building in my chest.

Nebraska's mother was whatever she was—I'd yet to figure that out. And her father was a contract killer and enforcer for the Bratva. So what did Charlie Michaels do? He basically led his daughter to follow in her biological parents' footsteps.

What the fuck?

"I can see you don't understand why I've done what I've done," Charlie murmured.

"Are you talking to me?"

"Yes, Mr. Spears. I had two choices when I took Nebraska in. Hide her away and do whatever I could to protect her until I died, which in my line of work could've happened at any time, or make her a worthy adversary. I decided it was best to give her the tools she'd need to protect herself against the enemies of her parents. I've been lucky, she's been lucky, and no one has made the connection. Pidge hid her pregnancy from Dmitri. She was successful in hiding her daughter for twelve years. The moment Pidge heard Dmitri was in the US looking for her, she faked her death and sent Nebraska to live with me. You can hate what I've done as much as I hate I had to do it. But you cannot disagree that Nebraska deserved to have all the tools necessary to protect herself."

I couldn't argue with that even if I disagreed with the tools he'd taught her.

EIGHT

There was nothing exciting about flying into Cairo International airport.

The landscape was brown.

Just brown.

From the buildings to the dust.

A few palm trees dotted the entrance to the terminal building but other than that, just brown.

That was until about twenty minutes outside of the airport and the iconic Waldorf Astoria came into view. The lush greenery and extravagance around the hotel looked out of place among the surrounding smaller buildings. Farther west of the airport the landscape changed once again giving way to high-rises and giant billboards advertising luxury condos and cellular companies. The closer you got to the river and downtown Cairo the buildings got taller, city buses added to the already hellacious traffic, and the highway became a maze of roadways that was nothing short of dizzying. In all of my trips to Egypt I'd never attempted to drive in the city. There was no such thing as rush hour traffic in Cairo. With a population of over twenty million jammed into the city the streets were packed 24/7. It was noisy and bright and busy—one in the afternoon or one in the morning, the people of Cairo seemed to never sleep. The streets were never empty, there was bumper-to-bumper traffic then there was slightly less traffic. And people thought New York City was insane. They'd obviously never visited Cairo.

By the time my taxi stopped in front of the Ritz-Carlton I could already feel the pollution coating my skin—not that I had much skin showing but the parts that were exposed were already grimy with sweat and dust.

After paying my fare, which included a five-minute standoff with my driver reminding him he'd already given me a price back at the airport and no I wasn't paying the "traffic tax" he was trying to persuade me into paying, we finally negotiated a price which was less than what I was quoted at the airport. With a wink and a smile I gave the driver a twenty-dollar tip—which was triple the cost of the ride. My generosity was met with a scowl.

What could I say, I liked to haggle, I liked sharpening my skills even if that meant wasting time on a busy street with a taxi driver and in the end still paying more than what I'd agreed to.

As a side note: there were three prices in Egypt—the local price, the Arabic price, and the tourist price. I always bargained for the local price but ended up paying the tourist price in the form of a gratuity.

After twenty-six hours in airports I just wanted to get into my room, wash off my day, and sleep. I'd worry about calling Amani tomorrow. I'd worry about Maddon and what he was up to after I met with Amani. Then I'd worry about what Zane and Kira were up to. Then maybe after that I'd give some time to ponder why I couldn't stop thinking about Easton Spears.

Maybe.

But probably not. I needed to focus. Easton was a distraction I couldn't afford. Not that he was so much of a distraction as he was a weird fascination. I was naturally curious, I couldn't sit in a restaurant without wondering about the lives of the people dining around me. I couldn't order a coffee without studying the barista or sit in a meeting without pondering how and why the man across from me had become who he'd become. I needed to understand people. Charlie had once told me I got my inquisitiveness from my mother. He'd also told me it was both a gift and curse. He wasn't wrong but I'd gladly embrace the curse if it was a gift from my mother. Though there were times, like with Easton, I wished I could turn it off. I'd probably never see him again, unless Zane figured out the truth —not that I'd recognize the truth anymore. What had started, had now morphed and changed into something I no longer fully understood. But I knew Zane's secret and when he figured out I was on his payroll he'd likely go ballistic. As amusing as it would be to watch the Almighty Zane Lewis find out there were things that he didn't know, I wasn't stupid enough to actually want to be present for the explosion.

Another reason I needed to forget about Easton and concentrate on what I could control.

One step at a time.

Before you can take control of a situation, you must first have control over yourself, Nebraska. Emotions kill. Distractions kill.

Charlie's long-ago lesson played in my mind as I approached the security checkpoint to enter the hotel.

Welcome to The Nile Ritz-Carlton, where one must pass through a metal detector to enter the lobby.

By the time I was in the elevator exhaustion had hit. When the doors slid open on the eighth floor my limbs felt sluggish and my eyes gritty.

Forget the shower, I just wanted a bed.

And to sleep for the next forty-eight hours.

I pushed open the door to my room, closed it behind me, secured the locks with no other thoughts than falling face first on the mattress when something caught my attention. The gauzy drapes were open, the exterior door ajar allowing warm air to fill the room, along with the unmistakable smell of the Nile River. But that wasn't what had my stomach clenching.

Nope, it was the man standing on the balcony. His hip and elbow rested on the railing, eyes on me looking relaxed —like he belonged there, like he was an invited guest, and not the intruder he was.

For a moment all I could do was stare.

Stare at a man who shouldn't be in Egypt. Who shouldn't be in my room. Who shouldn't be anywhere near me.

Yet there he was.

Easton Spears.

And worse, something inside of me calmed at the sight of him before unease took over.

Had Kira already figured out Zane's secret?

Was that why Easton had broken into my room?

Now was not the time for the big reveal, not when Maddon was still out there planning and plotting.

After I took out Maddon and stopped what Charlie called his end game, I'd face whatever censure Zane intended to dole out.

It was time for all the bullshit to end.

I was too tired.

I was done playing a game of Russian Roulette.

Dutch had warned one day he'd need to tell Zane the truth. I'd just hoped that when that time came, it would also come with me stepping out of the game completely. I was smart enough to understand in my line of work my usefulness had an expiration date.

Easton pushed away from the railing, his movements cleverly casual, laid-back, non-threatening yet still powerful. Movements that were intended to lull me into a false sense of security.

He was full of predatory grace, the kind that would strike when the time was right.

Masculine beauty—from his height, to his build, to his perfectly chiseled features, to his intimidating gaze.

There was something about him that threatened to reach down into my soul and expose all my vulnerabilities. Something that endangered my carefully crafted façade. Something that excited and scared me. Something I should've guarded against. But damn if I didn't want Easton to see the real me—not The Dove, not The Fixer, not The Mediator, not the woman Charlie had made me into but the woman I was supposed to be. I had no idea who that was exactly and I'd long ago resigned myself to the fact I never would. She'd been lost to circumstance and necessity. But whoever she was—that was who I wanted Easton to know.

I trusted one person completely—Charlie.

I trusted two men with my life—Charlie and Dutch.

Charlie had my love and admiration in a fatherly, mentor sort of way. I knew Charlie gave that love back in a very guarded, very cynical way. But no one outside of my mother had loved me totally and completely. It had been years since I'd felt that kind of love and now was not the time to yearn for it back. And Easton was not the man who should be making me crave it.

"Customs or traffic?" he asked.

"Huh?"

"Your flight landed hours ago. Customs or did you get caught in traffic?"

Was he insane?

"What are you doing here?"

"Here in your room or here in Cairo?"

No, he wasn't insane. He was playing a game.

"Let's start with Cairo," I suggested and for some reason Easton's lips twitched.

"Your dad sent us."

Us.

Craptacular.

And I was going to strangle my father.

"Who is us? Why did my father send you? And why do you sound amused?"

"You're a trip."

A trip?

Now what is he talking about?

"Listen, I haven't slept in like thirty hours, I have what amounts to the brain capacity of a snail right now. Can you please just cut to it and explain what's going on?"

"You're a trip," he repeated. "I thought for sure when you saw me on your balcony you'd either shoot me, scream, or throw a fit. So maybe you're not a trip, you're unpredictable."

Okay, it seemed like we weren't going to get to the point of his visit any time soon.

"As you noted, I flew here. I also entered through the metal detectors downstairs. A cavity search isn't on today's to-do list so I thought it best not to secure my weapons until after I left the city. Next, I don't scream. Screaming is reserved for the movies before the heroine decides to do something stupid and get herself killed or for men when they have their testicles in a vise—"

"Sorry to stop you but I just have to ask, are we still talking about the movies or have you witnessed this testicle thing in real life?"

"Both," I gritted out impatiently.

Easton took a step back and muttered, "Brutal."

He had no idea.

"I was going to add I'd never thrown a fit in my life, but seeing as I'm about to attempt my very first ever, that comment seems moot."

"Right. Your dad." He finally got to the point. "He came by my house in the middle of the night and felt it necessary for you to have backup."

The absurdity of Easton's statement penetrated my foggy brain.

"My father just came by your house? In the middle of the night."

"Well no, Zane brought him over."

Normally this news would have me running through all the possible end-of-the-world scenarios of why my father would fly to Maryland and risk Zane's wrath from a middle-of-the-night visit. Not one of those possibilities was good. Charlie would never make that trip unless something had gone seriously wrong. But right then, with Easton standing in my hotel room looking relaxed and carefree, and being as tired as I was, I did something I'd never done before—trusted someone outside of my immediate circle.

"Is the world coming to an end?" I inquired.

"Hopefully not tonight."

"Great. Then I'm taking a nap and I'll deal with you when I wake up."

Again his lips twitched.

"Shall I tuck you in before I leave?"

"Not if you like your testicles where they are."

This time his lips didn't twitch, they tipped up into a full-blown smile before he busted out laughing.

In my tired haze I forgot I wasn't supposed to be fascinated by the dangerous Easton and allowed myself to enjoy the show.

"Sleep tight," he called out, still chuckling as he made his way out to the balcony. "I'll be back in a few hours."

With that I watched him close the door behind him, then climb up onto the railing before he stepped around the stucco dividing wall between my balcony and the one next to mine.

We were more than eight stories above the ground.

The man was insane.

That was my second-to-last thought after I dropped my bag onto the floor and faceplanted onto the bed.

My last was, he had a really great laugh and I couldn't wait to hear more of it.

"NEBRASKA."

My name felt like a soft breeze over my heated skin. The calluses on his fingertips scraped over my sensitive nipple. Feather-soft, his fingers moved over the swell of my breast, down my ribs, over to my belly button, down to my hip. His thumb caught the elastic of my panties, and then they were being dragged down my legs.

I wanted to see him but it was too dark. I wanted to reach out and touch him, taste his skin, explore his body like he'd done to mine but all I could do was hold my breath and wait. Suddenly his hands were gone and his tongue was on the inside of my thigh. I spread my legs wide, giving him room to move where I needed him to go. I was so wet I was dripping. If I wasn't so far gone, I would've been embarrassed. I could hear myself panting. I felt my heart pounding in my chest. My body ached for release.

"Nebraska."

"Yes," I moaned. "Don't stop."

"Babe."

Why was he stopping? His mouth right *there*. It was so close all I had to do was lift my hips and I'd have him.

Then his tongue was gone.

So was the heat of his body.

But the pulsing between my legs made my entire body shake with the violence of my need.

"Nebraska! Wake. Up."

Easton's angry growl jolted my eyes open only to find him standing next to my bed scowling down at me.

Shit.

Shit, fuck, and damn it all to hell.

"Um," I mumbled.

"Seriously?"

"Uh..." I trailed off, not knowing what to say.

His eyes narrowed and one brow arched up in what I assumed was annoyance.

"I was having a bad dream," I lied. "I was being tortured." Not a lie. His hands and mouth had indeed been torturing me.

"Right, I'd believe that if you hadn't moaned 'don't stop'," he countered.

Normally I'd be quick with a better lie but in my fog I had nothing to say.

"Can we please forget you heard that?"

"No."

"No?" I continued to gaze up at him from my side wondering why I hadn't gotten out of the bed yet. It wasn't like I was a man and needed to hide an erection.

I started to roll but stopped and not only because Easton was crowding the bed, making it impossible for me to get up unless I wanted to look like a fool and scramble off the other side. The bigger reason was, sometime after I'd fallen asleep I must've woken up and kicked off my jeans.

The thin top linen was pulled up from the corner, barely covering my bottom half.

"Did you cover me up?" I amended my question to something more imperative.

"Yup."

My eyes slowly closed as my humiliation settled over me.

"Fruit of the Loom?" he asked.

Of course he would comment on my ugly undies.

"Everyone knows cotton wicks away sweat, Easton. Don't be a dick."

"Is it a requirement they be granny style to effectively wick away the moisture?"

Ugh.

He was annoying.

"You're still being a dick."

I blamed his smile for my moment of insanity. I tossed the thin blanket off, rolled three times before I hit the other edge of the bed, and tossed my legs over the side. When I was on my feet I whirled around and planted my hands on my hips.

"By the way, you're welcome," he said.

"I wasn't thanking you for being a dick."

Easton's smile turned into a smirk.

Did he think...

"And, I wasn't dreaming about you," I quickly denied even though I was pretty sure that was another lie. I didn't actually see the man who was touching me, though I'd never had a sex dream prior to meeting Easton, so there was a strong possibility he had fueled my nocturnal near-orgasm.

That stupid sexy brow lifted again.

"I think this is where I'm supposed to quote Shakespeare." When I remained silent, he went on, "You know, from Hamlet. 'The lady doth protest—'"

"Yes, Easton, I know the quote."

There was that damn smile again.

"But I was actually referring to covering you up. When I came in you were—"

"Is it possible for you to not be an asshole?" I seethed.

"Oh, good. You two are already at the name calling portion of the dance."

I jolted at the new voice.

Easton's eyes went over my shoulder and he smiled.

After I ascertained I wasn't going to be murdered in my ugly-ass granny-panties, I turned my head, found Smith standing in the open door to the balcony looking amused, and felt my temper snap.

"By all means, come in, make yourself at home."

Smith Everette's stupid smile was just as infuriating as Easton's.

"No time, we gotta jam."

Thank God they were leaving.

"Well then, don't let me keep you—"

"You're coming with," Easton interjected.

Like hell I was.

I had no idea why my father went back to Zane for help. I had no idea what made Zane change his mind and send Easton and Smith to Cairo, but I didn't trust it.

And this was *my* mission.

"That's not—"

"It is," Easton insisted firmly. "You've got two choices:

get dressed, grab your gear, and motor, or I dress you, Smith grabs your shit, and I carry you out of here. Maddon's on the move. Your meeting with Carver has changed. If you want to make it to the new location in time, you have five minutes to get ready. You have ten seconds, make your choice."

There was a lot to unpack from his succinct explanation of the situation but I was stuck on the ten-second mandate.

"Are you actually going to count to ten?" I snapped back.

"Five seconds."

"Asshole."

"Three."

"If you come near me, I'll punch you in your dick."

My threat was met with a grin.

"Was that a threat or talking dirty to me?"

"You're—"

Easton was on the move when he announced, "Time's up."

This was crazy.

But the crazier part was I wanted to see if he'd actually dress me before he tossed me over his shoulder and carried me out of my room.

NINE

"Your head's in the clouds."

I glanced up from zipping up my backpack and looked over to Smith waiting for me by the door.

"Huh?"

"No, correction, your head's full of beautiful brunette."

He wasn't wrong but still, I wasn't tracking his point.

Thankfully he continued before I had to ask.

"I've been talking to you. You've been nodding but you're not hearing me."

Fuck.

I had yet to manage to get Nebraska's long, bare legs out of my mind. Or more to the point the way she was clenching and rubbing her thighs together when I entered her room. Add in her soft moans and my dick hadn't fully recovered from the incident. Not even her getting stubborn and throwing an abundance of attitude at me about losing control of her mission had put me off. If anything, watching her dig her heels in only turned me on more.

Fortunately or unfortunately depending on how I

looked at it, she decided to dress herself. The fortunate part was she'd put her pants back on. Not that I particularly wanted that, but with Smith coming into the room I wasn't all that happy she was standing in her underwear facing off with me. And it was *underwear*. No way in fuck could I call the abomination of undergarments *panties*. The unfortunate part was, I didn't get to help her. Though that was arguably for the best, seeing as my hands were itching to touch those long legs.

I ignored Smith's observation and asked, "Did Kira find where Maddon's staying?"

"So...we're not discussing what I walked in on?"

"Nothing to talk about," I returned as I hitched my pack over my shoulder.

With a shake of his head and a grin that clearly said he wasn't buying my bullshit he opened the door.

"The St. Regis. And before you ask, he booked it in his name."

"He wants her to know he's here."

My statement was met with my teammate's agreement, "Yup."

Fucking hell.

It was time to talk with Nebraska.

"Anna?" Smith quietly asked before he exited the room, holding the door open for me.

One word, not that I needed more to understand what he was asking.

"We wait."

Smith's sharp shake of his head spoke to his disagreement.

"Is it smart to start, whatever it is you're starting on a lie?"

I could pretend I wasn't following his logic but Smith had already let my subject change slide; he wouldn't allow it a second time.

"Probably not, but the mission has to come first."

As soon as the sentence left my mouth it felt wrong. So wrong, my gut clenched and my feet stopped moving.

"Yeah, that's what I thought," Smith rightly noted my unease. "Don't sit on it too long, Easton. Or there might come a time when she won't be able to forgive you for keeping something as important as this from her."

I knew he was right. But telling her too soon could be just as bad.

Before I could respond—not that I had much of anything to say about Nebraska's mother being alive besides Charlie being a spineless asshole for not telling her himself—Smith turned his head and looked down the hall.

With a lift of his chin he greeted, "Good timing."

"Ready?"

I watched Smith crack a smile and shake his head, clearly not taking offense to her snappy tone. He also moved out of the doorway so I could move out into the hallway.

The only question Nebraska asked on our way down to the lobby was if we needed to call a taxi or if we had a rental. Once Smith told her we had a car, she looked away and kept her expression neutral as we made our way to the car park beside the Ritz. She only mumbled thank you when I held open the door for her as she slipped into the back seat. She didn't speak again until we crossed over the

6th of October Bridge to the West Bank of the Nile and entered Giza.

"Has Maddon checked into the St. Regis yet?"

Her question had me turning in the passenger seat to stare back at her.

We hadn't told her where Maddon was staying.

"What makes you think he's at the St. Regis?"

With an uncharacteristic roll of her eyes that communicated she thought I was an idiot, she went on to use words to convey her sentiment.

"If Maddon is in Cairo he always stays at the St. Regis. He's here and he wants me to know he's here, so he won't deviate. If he wanted to fly under the radar he'd stay at Zuberi Shamel's compound in New Cairo City just outside of District 5."

"Why do you think he wants you to know he's here?"

Another look that left her thoughts on my intelligence or lack thereof clear on her face—though this time, she kept her eyes firm on me when she answered, "He flew here using his real passport."

"Is that the only reason?"

"Isn't that enough?"

"It is but there's another reason."

Nebraska's eyes narrowed and she reluctantly shared, "If Maddon was staying at Zuberi's compound, Zuberi would've called. He hasn't. And I know Maddon. I know he wants me to know he's here and keeping an eye on me. He thinks he has the upper hand."

"Doesn't he?"

Nebraska shrugged her slim shoulders.

"For now he does," she conceded.

"You don't seem concerned."

"I'm not."

I was mentally debating whether or not I found her nonchalance commendable or foolish when Smith broke in. "It's not smart to underestimate your opponent."

"It's equally unsmart to assume," she pointed out. "I am well aware of what Maddon is capable of. Likewise I have a healthy dose of respect for his competence, especially when it comes to playing the long game. I'm not concerned because I know who I'm playing the game with. I know *him*. His mistake was teaching and shaping me into the player I am, then underestimating the skills he gave me. I learned by watching but also I've sharpened those talents. Unfortunately for him he wasn't paying attention until it was too late. I know my father thinks Maddon's in the dark, but I know he knows I've caught onto his game. Insisting I approach Zane was a distraction. I played the hand he forced me to play. Now I'm playing the game he wants me to play. With that he has the upper hand. But while he's busy running me around, he won't see the blade at his throat until I deem it's time to end him."

The woman was serious. She was going to slice Maddon's throat.

Again I was working out my thoughts on her planning to murder Maddon when Smith continued, "Why would Zane be a distraction?"

"That's not my story to tell."

I glanced at Smith.

Like me, his jaw was clenched. I knew my friend well enough to know we were having similar thoughts. Despite what Charlie had said, it sure sounded like Nebraska knew her mother was alive.

"Whose story is it?" I asked.

"Not mine."

Dead end unless I wanted to bring up Anna.

"Why did my father visit you?"

"Badger called him—"

"Let me guess," she interrupted. "Maddon called Badger to tell him I'd turned."

Well, fuck me.

"How'd you know?"

"I told you, I know Maddon. Under different circumstances that would've been a smart play. Tell the man who has a bevy of mercenaries at his command that your mediator had turned and could no longer be trusted. Badger would have no choice but to send someone to take me out. Saw that play coming. Badger and Dutch are aware of what's going on. My father's already taken precautions should he or I get taken out. Badger has all he needs to continue."

"He mentioned that. He also handed the intel over to Zane."

Nebraska visibly stiffened.

"Is there a problem with that?" I pushed.

"Not for me there's not."

"Care to explain that?"

"Not my story."

I figured that was going to be her answer.

So I was shocked to shit when she went on, "Zane's Maddon's backup plan."

"How so?" Smith inquired before I could.

Nebraska shifted in her seat but remained quiet. Her silence lasted long enough I righted myself in my seat and was scanning the apartment buildings that lined the street when Nebraska finally answered.

"Maddon's banking on the truth ruining Zane."

Apprehension unfurled in my gut.

Before I could press what the fuck she meant by that her phone rang and she announced, "My father."

I glanced at Smith. His jaw had yet to loosen. When he felt my stare he turned his head, gave me a 'what the fuck' look before his eyes went back to the road.

Then I listened to a one-sided conversation that was nothing more than Nebraska responding with "yes" or "no." Until the end when she proclaimed, "I'll call you after I sit down with Amani. However, I'd just like to point out, you're speaking to me like I'm twelve. But more than that you're treating me like I don't know what I'm doing when I've more than proven I do. Another point, Father; if you didn't trust my judgment you could've told me to come home after I met with Zane. You knew what would happen. You knew he'd have his people dig. But they didn't need to dig, did they? You just played into Maddon's hand and handed everything over. Now not only do I have to hope Amani believes me and doesn't turn this around as a sign of disloyalty to Maddon, which will make me look untrustworthy, but I also have to worry about Zane Lewis going all Viper on me. Charlie, out of all the players Zane scares me the most and not because I'm at the mercy of two of his men. You know, when he has his talk with Dutch and Dutch comes clean, it'll be me that pays the price. Not only that, we've put Zane in a tight spot and I'm positive that's not a spot he'll be happy to be in. Which means he's going to lash out. At me. At us. At Dutch. We don't need this. We need to be a united front until Maddon's stopped. Now, that will be impossible."

Throughout Nebraska's soliloquy there was no inflection, no anger present, no attitude. She spoke in a calm, even tone despite her words conveying just how pissed she was.

Interesting.

The woman had tossed attitude at me for far less.

There was a pause on her end before she finished with, "I hope that's the case, Father."

I waited a few beats before I craned my neck and looked back.

"Wanna explain that?"

"No," she whispered.

I took in her hunched shoulders and grim look and decided I didn't like how she'd folded into herself.

"Zane sent us here to protect you," I reminded her.

Nebraska's blue eyes lifted to mine and I nearly flinched at the defeat I saw.

"Okay."

"He won't hurt you."

"Okay."

"He won't," I pressed.

"You don't know what I know," she softly murmured and looked away.

And she didn't know what I knew, at least that's what we'd been told.

So many secrets.

Secrets that had the potential to ruin lives.

Or worse, kill.

I turned back to the front leaving Nebraska to her thoughts.

Later.

I'd get all of her secrets later.

Then I'd tell her mine and hope like hell when she learned her mother was alive she didn't kill the messenger.

Fucking Charlie Michaels.

TEN

"Dove." Amani stood and greeted me with a smile. "Always beautiful."

The man looked out of place in his suit. Though, with how well he dressed, his freshly shaven face, his close-cropped dark hair, every time I'd met with him he'd looked like he didn't belong. Not in a swanky hotel lobby and certainly not in this dinky little house with crap furnishings.

"Mr. Carver," I returned with one of the professional smiles I'd mastered. "Thank you for meeting with me. I'm sorry for the inconvenience."

"I believe I have inconvenienced you a time or two," he said, looking over my shoulder. "Shall we sit?"

I glanced at the rickety chairs and wondered if they were sturdy enough to hold up under the weight of the hulking men in the room. Although I knew from experience Amani's three bodyguards wouldn't sit; they'd strategically position themselves around the room.

"Let me introduce—"

"Easton Spears and Smith Everette," Amani interrupted. "Yes, Mr. Lewis warned me they'd be joining us."

I wasn't sure if that was good or bad. What I did know was I was extremely annoyed Zane had made the call without informing me. Not that I wanted a phone call from Zane.

Amani skirted around a beat-up, splintering wooden table that once upon a time might've been a decent coffee table but now looked like its best use would be for firewood. He sat in an equally tattered chair minus the splinters.

Once I was seated, Easton standing behind me to my right, Smith the same but to my left, Amani launched straight in. "It seems you have a problem."

Boy did I.

One of those problems was Easton's hand resting on my shoulder.

My second, bigger problem was I didn't know how much Zane had shared with Amani, which meant I was unprepared, something that never happened. I always knew the state of play before I entered a meeting. I always knew who the players were, their motives, and had already worked out several possible outcomes.

This time, I was flying blind.

Before I could respond, Easton did. "Have you looked over the files Zane sent over?"

Files?

Zane sent files.

The vastness of my irritation grew to extreme anger.

Amani pinned me with a sharp look that made me uncomfortable. "I wasn't unaware Maddon Judd was playing both sides."

Well, fuck a duck.

Amani went on, "I'm not unfamiliar with people underestimating me. Actually, I prefer it. That is precisely how and why I remain as successful as I am."

He wasn't wrong about that. I picked up on that easily during our first negotiations. Amani sat quietly throughout the meeting and allowed the other party to speak to him as if he were some uneducated desert nomad. When in reality he went to the best schools in Egypt before he finished his secondary schooling in London then went on to study at Harvard. I pushed aside thoughts of his successful business dealings because they weren't something to be proud of or something I condoned. But my job wasn't to judge or stop the criminal activity. It was simply to keep it contained. Right or wrong, Amani Carver was a reasonable man.

"The problem, Dove, is not me. It's you."

"Me?"

"Yes, you."

I felt Easton's hand on my shoulder tense.

"Care to elaborate?"

Amani's gaze shifted to Easton when he answered.

"I'd like to understand why Mr. Lewis has entered the game," Amani demanded, though his easy posture suggested it was a request when in reality it was anything but.

"That's not up for discussion," Easton bit out.

Amani's eyes dropped back to me. A brow rose and his fingers drummed on the cracked wood of the chair arm.

"Maddon needs chaos," I rejoined. "He sent me to Zane to offer him assurances Bridget Keller was in no danger. As a show of good faith, I was to give Zane the news the sale of the drone plans had gone through and you were in possession of the prototypes and had a team of engineers working through the glitches."

"Dirty work," Amani muttered.

"Yes. Maddon has GB team at the ready to take you out if Zane didn't bite."

Amani didn't flinch at the news. Neither that Maddon had a team of highly trained CIA trigger pullers at the ready to kill him, nor that I was sent to enlist Zane to take him out.

Such was the life of a man who was essentially a terrorist.

"This meeting is what?" he prompted.

"A warning," I went on. "You are the last person alive who can connect Peter Brady as Maddon Judd. The rest of the men he had face-to-face meetings with have been taken out."

At that Amani cracked a smile.

"For a man as arrogant and prideful as Maddon is, it is ridiculous he uses a name from a poorly written television show."

It was ridiculous, but if you knew Maddon the way I did, the absurdity made sense. He believed he was clever. He liked knowing he could run powerful men using a name that was associated with the not-so-smart middle-child.

"Undervaluing Maddon's reach would be a miscalculation, Mr. Carver. He's becoming impatient. He has other plans he wants to set in motion but cannot until he ties up the loose ends and you are the last of those tethers he needs to dissolve. As you're aware, desperate men are unpredictable. Impulsive and arrogant is a dangerous combination."

Amani relaxed in his chair.

He also didn't shift his stare even though I knew he was addressing Easton.

"You'll keep Dove safe?"

Easton's fingertips curled tighter and dug into my shoulder.

"Yes."

Three letters strung into one word that he vowed through gritted teeth.

I didn't know why my belly did a strange flip-flop and my chest grew warm. I'd never had anyone make an oath such as Easton had. And make no mistake; that one word in that tone was a promise. I shouldn't have felt the flip-flop or the warmth, but I did, and try as I might not to acknowledge it I could not. It was there. I felt it, along with his strong hand anchoring me, claiming me in front of a man whom he'd viewed as a threat to my safety.

Interesting.

No, not interesting, alarming.

I couldn't allow myself to get involved with Easton or any man.

My life was not mine.

Plus it was dangerous.

There would never be a time when I would be free to be loved.

Not that I knew what that meant exactly.

Amani nodded and held my eyes.

"Word is Maddon has put out a bounty on you."

That warmth in my chest turned frosty.

"You and your father," he went on.

I wished I could say I was surprised but I wasn't. However, I didn't anticipate Maddon going to the extreme of a bounty this soon. This wasn't good. This meant he'd cottoned on to my plan earlier than I'd thought. He'd need time to plan, time to get the right people in place, time to whisper in the right people's ears I had defected. It wouldn't do for him to put a hit out on the Mediator without reason. I was well liked and trusted. I had been for years. A bounty out of the blue would draw suspicion. And Charlie, his best friend? That widely known relationship would be even more dubious.

"Thank you for that information."

Amani dipped his chin.

"Do you have anything else for me?" he asked.

"He'll hit you from the inside. He doesn't like to get his hands dirty. He knows you're untouchable so he'll find your weak link and set the trap to find himself a rat. My advice is to close ranks to only your most trusted men." I paused and drew in a breath knowing this last piece of information was going to anger a man I had no interest in angering. "The sparrow prototype has a tracking device embedded in the software. Tracking and listening."

A ruddy color tinged Amani's face.

Yup.

Angry.

"CIA?"

"No. Maddon."

Amani nodded. "Out of respect you have one week to handle this situation. After that, I will step in and take care of our problem."

I knew there was no use in arguing.

"That's—"

"That's appreciated," I cut Easton off. "I'll be in touch. Until then, stay safe."

Amani stood.

I followed suit and extended my hand. Amani's eyes dropped to my offering and he frowned. I knew why, I'd never shaken the man's hand before. I never touched him in any way. The truth was, I didn't offer any external signs of respect when I was mediating a situation.

I was neutral.

Switzerland.

Amani finally accepted my hand and squeezed.

"Please be careful, Dove. There are some who would be all too happy to have you taken out. Without you in play, Dutch and his team would have to rebuild. The chaos that would ensue could mean the end of Black."

Good Goddamn it.

I needed Amani to stop talking. He was dangerously close to saying too much.

Not that he knew Zane was behind the Black Team. The face of the team was Dutch, always had been. But Easton and Smith would have questions.

Ones I was never going to answer.

ELEVEN

It was time for answers.

The thirty-minute drive from the apartment we'd met Amani at to our safehouse was tense.

Tense and silent.

I was under no illusion Nebraska was using the silence as a way to digest what Amani had told her. Nope, not The Dove; she was scheming. Using the quiet to come up with her next play. She was smart, cunning, resourceful. She knew she would be drilled as soon as we got to where we were going. She'd sat in the back of the car and made good use of her time.

As soon as Smith closed the door behind us, I went at her. "Who's Badger?"

Her right eye twitched.

She was expecting me to start with Dutch.

"The last person you want to see."

I'd heard something similar to that already.

"Yeah, your dad already gave me that. But who is he and why doesn't Zane like him?"

Nebraska averted her eyes under the pretense she was taking in the small living room.

"Nebraska," I called back her attention. "Badger?"

"Can we sit?" she stalled.

"We can sit. We can stand. We can eat, drink, do fucking handstands for all I care as long as you start talking."

Her eyes whipped back to me and narrowed.

"Not only are you a dick but you're a sarcastic one, too."

Smith chuckled and tossed his backpack on the smaller of the two couches.

There was a lot of furniture shoved into the small area. A two-seater couch, one that sat three, two armchairs, and three stuffed squares I'd heard called poufs. There was also a rectangle table that ate up too much space between the seating selections, meaning anyone over five-foot would have no leg room. None of this furniture matched. The fabric and colors were anything but complementary. At least the white walls didn't add to the dizzying ugliness.

"I can show you my—"

Nebraska's hand came up, palm out in my direction, to stop my threat.

I ignored her hand and Smith's renewed laughter and went on. "I was going to offer to show you just how sarcastic I can be but you went straight to thinking I was offering to show my dick. So, once again, I have to ask—"

Nebraska's cute girl growl cut off the rest of my taunt.

As much fun as it was knocking her off balance, I was more interested in Badger. And why Carver mentioned Dutch. And who Black was.

"If you don't want to talk about Badger you can tell us about Dutch. Or why Maddon thinks the truth will ruin Zane. Or you could explain who Black is."

Nebraska's shoulders stiffened.

Bingo.

"Why would chaos end Black?" Smith joined. "And what would Dutch need to rebuild?"

For the first time since I'd met Nebraska she looked genuinely scared.

Trapped.

Her eyes were her tell. When she was taken off-guard her right eye twitched. When she was backed into a corner they became blank, almost unfocused.

Smith's phone rang, pulling Nebraska from her trance. Stark relief shone in her eyes.

"Zane," Smith muttered.

The reprieve she was hoping for vanished and her whole body went back on alert.

I knew that feeling.

The one where your muscles strain to keep you upright and you mentally brace for the worst.

What was her issue with Zane? He wasn't the friendliest man. He could be a supreme asshole if you rubbed him the wrong way. He was a lot sarcastic, which was one reason we got along so well. And he could be downright lethal if you crossed him. But that didn't explain why Nebraska looked terrified of him.

Unless she'd sold him out and we just didn't know it yet.

Fuck.

"Yo," Smith answered his phone. "You're on speaker with Easton and Nebraska in the room."

Nebraska smirked knowing Smith had included my name only to lessen the sting of warning Zane Nebraska was listening.

Smart woman.

"How'd the meeting go?"

Zane's question wasn't unusual but his tone was all wrong.

It was too professional.

Too guarded.

Smith's head tipped to the side.

He heard it, too.

"Confirmation there's a hit out on Nebraska and Charlie," Smith informed our boss.

"What else?"

What the fuck?

No ill-humored comeback? No off-colored joke?

Something was seriously fucking wrong.

"He warned her to be careful," I jumped in. "Went on to tell her that if something happened to her, Dutch would have to rebuild and that could be the end of Black."

The utter silence was the last straw.

"Who's Black?" I pressed.

Nothing.

"Zane?" I prompted.

But it wasn't my boss who spoke, it was Nebraska and she was holding out her phone.

"It's Maddon."

Goddamn motherfuck.

Was it too much to ask for the fucking truth?

"Answer it," I told her. "On speaker."

I thought I heard Nebraska mumble 'dick' under her breath before she angrily jabbed at the screen. Her insult wasn't the insult she thought it was. My dick took no offense to her frequent mentions. Which meant when she answered the call my mind was filled with all sorts of filthy things I wanted to do to her.

"Maddon," she purred.

Fake as fuck.

"Ah, my Dove. How's Cairo? Busy day, yeah?" Maddon returned the fake sentiment.

"Productive. How's your stay?"

"Same, my dear."

After that neither spoke. Nebraska simply stared at her phone, patiently waiting for Maddon to get to the point of his call.

I glanced from Nebraska to Smith still holding his phone screen up. Zane was still on the line listening. In all of the time I'd worked for the man I'd never known him to be anything other than straightforward and to the point. He didn't prevaricate or evade questions. If he didn't want to answer or didn't want to elaborate or didn't want to talk about something he said that straight. He didn't hide behind niceties, he didn't worry about offending someone. The man was honest and his honesty normally included a hefty dose of impolite, foul words.

Now he was being shifty.

He was hiding something.

The truth will ruin Zane.

Dutch, Badger, or Black.

One of those three held the answer.

My guess was Black was the bomb that would discharge.

However, I couldn't press for answers until Nebraska was done with Maddon.

Finally Maddon broke the annoying silence, "It would seem I was correct."

Nebraska's lips twitched.

It was then it dawned on me, the game she'd played and won. She hadn't filled the void, she'd waited Maddon out, made him lead the conversation, giving her the upper hand. Not only that but it made it so she could hold her cards close to her chest.

Smart.

"About?"

"Viper."

Nebraska's eyes darted to mine, then sliced to the phone in Smith's hand.

"It would seem his desire to keep a woman who is under his protection safe outweighed his long-standing hatred for the Agency."

Maddon's loud laughter came through the speaker sounding forced and ridiculous.

The idiot might've been going for sinister but instead it came across as bad acting.

"You think I'm a fool," Maddon accused.

"I think you are a lot of things, Maddon. However, a fool is not one of them. You knew what you were doing when you sent me to visit Mr. Lewis. You knew what the outcome of that meeting would be. And you knew it would be the distraction you were hoping for."

"You know I had high hopes for you. From the very

beginning you reminded me of your mother. Like you, Pigeon's clever."

I couldn't pull my eyes off Nebraska as she absorbed that blow. And she had yet to recover when Maddon twisted his knife deeper.

"But, unlike you, your mother's willing to do what needs to be done. She doesn't quibble over stupid things like morality. When there's a job to do, she simply does it."

Nebraska might not have been literally bleeding out, but figuratively speaking the woman was hemorrhaging. Her hands trembled, she blinked rapidly, her eyes darted around the room looking for something to focus on.

She caught the present tense.

Good fucking Christ.

I made quick work of getting into her space and when she still hadn't looked at me, my hand went under her chin to force her attention to come to me.

Blue eyes swirled with uncertainty and pain.

I gave her a sharp shake of my head and held her gaze, willing her to regain her strength.

I knew she found it when her shoulders stiffened and she said, "Sorry to disappoint you."

Her words almost came out steady.

But not quite enough for Maddon not to have heard the shakiness.

Seeing as the jackhole knew her well, he pounced. "Oh, dear, that's right. No one's told you."

My hand went from under her chin to cupping the side of her face.

Any doubts I had vanished.

Nebraska had no clue her mother was alive.

None.

And right then, as her world shattered before my very eyes, she was dangerously close to breaking apart.

"Stay strong," I mouthed.

Her nostrils flared. Her eyes widened. Her breath came out in choppy pants.

"It would seem ol' Charlie Buck's got some explainin' to do."

With that the motherfucker disconnected.

"Fucking asshole," Smith growled.

I kept hold of Nebraska's face and her gaze.

"Need answers, Zane," I stated the obvious. "But first I need to see to Nebraska."

"Dove," Zane called out.

She didn't even blink when in a bleak, dead tone she answered, "Yes?"

"You might not get it right now, why people do what they do, especially when they're backed into a corner. But you will. One day, you'll get it and understand that some of the most fucked-up lies told are the ones that are selfless and shrouded in love and protection."

Then Zane disconnected as well.

"Did that sound like a preface to you, too?" Smith asked.

"If by that, you mean him setting the stage to come clean, then yes."

"She's alive?" Nebraska whispered.

Fuck.

My gut felt as hollow as her eyes looked.

"Yeah, baby, she's alive."

She sucked in a sharp breath.

"You..." Nebraska trailed off and stepped back, hitting the back edge of the couch. She grunted, skirted around it, and continued her retreat.

Fuck.

"Nebraska—"

"Pigeon..."

"That's her—"

"I know that name," she hissed. "I've heard it. I've heard stories. I thought she was... I thought... Dove, Pigeon." Nebraska's head shook wildly. "They knew. They all knew."

I wasn't tracking.

"Who's they?"

"Zane, Dutch, and Badger. They had to have known."

Goddamn it.

She was losing it.

Not that I blamed her but fuck, it killed to watch.

"Babe—"

"Charlie," she seethed. "My *father*."

I needed to guide her back to a place of relative calm where I could explain what I knew then hopefully guide her to a place where she could have a conversation with Charlie so he could give her what she needed. When she started pacing I knew she wasn't ready to have any sort of civilized exchange.

"He knew. Maddon knew. My team knew. You knew. Everyone fucking knew. But...*me*," she finished on a shout then continued to yell as she raged, "I was twelve when I went to my mother's funeral. I was twelve when I went to live with a stranger. I was a fucking child and my mother faked her death. Did she want to get rid of me so desperately she *faked her own death—*"

"Stop," I cut in. "You have every right to feel exactly how you feel but you're going down the wrong path."

"Oh, really, I have the right to feel what I'm feeling? Thanks for the permission, asshole." She heaved in a breath. "No shit, I get to feel what I'm feeling. I was twelve when my mother left me with a stranger. I was a child and she gave me to Charlie so she could what? Go live her life without me tying her down? She could go back to being Pigeon without the annoying little—"

"Enough!" I shouted over her. "Don't do that."

"Do what?"

I didn't answer her because I didn't know how to say what I wanted to say without giving her more than she was ready to hear. I also couldn't tell her that hearing her call herself an annoying anything made me want to throat punch her mother for making her feel unwanted, and strangle the life out of Charlie for allowing this to go on for as long as it had without giving something away I didn't fully understand.

But I had to give her something.

"Zane was unaware you didn't know about your mother until Charlie admitted you thought she was dead the night he came to visit."

"You thought I knew and I was playing along with the *fucking lie* so you were keeping that information to yourself until you could use it to your advantage."

Damn, that stung.

"No, none of us were holding onto that information to use against you."

She nodded and pinched her lips, telling me without words she didn't believe me.

"But you thought I knew even though Charlie told you I didn't."

In that moment I wished Nebraska wasn't as smart as she was.

"I wasn't sure," I admitted.

"Right," she grumbled.

"Can you at least understand this is complicated? There're layers and we're all treading cautious? I wasn't going to keep the truth from you for long, but I need to understand the scope of what we're dealing with. Which I'll point out, I still don't understand. But if I'd known Maddon was going to blindside you with that information, I would've told you."

"Right," she grumbled again.

That pissed me off.

"You really think I'm that much of a motherfucker I'd let that piece of shit gut you like that? Jesus, Nebraska, I don't expect you to trust me, but fuck, woman, that's some lowdown shit right there."

She said nothing.

Not that she needed to, the scathing look said it all.

So did her departure.

She thought I was a motherfucker who'd purposely allow Maddon to harm her.

Good to know.

TWELVE

I was on my back in a strange bed and my world was spiraling out of control.

I felt like I'd been on a week-long bender—not that I'd ever actually been on one but I suspected this was what it would feel like. The room was spinning, my stomach was queasy, my muscles hurt, and I was hot all over. In some faraway place in my mind I wondered if this was my body's way of protecting me. If the physical pain I felt was masking the soul-crushing emotional agony I wasn't ready to deal with.

Physical was easier.

Physical I could get over.

But the other stuff, the way I knew my heart was shattering and my soul was crying I wasn't so sure.

Everything had been a lie.

Every. Thing.

Since I was twelve every single day had been a betrayal.

And the one person I trusted and loved had perpetrated the worst of it.

Charlie wasn't my hero.

He was the devil.

A chill slithered down my spine, cooling my overheated skin. Making me simultaneously hot and cold while at the same time making me vibrate with overwhelming rage.

I'd given up everything to be who Charlie encouraged me to be.

He'd molded me after Pigeon.

He'd told me she was the best mediator he'd ever seen.

There wasn't a deal she couldn't swing, a situation she couldn't negotiate, a man who hadn't respected her.

She was magnificent, Nebraska. Calm under pressure, persuasive, fair but tough when she needed to be. But most of all she had an iron will. No one crossed Pidge.

I heard the stories.

What Charlie failed to mention was he was telling me stories about my mother.

The same mother who was alive.

I was going to be sick.

Or cry.

I wasn't sure which.

But I knew I'd rather puke until I passed out than shed a single tear for the assholes who'd betrayed me.

I couldn't break.

Not yet.

Maddon had to be dealt with and now more than ever I was determined he would die by my hand.

I couldn't hold back the first tear and once it escaped the floodgates opened.

There in a room that was not mine, in a country far away from my home, I stared at the ceiling wondering how

I would pick up the pieces of my life as the sting of betrayal leaked out of my soul and ran down my cheeks.

I WAS HOT ALL OVER.

Not just hot, sweltering.

I opened my eyes to a dark room. I immediately knew where I was. And just as immediately I remembered.

Before I could roll away from the heat source I felt strong, calloused fingers wrap around the back of my neck then heard a rumbled, "You okay?"

Easton.

In bed with me.

What in the hell?

With great effort I forced myself to relax.

"Why are you in here?"

The fingers at the back of my neck pulsed.

"Babe," he murmured.

"Is that an answer?"

I laid perfectly still when the bed moved. I stopped breathing when I felt that heat get closer. I fought back a whimper when Easton's forehead gently hit the back of my head.

"I heard you, baby."

I wasn't sure what he heard other than me being a total bitch to him after I found out everyone in my life whom I'd once trusted lied to me. But that didn't explain why he was in bed with me.

"Easton—"

"I heard you crying."

Ohmigod.

My eyelids drifted closed as if by doing that I could block out the mortification.

"The walls are thin," he went on quietly. "Heard you. Waited. Then I couldn't take it and came in here. When I got into bed with you, you quieted."

Okay, that wasn't mortifying, that was mortification times a thousand.

"You had a rough day." He made an easy excuse for my mental breakdown and sobbing fest.

Rough didn't cover finding out you were living a big, fat lie.

But I didn't correct him.

"Tomorrow's gonna be a long day. Try and get some more sleep, yeah?"

Easton was still murmuring softly. If I was in my right mind, and not trapped in the fog of having him so close touching me I would've contemplated his kindness. He was being gentle with me after I'd been nothing but a royal bitch to him since I'd found him in my hotel room. I'd lost count of how many times I'd told him he was a dick or called him an asshole. Yet, there he was in bed with me, offering me comfort as my world shattered apart. He'd heard me crying and came to me *after* I'd been nothing but ugly.

I needed to apologize.

I should've told him I appreciated his kindness but I was fine, and let him off the hook so he could go back to his own bed.

But my voice caught in my throat.

It had been many, many years—so many of them, they

could be measured in decades since I'd felt... well, safe. Not in the physical sense but emotionally. I hadn't been allowed to have an honest, emotional reaction in so long I didn't know what to do with how I was feeling. Nor did I know how to allow myself to feel it.

Since I couldn't speak, I nodded.

Easton's fingers gave my neck another squeeze before his hand slid to the side, down my shoulder, arm, and finally rested on my hip.

I was still in my loose linen pants and cream button-up shirt. My hair was still twisted up into a messy bun though I figured it was now messier than it was when I'd pulled it up that morning. I'd already kicked off the ballet flats I'd worn that day when I first crawled into the bed.

All of that to point out I was fully dressed and I assumed Easton was as well.

Yet, I'd never felt more naked in my whole life.

THIRTEEN

I knew Nebraska was awake before consciousness hit her and she stiffened in my arms. At some point late into the night or early morning depending on how you looked at it, she'd turned, pressed her head into my throat, and cuddled close. That meant right then as she was coming fully awake Nebraska's cheek was resting high on my pec, her right arm trapped between us, her left over my hip, and to round that out my arm was holding her close.

To stop her from rolling away I slid my hand from her hip to her lower back and kept her pinned to me.

"I know you're awake," I told her.

Her already stiff body turned to stone.

"Nebraska?"

Still nothing. No movement. Not even a breath.

"Baby?" I pressed my hand deeper.

Finally she blew out a breath and admitted on a whisper, "I don't know what to say."

She didn't need to say anything for me to feel her pain.

Just like last night, when I could take no more hearing

her whimpers through the thin-ass walls, and crawled into bed next to her I could *feel* the pain. It radiated off her in waves of anguish. It filled the room with thick, noxious poison that made it hard to breathe.

Then and now.

It hadn't diminished—not a fraction of the agony had been shaved off by sleep. Not that I thought a few hours of shuteye would lessen the betrayal.

Apparently she did know what to say. And it was no less excruciating to hear it a second time.

"I went to her funeral."

Jesus fuck.

"I didn't want to go. But my mom's friend, Lori, told me I'd one day regret it—not going. Not saying my goodbyes. So I went with her. Now...I regret it. All of it. Wearing the stupid black dress Lori picked out for me. Sitting through the memorial service at the funeral home. Listening to all of my mom's friends tell stories about how sweet she was, how she'd do anything for anybody, what a great mom she was. I regret sitting there in that front row watching her casket being lowered into the dirt wondering if I'd die if I jumped in after her. Would I die and be back with my mother."

She didn't sound like she regretted attending her mother's funeral, she sounded like she was being tortured by the memory.

Christ.

"I cried for weeks. I couldn't *stop* crying. I had nothing. I wanted nothing more than to never wake up again. I wanted my mom. And it was all a lie..." she trailed off and sucked in a breath. "All of it. Everything. How..." she petered out again, took another breath and restarted. "I've seen a lot of evil. I've sat across from the vilest men on the planet and still I can't wrap my head around their cruelty."

Well, fuck. I had to end that line of thinking but in doing that I risked causing her more pain.

"Can you take more?" I asked.

"More?"

I loosened the pressure on her back but only so I could shift away enough to tip my chin and look at her. Instead of looking up at me, she dipped her head, pressed her forehead deeper, and hid.

I understood that play, not wanting to look at me, so I didn't push when I asked, "Did your mother ever talk to you about your father?"

"My father?"

"Your biological father."

That pain swirling around us, radiating off Nebraska, *suffused* the room. It was so big, so ugly she shook with it.

"Don't tell me, he's alive, too." The thread of anger in her voice was nothing more than a front to cover the hurt.

"It fucks me to tell you this, baby, mostly because I know you're already suffering and adding to that isn't something I feel real great doing. But, you need to know."

"Know what?" she asked before I could figure out a way to soften the next blow.

"There's no way for me to—"

"Just tell me."

Right.

Just tell her.

Slice her open then hope like fuck I have the tools to stop the bleed.

But first I needed to know what she'd been told.

"What do you know about your father?"

"Nothing. He died before I was born. Car accident."

It was coming clear—no one in Nebraska's life told the truth.

Lie after lie then more lies to cover the lies they'd told.

That ended *now*.

Even if the unraveling of the truth was going to slice her to shreds, I'd make goddamn sure she knew it all.

"Your father's name is Dmitri Zenin—"

I got no more out. With a heave, Nebraska pushed away, rolled, and was out of bed on her feet before I could blink.

"Are you fucking kidding me?" she shouted.

Welp. If Smith was still asleep he wasn't now.

I found my feet, hit the light on the bedside table, and when I did Nebraska whirled.

I should've left the room dark.

Just like yesterday she couldn't hide it—not any of it, not the fury, not the hurt, not the confusion.

I now fully understood Charlie Michaels.

Seeing all that I was seeing, I understood not wanting to be the one to witness her ruin. But the man was still a coward. He'd participated in the lie that was her life. He should've found a way many, many years ago to explain everything to her.

He had not.

He let his daughter swing.

The results of that betrayal were right then horrifically playing out in the most catastrophic of ways.

Nebraska didn't look gutted—she looked destroyed.

"Oh my God," she wheezed as she tore her hands

through her hair, ripping the elastic band free. "*Oh my God.*" With the repeat she fisted two handfuls of her thick, shiny brown hair and yanked.

"Nebraska—"

"Two years ago, there was an issue. A new player stepped into the game and was threatening to take over some well-established territory. We kept an eye on the situation hoping we wouldn't have to step in. It was getting ugly, but there were no outside casualties so we waited. Then a restaurant was hit and everyone inside died—the target and ten innocent people including an infant and a three-year-old. That's when we got involved. Charlie was in charge of making the meet. Both organizations agreed to the sit-down. But at the last minute I was pulled and another mediator was sent in my place."

There were a few things to note. The first: Nebraska's tone had completely changed. No threads of pain or anger. She rapped out the information like a briefing. Second, she'd shut her emotions off so completely I wasn't sure if I was impressed she could make the switch that fast or if it was highly concerning she'd flipped so quickly.

"Another mediator?" I inquired. "I thought you were *the* mediator."

"No, there are a few of us."

Now we were back in dangerous territory. The zone in which I was still in the dark, since Zane was being shifty and Nebraska wasn't talking.

"Let me guess. The others are wrapped up with Dutch, Badger, and Black."

At that Nebraska jolted.

Yep, I was on the right track. However, the question

was: did I want to push while she was under emotional upheaval. With anyone else, I wouldn't hesitate. I'd take full advantage of the situation and use the turmoil to get the answers I needed. But with Nebraska it felt wrong to use her vulnerability against her.

"Forget I said that. Why were you replaced?"

Her shoulders lurched back again but with the jerky movement her eyes widened.

"What do you mean forget you said that?" she returned.

"What do you mean, what do I mean?"

Nebraska's head tilted to the right and those wide eyes studied me.

"You have me in a corner. I'm all over the place. I can't keep a straight thought. I'm furious. My loyalty to the people I trusted could be called into question. I'm confused and would likely slip up. Yet you're going to let the opportunity to get the answers you want go?"

That about summed it up.

"Yep."

"Why? You have me where you want me. I'm a freaking mess."

I didn't have her where I wanted her. Though a few minutes ago, when she cuddled into me I certainly had her where I wanted her. No, correction—I had her where I almost wanted her. If I truly had what I wanted she wouldn't have been wearing yesterday's clothes—or any clothes at all while she was curled into me.

"I know you think I'm a dick, but seriously, Nebraska, do you really think I'd play you?"

She seemed to think about her answer before she spoke.

"I don't know... yes? Why wouldn't you?"

Jesus.

"Straight up, it feels like I just had battery acid poured down my throat the way my gut is churning hearing you say that. Not because I've given you reason to trust me but because you've been taught not to trust, and that happened way before you found out the people you loved fucked you over. I'll give you this; if this was an interrogation and I had my target where you are, I'd play them and do it until I wrung every last piece of intel out of them, uncaring I was twisting the knife. But this is not an interrogation. You are not a target. But even if this was and you were I still wouldn't be able to cause you that kind of harm."

It was comical, the look of complete and total confusion on her beautiful face. Comical in the sense it was completely and totally fucked up.

Had no one ever shown her any concern?

Unfortunately she answered my unasked question.

"Charlie sent me to meet with Zane."

Not the worst thing that man had done to her, but not very thoughtful considering Charlie knew Zane would chew her up and spit her out as soon as he got a look at her files.

Then there was the part about Zane having a past with her mother—something Charlie likely knew about. Which meant he'd sent Nebraska down the path of secrets being exposed without preparing her first, and that was fucked up.

"When I texted him after the meeting went bad and told him I was coming to Egypt his response was 'be safe.' Nothing else. Just that."

Another asshole maneuver.

"Since as far back as I can remember, I was taught how to be the mediator. When I was a teenager, the lessons were masked as advice on how to deal with bullies and high school mean girls. But the older I got, the more overt they became. He was molding me into who he wanted. I thought that was me joining the CIA like him. But he quickly disabused that notion. He had bigger plans for me. So you see, I'm nothing more than a pawn in a game that's centuries old. Crime. War. Greed. The game always remains the same, the players just change. With all of that, knowing I'm just a piece to move around the board when I need to be used, why would I think now was any different? That you were any different? Everyone uses me—"

"Please stop."

"Easton—"

"You're breaking my fuckin' heart," I groaned.

Her eyes did something strange. First, they went soft and unfocused, then after she blinked they remained soft but gained clarity. It was like she was seeing me for the first time, the way her stare turned sharp and acute. This wasn't the first or only time I'd noted she was observant, always watching and assessing. But this time it was different. Alert in a way that wasn't so much assessing as it was reflective.

Sadly, if not tragically, the softness vanished when three loud bangs came at the door accompanied by Smith shouting, "We gotta jam, company's inbound."

Fuck a motherfucking duck.

"Nebraska—"

"Later," she returned and sprang into action.

Obviously the woman was no stranger to bolting on a

moment's notice. She had her shoes in hand and was shoving her feet into one of them before I took my first step toward the door. When I got it open I stopped only to warn, "Our conversation's not over."

"Copy."

Clearly, I'd lost her. She was back to all business—mission first. Nebraska was gone, and Dove was back in full force.

As soon as I was out of Nebraska's room Smith was there, his expression a mixture of apologetic that he'd interrupted, and pissed way the fuck off.

"Kira called," he started. "Maddon's been busy."

No shit.

I kept that to myself and instead asked, "What now?"

"His latest cable back to Washington included an aside he was worried Amani Carver had passed the engineering plans of the drone off to Nebraska. His report included pictures of Carver entering the apartment, Nebraska entering, then her exiting."

"Just her?"

"Yes."

It would be impossible to have a shot of just Nebraska. Neither Smith nor I ever left her side.

"He doctored the images to remove us? Why?"

"No clue, brother. Kira's guess is Maddon doesn't want to piss off Zane by dragging us and by extension the company into whatever game he's playing."

Maddon wouldn't give the first fuck about pissing Zane off. First, it was his idea to send Nebraska to Zane, meaning he knew he'd already pissed Zane off. Second, he *wanted*

Zane pissed and playing defense. That was part of his strategy.

"No. He doesn't want any mention of us or Z Corps in the report because someone would see the name, know his connection to POTUS, and alert him. That would give Zane the opportunity to brief POTUS on the entire situation. And if Zane hasn't gone to him yet there's a reason why. But still, it would make Maddon vulnerable to expose Zane's involvement at this point."

Smith dipped his chin.

"I'll call Kira back."

"Who's comin' our way?"

"A GB team."

Good Christ.

That was the worst-case scenario—a team of good guys who'd been told Nebraska was the enemy and we were providing protection on their way to take her in. There would be no talking our way out of the situation, there'd be no reasoning with these men. They had their orders and they'd follow through by any means necessary. That's what they did, they were trigger pullers, door kickers. They wouldn't deviate.

I'd once been one of them, and so had Smith.

"The fucker picked well," Smith finished and peeled off to grab his shit so we could hit the road.

He wasn't wrong.

Maddon's play was a bullseye. He knew damn well neither of us could live with taking out any of the men he'd sent our way to the extreme one of us would sacrifice ourselves to protect a comrade. So, yeah, the fucker had picked well sending his GB team our way.

WE WERE IN THE CAR, Smith behind the wheel, when Nebraska broke her silence. Since I'd left her in the bedroom she'd locked herself away and hadn't spoken. That was twenty minutes ago. And in that time she might not have said a single word but she'd been mulling over something.

I knew I was right when she announced, "I need to call in Badger."

Badger, the last man you see before you meet your maker.

"You don't think *we* can protect you?"

That I can't *protect you?*

"This isn't about protection, Easton," she snapped back. "He needs to be aware Maddon's jumped the gun. I planned for this. I'd bet he's already got word to Langley I met with Amani. He'll make me look like I'm an accomplice. He'll have told his team he wants to interrogate me. They'll follow his orders because that's what they do, not knowing they're being used. I knew he'd play it this way, I just didn't think he'd do it so soon."

"Well, fuck," Smith muttered.

"He contacted Langley," Nebraska rightly surmised.

"Yes. He also sent pictures," I told her. "Though Smith and I were taken out of the images, they just show you walking into Carver's apartment."

"That tracks."

I shifted enough to glance in the back. Nebraska was behind Smith so I had a clear view of her hands clasped in her lap, knuckles white.

Her voice didn't denote the white knuckles.

But she was anxious and doing a damn good job of masking it.

"How does that track?"

"He knows better than to bring Zane into the mix just yet. President Graham might not be to Zane what President Anderson was and contrariwise Graham might not have that bond with Zane that Anderson does. But it's still no secret Zane has Graham's respect, and more importantly his ear. Maddon's not ready to tip the scale."

It was impressive, all of it, how deeply Nebraska understood not only Maddon but the strategies of battle. It was one thing to know a person, their motives, and because of that predict their next move, and seeing the bigger picture —the battlefield as a whole and with that the tactics.

Nebraska saw everything.

"What's he waiting for?" I asked.

"Chaos."

She'd said that before. And this time it was no less helpful than the last.

"What kind of chaos?"

"The kind that sends Zane scrambling."

I'd heard that before, too.

We were back to riddles and word games.

I wasn't a fan.

Nebraska must've read my expression because hers changed.

That meant when she muttered, "I want to tell you but I can't." Her face softened and I almost believed her.

Almost.

"You can—"

"I can't, Easton. This is what Maddon wants. This right here. He put me on this path; it's a no-win for any of us. You want the truth, I can't give it, so you continue not to trust me. I keep you in the dark, you don't have the full scope, it puts you at a disadvantage. The other option is I tell you everything in an attempt to win your trust, prove I trust you and I'm the one who causes the war. Lose-lose for me. Win-win for Maddon."

Yep, she fully grasped tactics.

"War?"

She nodded.

My gaze dropped back to her hands. Her knuckles were no longer white but only because she was now pulsing them together. Anxiety had turned into apprehension.

She was nervous and couldn't hide it.

I turned back, pausing to take in Smith's profile. He was concentrating on the road but his jaw was set to pissed.

Me, too, buddy. Me, too.

FOURTEEN

Eight hours in a car meant you had a lot of time to think. Loads of time to ponder life, regrets, all the things you wished you'd done differently. Tons of time to ruminate over the lie that was my life.

And that was the truth—my whole existence was a lie.

My once beloved mother was alive.

A-*fucking*-live.

There was so much to that it would take more than a scary drive to Luxor to unpack all I was feeling. Compound that bombshell with my father being a notorious Russian enforcer and I was the poster child for screwed. Since I didn't have enough time to process what all that truly meant I did what I'd been taught to do and set it aside. No, I shoved it into a mental box, padlocked that cargo container full of messiness, and buried it behind all the other messy emotions I wasn't ready to deal with.

In exchange I spent the hours fuming. As the minutes ticked by my anger at Charlie grew to an irrational state of wrath with a healthy dose of resentment and bitterness.

He knew.

He knew my mother had faked her death.

He knew why.

He knew she didn't sell insurance like I thought she did. As the story went that was how they first met; she sold a policy for an art collection he'd helped secure for a wealthy buyer. Then as the years went on, they'd become close. Brother-sister close though I always wondered if at some point during their friendship Charlie had fallen in love with her and that was the real reason he'd taken me in. Love made you do stupid shit—Charlie had pounded that into me. He'd said it so often, I'd lost count.

He knew who my father was.

He knew every-freaking-thing and allowed me to mourn a not-so-dead mother for over a decade.

He also told me stories about Pigeon. About a woman who commanded respect. A woman who could outsmart, outplay, outmaneuver anyone. He'd just failed to tell me those stories were about my mother. He failed to tell me he was molding me into her.

For some reason, that betrayal hurt the worst.

It hurt so bad, it twisted in my belly until it formed a ball of hate. And the more I thought about the life lessons, the birthday cakes he bought me, the times he'd watched movies with me, the hugs goodnight, the sadness I saw when he dropped me off at college, the daily phone calls while I was away to keep us connected, that ball grew and grew and grew some more until it was an ugly knot of loathing.

In all of Charlie's teachings he forgot to educate me on one thing—emotional maturity. I was not equipped to deal with this kind of betrayal, not from the one person I loved unconditionally. I didn't have the tools necessary to work through my pain. So I shoved all that was Charlie into a separate box and locked that up as tightly as I could, marking it—*never, ever open*. I mentally penned that with blood.

But it was too late. I'd spent eight hours contemplating my life so the damage was done. I hadn't compartmentalized fast enough.

When you learn how to transmute pain and fear into strength you become unstoppable, Nebraska.

Clearly, I had yet to learn how to do that.

But I was going to.

I was going to use my pain and fear and turn it into strength.

I had no choice.

Then I was going to do what I should've done when Charlie put me forward as the Mediator—run and disappear.

Fuck this life.

Fuck what Charlie wanted for me.

Fuck Maddon.

Fuck Zane Lewis.

I wasn't entirely sure why I was angry with Zane, but as I said I was irrationally irate.

So, it was seriously unfortunate my phone vibrated in my hand at the very moment Smith was unlocking the front door of what was undoubtedly one of Zane's many safehouses—I couldn't know for sure because I hadn't asked. I'd opted to wallow in self-pity rather than ask questions about where we were going, why, and what the plan was.

Unfortunate in the sense when I saw an unknown number on the screen with a Maryland area code I had a gut feeling I knew who it was so I answered.

Unfortunate in the sense I didn't guard my words.

Unfortunate in the sense, in my extreme fury, I was prepared to burn the world to the ground, consequences be damned.

I forwent pleasantries and snapped, "Just the person I wanted to talk to."

"Figured it was time for you and I to have a chat," Zane's deep voice rumbled.

Any other day, I'd take that rumbly tone for what it was —a warning.

Today was not that day.

"I quit," I told him.

"Come again?"

"I. Quit. Effective immediately."

"You can't quit. Seeing as I just found out you're on my payroll I was calling to fire you."

Later, much later, when I had my wits about me, I'd be happy he'd learned I was on his payroll during an emotional drama to end all emotional dramas. For years I'd dreaded the day Zane found out the truth.

Now?

Now I gave two shits less than the zero fucks I gave about him going nuclear at the news.

He could do his worst. There was nothing more he could take from me. I'd already lost it all.

"Great. I accept your termination. Does that mean I'll be receiving a severance package since you have no grounds to fire me since I'm the best mediator Dutch has and the best fixer and the best at going in and getting the job done when the rest of the team can't?"

"Jesus, woman, did you take a single breath—"

"Tell Dutch he can wire my last paycheck into my account and we'll part ways now. Maddon's a freebie. I don't want payment for him."

"Nebraska—"

"Did you know?"

There was a pregnant pause.

I could read the silence. Either he was formulating a response or he was planning my execution for interrupting him.

"I knew Anna was alive. I know her also as Pigeon and throughout the years I've heard Pidge is still working."

My eyes drifted closed.

I didn't startle when I felt a hand on my lower back. I didn't stop myself from being pushed into the house. I didn't open my eyes again until I heard the door close. I didn't take in my surroundings.

I was too busy using up the rest of my strength to stay upright.

"Though, I didn't know you'd been led to believe she was dead until Charlie told me and Dutch confirmed."

Red hot fury washed over me.

"So, Dutch did know?"

Another name to scratch onto my People I Hate list.

"He did," Zane confirmed. "He had his reasons for keeping that secret. Reasons I'll let him explain. I can't say he made the right call but he had his reasons, and, Nebraska, those reasons were to protect you."

No they weren't.

They were to control me.

"Whatever," I snarled. "I have no interest in listening to more bullshit lies. I'm done. Out. No more. Dutch can take his reasons and shove them up his—"

"I'm not positive, I've never asked, but Dutch doesn't strike me as the kind of man who enjoys things forcefully shoved up his ass."

Even though Zane was over six-thousand miles away and couldn't see me my eyes still narrowed.

"You think this is funny?"

"No, Nebraska, there's not a damn thing funny about the way you've been treated. There's not one fucking thing funny about those who were supposed to protect and love you betraying you the way they have. I've met your mother. She's wicked smart, cunning, calculating, a master of her craft. She fucked me and Dutch, fucked our op, and landed us in jail. Yet I still cannot believe she has it in her to leave you unless she had no choice. Why no one told you when you were old enough to process and keep the secret, I don't get. Especially because you're in the life, you do the work you do and Pidge does what she does. How you haven't found out before now is a miracle. I'm not happy Dutch kept you from me, but I understand why he did. I would've cut you loose. No way in fuck would I have allowed Agency ties, even loose ones, to infiltrate Black."

He abruptly stopped speaking so I took my opportunity to remind him.

"No need to worry about those ties anymore. I'm gone."

"I don't accept your resignation."

Was he nuts?

"You fired me," I spat.

I heard an exasperated grunt come from beside me. When I glanced over, I saw Easton was much closer than I thought he was.

Damn, he was a good-looking man.

But furious... he was hot.

Another reason to hate Charlie.

He'd taken away my choices. He'd forced me to live in a world where Easton Spears wasn't an option.

Easton verbalized his grunted annoyance by growling, "What the fuck?"

Oops.

Shit.

"I can't deal with you right now, Easton Spears." I underlined this by putting my hand up in his direction. "Take your growly hotness somewhere else."

Two things happened at once. No, correction, three: Smith busted out laughing, Easton blinked—rapidly—but most confusing and frankly scary, Zane grunted.

"Not this again. Tell Easton since I sign your paychecks, I'm the boss of you."

The boss of me.

No one ever again would be the boss of me.

"I'm not telling him that and you don't sign my paychecks, your accountant wires me money. And you *fired* me. So really, after my separation package—which I expect to have a big, fat, hefty pain and suffering bonus included— you won't be paying me at all. And just to point out, you've never been my boss."

"I'm everyone's boss," he returned, sounding like he believed he was on the top of the pyramidal hierarchy of the world. I was proven correct when he finished with, "Think of me as the Big Boss."

I didn't get a chance to reiterate to the egomaniac he was not my boss, technically Dutch was, but he wasn't that anymore since I'd quit-fired. I quit while at the same time Zane fired me hence the *quit-fired*. Though, I was taking the termination and the separation package and I was moving to some small Greek island where there was no phone service or internet and living out the rest of my days in peace. That was if some unconnected island existed in this day and age. If it didn't, I would find myself a small seaside cottage and wouldn't connect either service. Neither would I purchase a car. I would buy a bicycle with a white basket on the handlebars and purple tassels hanging from the grips and pedal everywhere.

Peace.

Yes, that was what I needed. Total isolation. Maybe then I could unbox all the emotional trauma. Or maybe not. Maybe I'd just leave it all where it was and pretend I'd lived a perfect, charmed life and living the rest of my days on a Greek island was the spoils of such a life. I hadn't decided yet but I was leaning toward the latter.

My musing was cut short when I realized I was no longer holding my phone to my ear. Easton had confiscated it.

He tapped the screen a few times then announced, "You're on speaker."

Zane wasted no time—as in he launched straight to the point without preamble.

"Last night I found out that for the last three years,

along with her freelance work, Nebraska has been employed by Z Corps."

Easton pinned me with a scorching look.

I pinched my lips.

"How is it possible you didn't know she was an employee?"

No, *now* Zane got to point, or actually to the meat of the confession I wasn't sure he was ready to reveal.

With a long-suffering sigh that wasn't so much suffering as it was highly annoyed, Zane went on.

"I've been keeping something from the team."

Since I was staring at Easton, I saw it happen in real time. The way his shoulders drew up, the way his back straightened, the tightness that suffused his body.

Shit.

This was going to be bad.

Really bad.

I didn't think. No, I didn't have to think, I knew now was not the right time to share.

"I don't think—"

"It's time, Nebraska. The truth's out, they all need to know."

Easton's gaze turned into a glare.

When I could take no more I closed my eyes.

And waited...

FIFTEEN

"It's time, Nebraska. The truth's out, they all need to know."

Nebraska looked like she was ready to come out of her skin.

And when her eyes closed, Zane's warning hit me square in my chest.

Don't let those pretty blue eyes and all that soft you think you see under her hard exterior fool you. She's a fixer, same as her mother. She'll sell her services to the highest bidder. Women like that have no loyalty. And right now, she holds more power than I'm comfortable with.

All that soft you think you see under her hard exterior fooled you.

I'm just a piece to move around the board when I need to be used.

I'd fallen straight into her trap.

Everyone uses me.

I should've pushed for answers when I had the chance,

but I'd fallen for her shit. I'd backed off when I should've gone hard to get the truth from her.

I would not make that mistake again.

"Tell me, Nebraska, that shit you spewed in the car—"

"Easton," Smith interrupted. "Patience."

Nebraska's eyes snapped open.

Fuck patience.

"What shit?"

Smith stepped between me and Nebraska, which was to say he came chest-to-chest, eye-to-eye with me and lowered his voice to say, "Think carefully about the next words that come out of your mouth, brother. Sometimes there are things that can't be unheard or forgiven. We haven't heard what Z has to say."

I bit the inside of my cheek to stop myself from lashing out at my friend. He'd know a thing or two about saying shit in anger you couldn't unsay. Shit that was unforgivable no matter how much you loved the other person. But this was nowhere near the same situation. Nebraska wasn't my fiancée. I didn't claim to love her and I certainly hadn't made any promises to her.

But he was right. We hadn't heard what Z had to say, and right then, the mission was more important than my pride being stung and my feelings being hurt. The last bore contemplation. How in the fuck could a woman I barely knew hurt my feelings and why in the hell would her not telling me she worked for...

"*Black*," I ground out.

Smith's brow winged up before the same realization I'd just had hit.

Zane obviously heard.

"Haiti was a learning experience," Z started. "For me more than for Dutch. He'd been in longer, he understood the game, he'd long since stopped looking for the good. The missions we went on, the people we dealt with both in the field and the assholes who sat behind a desk, everything was bad or worse."

Once Zane had started speaking Smith had stepped away—not far but away enough I now had eyes on Nebraska. She no longer looked anxious, nor did she look like she was paying attention to the conversation—all of her concentration was homed in on shooting daggers at me.

Ten minutes ago, before I heard her rant, I would've been concerned at her worry. Now, not so much. She could stare at me all she wanted.

"But it was the next op that killed whatever belief in justice I had left. True justice, not this bullshit we think is justice."

"What was the op?" Smith asked.

"Africa. UNICEF aid was being hijacked. The suits knew who was seizing the packages. Dutch and I were sent in to negotiate a deal. In other words, we were sent in to hand over large sums of cash to a warlord to buy safe passage of food, water, and meds. The deal was done. The next UNICEF delivery was hijacked. The warlord had gone back on his word. The suits' brilliant plan was to hand over more cash and ask again. Dutch pitched another plan —take out the warlord and call it a day. But the problem is, that doesn't solve shit. Take out one and five more are ready to take their place. The merry-go-round continues. Shit needed to change. So we found a way to change it and Black Team was formed."

Black Team.

"How does that work and where do they fit with Red, Gold, and Blue?" Smith carried on.

The three flagship teams until me, Theo, Smith, Jonas, Cash, Kira, and Layla came to work for Z Corps and Silver Team was formed.

"Until last night, no one but Lincoln and my wife knew Black existed."

There it was, the truth.

Zane had a team no one knew about.

"This is the secret you said would cause a war?" I asked, not understanding the drama.

Nebraska's stare became acute and assessing when she addressed Zane. "How pleased are you right now you were forced to divulge something you weren't ready to reveal?"

"Murderous."

She nodded like she knew that would be the answer.

"And how pleased are Red, Gold, and Blue you've been keeping this secret from them?"

"Pretty fucking unhappy," he grunted.

Another nod.

"That was what Maddon wanted. Disorder within the teams. Dissention. Suspicion. Men distrusting their leader, because if he didn't tell them about Black what else isn't he telling them? It is no secret when Viper feels threatened he strikes. Maddon's hope is, with Zane's company in turmoil and no one there to talk him down, Zane will act out of emotion and activate Black. Dutch will follow orders, Badger will back that play because he's been jonesing to take out Maddon for months. Three powerful men, reacting instead of planning. That's chaos. That will lead to someone getting killed."

She paused, brought her hands to her hips, and shook her head.

"Maddon sent a GB team to take me in. Now imagine Black in that same situation, having to take out a good guy to protect themselves, to protect me or Zane or you. They'd do it. Their loyalty is with Black. But they'd die a thousand deaths and have to live knowing they took out a good man, who was just misguided."

Fuck.

She wasn't wrong about any of that.

"More chaos. More reacting. The war Zane would wage would be bloody. There would be no winner, just a bunch of good men dead for no fucking reason."

"And you?" Smith rejoined. "Where do you fit in?"

"I'm inconsequential—"

"That's a lie," I cut in. "It seems to me, all of this revolves around you."

"Does it, Easton, does it all seem to revolve around me? Because where I'm standing it looks a hell of a lot..." she trailed off, her head jerked to the side, and she got a faraway look in her eyes.

I glanced at Smith. He was studying Nebraska, eyes narrowed, looking just as perplexed as I was.

"Looks a hell of a lot like what?" I prompted.

"Where's Badger?" she asked instead of answering.

"Hunting."

Nebraska was rapidly shaking her head at Zane's announcement. There wasn't that much room separating us in the small living room but whatever space there was she quickly closed and stopped right in front of me.

"Call him home," Nebraska demanded as she reached up and curled her hand around my bicep. The hand curl was an unconscious reaction to whatever had her so scared.

"As you're well aware, that's not my call," Zane returned. His tone clearly communicated even if it was his call he wouldn't make it.

Nebraska might've been aware, however I was not.

"Why isn't that your call?"

"Black Team might fall under the umbrella of Z Corps' protection but it is not my team, it's Dutch's. As you're very aware it's his team, his call."

Nebraska's fingers dug into muscle, her grip getting tighter and tighter as she continued to shake her head.

"Dutch will listen to you," she disagreed. "You know he will. You're his moral compass."

Well, fuck. If Zane Lewis was this Dutch dude's moral compass we were all fucked. Not that Zane didn't have one, he did—his pointed *true* North. The problem with that was Zane's North tended to be other people's South. Zane didn't have moral dilemmas; the code he lived by didn't allow for such things. There was honor, integrity, and loyalty. When you lived by those principles there were no dilemmas.

"Dutch is—"

"He's playing into Maddon's hands," she interrupted Zane in a panic. "He'll be ready for Badger. He'll hide behind—"

"Do you know what your problem is?" Zane calmly cut in.

My arm jerked with Nebraska when she rocked back clearly unprepared for Z's question. "In all this shit those two assholes taught you, they left out the most important lesson. They groomed you to be the best Mediator, the fixer they needed. I can't say they didn't do a damn good job leading you to home in the skills your mother passed down to you. You are the best Mediator the Black Team has. You earned the respect of powerful people. You were fair in your negotiations. You're fucking smart as hell and you see the field clearly. You understand the board, and move your pieces accordingly. It's impressive. But you lack two skills and I suspect it's because they lied to you and told you they were weaknesses. Trust and family."

Nebraska looked like Zane had slapped her and in doing so she swayed back. I twisted my arm from her grasp in order to reach out and reverse our positions. Now I was holding her steady. Which turned out to be the right call since Zane wasn't done with her yet.

"Maddon's play didn't work. It never would've worked because nowhere in that fucked-up head of his does he truly grasp loyalty, trust, and family. He thinks loyalty is something you buy instead of earn. He thinks trust is a vulnerability. He thinks family is a liability. A man like him will never understand without those three things you have nothing. Sure my *family* was pissed at me. I lied to them and I've been doing it from the beginning. But they know me down to my soul because I trust them, *explicitly*, and have given them every reason to trust me. It took less than an hour of them giving me shit to burn themselves out and come to the conclusion I had my reasons for not sharing. That's done. We're moving on. That's what family does.

And there's the fatal flaw in Maddon's play. He has no fucking concept of family. Let that be a lesson to you, Dove, before it becomes your greatest failure. Without family, trust, and loyalty you've fucking lost."

Zane's aim was true. Every word he'd said was a bullseye.

I wasn't sure lecturing her about family and trust when the sting of betrayal was still fresh was the way to go, but in true Zane fashion, when he had a point to make, he made it.

"The lesson you need to learn and learn really fucking fast is family isn't perfect. Sometimes what was meant to protect, hurts. Sometimes decisions are made for the right reasons even though from the outside they look wrong. Sometimes you have to trust what you know rather than what you feel. Sometimes you have to go with a gut feeling when all your intel is showing you something different. You're correct in your thinking. Maddon wants chaos. He needs it for his plan to work. But you were wrong in your assessment. I'm not the chaos, Dove. You are."

Since I was still holding Nebraska's phone I couldn't stop her from stumbling back. Smith saw her start to go down, took the phone I was holding out to him, and did it quickly so I could use both hands to pull Nebraska to my chest and keep her upright.

It was then Zane delivered his final blow.

"Badger's not headed Maddon's way. He's out looking for Pidge."

Nebraska's reaction was so violent my body jolted with hers. With her tight against me, I heard her swift intake of air. Though if I was standing across the room from her I wouldn't have been able to miss it—I knew this to be fact when Smith didn't miss the sucking in of breath or whimper she made doing so. His face went hard—harder still when he watched her burrow so close. Just like she'd done when she'd woken up, only this time it felt like she wanted me to absorb her.

She'd either missed her calling as an Academy Award winning actor or her performance wasn't a performance and the pain she was feeling had once again overwhelmed her. There was no other excuse as to why she'd seek me out unless what she was feeling was so huge she didn't have it in her to beat it back alone.

I was leaning toward the second.

If she was acting, I needed to quit my job.

SIXTEEN

It was official, I could take no more.

The man I grew up thinking of as an uncle turned out to be nothing short of a bastard who was plotting a terrorist attack with the Chinese. The man who'd raised me had been lying to me since the day I'd met him. The man who'd donated his DNA to make me was a well-known Russian enforcer. The mother I'd mourned for two decades was really alive and had abandoned me.

If that wasn't enough, I'd screwed up. Not just a little screw-up—not that there was such a thing in my line of work but on a scale of one to ten I'd *royally* fucked up. I'd miscalculated. I hadn't considered I was the pawn until Zane pointed it out.

Then to round out the suckage of my life, Easton was witnessing my downfall. That should've been the least of my worries, however for some reason it mattered *way* more than it should. A lot more than it should, so much so I couldn't stop thinking about it when I should've been focused on Maddon and how I'd misjudged his plan. Or how Dutch had sent Badger out to find my mother. That last was a hit to my heart.

Badger would find her; then what?

Another mental breakdown?

Would Easton be there to see that, too?

Would he hold me through it like he did last night?

Did I want him to?

More than my next breath.

And speaking of breath, I felt a pair of strong arms that were already tight around my middle, squeeze. I forced in a lungful of air and mentally came back to the room.

"Babe," Easton called.

Damn, I really liked when he called me 'babe.' I wasn't so delusional I didn't know that for a man like Easton it was nothing more than a throwaway name, not an endearment. But still, no one had ever called me that, or baby. He'd called me both. I liked 'babe' but when he called me 'baby' it did crazy things to my insides.

"Hey," he called out again.

"Huh?"

His arms loosened, his back arched so he could dip his chin, mine tipped back, and when it did I caught his eyes.

Realization hit full force. Easton holding me, how close we were, how natural it felt to go to him, to reach out and touch him when I needed strength.

"Did you hear Zane?" he carefully asked.

Shit, I'd totally zoned out.

I shook my head.

"We're headed back to the US."

I glanced to one side, then the other, to find Smith missing from the room.

Damn, I'd seriously zoned out.

"Why?"

"Regroup."

Right. Regroup. That made sense.

Disorganization is the same as defeat, Nebraska. Never go in unprepared.

I could go to Florida, or better yet go to Wyoming to The Ranch outside of Evanston. Connect with Dutch, give him a piece of my mind, and regroup there. Maddon wanted my thoughts and emotions muddled. He needed me confused and in pain. The more disoriented and distracted I was the better.

"When do we leave?"

"Tomorrow morning."

I nodded and tried to step back—the tried part of my attempt was denied. Easton held tight while he stared down at me. I wasn't short, neither was I tall. It was just that he had inches on me, at least six of them. I wasn't going to think about how much I liked the height difference, how safe I felt with his arms around me, how I'd have to roll up on my toes to touch my mouth to his, how he could tuck me under his arm and how I'd fit perfectly there.

Nope.

I wasn't thinking about any of that.

Further from that I wasn't thinking about how much I'd miss him when we parted ways. I was blocking that out because it was crazy.

"Are you hungry?"

"Hungry?"

"Two protein bars and a sticky bun from an ENOC station isn't enough to sustain life."

"Says who?"

I wasn't so far gone in my seriously shitty situation I missed the way Easton's lips twitched. Actually my awareness of his nearness was so acute I *couldn't* miss the way those kissable, full lips, surrounded with a few days of stubble, tipped into a panty-melting grin.

"Says me."

"I'll have you know finding a sticky bun at a petrol station in the middle of Egypt was a once in a lifetime find."

His smile widened, ratcheting up the hotness quotient tenfold.

"So I bought three," I continued.

"I know, I was there."

And he was there, right by my side. He hadn't let me go into the station without him. He'd also stood outside the bathroom door the four times we'd stopped to gas up and use the restroom.

"I only ate one."

"Right. So what you're saying is your dinner is going to be two sugar rolls."

"Two gooey rolls, drenched in brown sugar with pecan bits," I corrected. "Yummy goodness that undoubtedly will give me a stomachache but it'll be worth it."

"How about I feed you something that won't give you a stomachache?"

I used another mental stop sign and blocked that out, too.

I wasn't going to process how much I liked him wanting to feed me. Neither was I going to expend the energy of trying to remember the last time someone cared enough to make sure I ate.

Something so small—silly really—yet at the same time huge. At least for someone like me, who'd never had anyone give a shit if I was taking care of myself.

"Fun fact about me, I don't eat MREs."

Another twitch of his lips.

God, he was killing me.

"Can't say I blame you, they suck."

"So I'll pass and stick with my—"

"Yummy goodness," he finished for me.

Okay, now he was just twisting the knife in my heart.

Hot then cold.

Jerk then kind.

One minute he made it clear he didn't like me, the next he was being sweet.

In all fairness, that hot and cold ran both ways and I had yet to apologize for the name-calling.

"Listen, Easton, before we part ways I need—"

"Part ways?"

"You said we were going back," I reminded him.

"We are. You're coming with me."

"Yeah, I know back to the US. Then parting ways. Regrouping."

His head tipped to the side at the same time his eyes narrowed.

"I didn't say anything about parting ways. You're coming with us back to Annapolis."

Oh no.

That wasn't good.

I needed to get away from Easton before I did something really dumb and got more attached to him than I already was. Not to mention, I was a coward and didn't want to face the rest of Z Corps.

I shook my head but didn't get a chance to speak before Easton continued. "You're coming with us. That's non-negotiable."

Not this again.

"Non-negotiable? What, are you going to count to ten and threaten to throw me over your shoulder again?"

"I don't know, are you going to threaten to fondle my dick again?"

Now I was remembering why I hadn't apologized for the name-calling.

The man was infuriating.

"I didn't threaten to fondle. I threatened to *punch* you in your dick."

"Same thing." He shrugged.

It was nowhere near the same thing.

The smug grin he sported made my next question rhetorical.

"Are you enjoying this?"

Yet he still answered, "Not as much as I'd enjoy—"

"*Asshole*," I hissed and turned on my heel to find a bathroom so I could shower off the eight-hour drive and the news that Badger was out there somewhere looking for my long-lost-still-alive-mother.

"You wanna change it up and play it that way, I'm game."

For my sanity I kept my retort to myself.

It wasn't until I was in the shower alone that I smiled.

As irritating as Easton was, I couldn't deny I liked the banter.

Another reason it was time to cut ties and retreat back to The Ranch.

Easton was the distraction I couldn't afford. The man was lethal. He would be the diversion that killed my mission.

SEVENTEEN

Smith appeared in the kitchen, hair still wet from his shower, face set to contemplative.

"You good?" I asked as I flipped the grilled cheese I was making for Nebraska and finished by waving the spatula in the direction of his food. "Yours are on the plate."

"I was coming in here to ask you that."

By the time I looked up from the pan, Smith had already stuffed his face with grilled cheese. "Who hooked us up with real cheese?" he asked around a mouthful.

"Probably Ivy. Kira's idea of cheese is that block of soft yellowish shit she melts."

Smith nodded and took another bite.

I went back to the pan.

"Silence. That's telling," he taunted.

I would much rather talk about Kira's fake cheese preference than try to put what I was feeling into words.

"I'm not pissed at Zane," I told him. "If he kept Black a secret he had his reasons."

"Agreed. But that's not what I'm talking about and you know it."

Fucking Smith.

He never let shit go.

"There's nothing to say," I evaded.

"That's bullshit."

I dumped the sandwich on a plate and gave Smith my full attention.

"What do you want me to say? She confuses the fuck out of me. I don't trust her yet I can't stop myself from wanting to get close. Her attitude drives me around the bend. She's smart as fuck yet dangerously vulnerable and I can't stop myself from wanting to shield her from all the shit swirling around her. Part of me wants to tie her ass up and take her away from all of this and not let her free until you and the team take out Maddon. The other part of me wants to watch her take him down. She impresses me and pisses me off, both of those at the same time. The way she shuts down makes me insane but when she opens up and gives me a glimpse of the real her I want to protect her with my life. I've never met a woman I wanted to run from, yet when she said something about parting ways my gut clenched to the point of pain. So with all of that, brother, I'm at a loss. There's nothing to say because there's nothing to be done."

"Nothing to be done?"

"Did you miss the part about me not trusting her or about how crazy she makes me?"

Smith's response was to smile.

I shook my head thankful the conversation was over and grabbed Nebraska's plate.

"I didn't miss shit, brother. Certainly not the part about her driving you crazy. Your problem is you're ignoring the important parts."

It was official. I was seriously fucking over riddles. From vague answers from Nebraska to Zane acting like a shifty bastard. Now that the big secret was out I'd hoped the ambiguity would no longer be a factor. However, it would seem it was Smith's turn.

"And what are the important parts?"

"Maybe she drives you crazy because you're crazy about her."

"Yeah, Smith, she's crazy, she drives me crazy, and I'm crazy for liking it. That's too much crazy."

The idiot just smiled.

"You know another word for crazy?" he pressed.

I knew a lot of other words for crazy but the two I would use at that very moment were—*this conversation.* That's what was crazy. I was participating in this insane conversation. And not only that but my participation was encouraging Smith to continue.

When I didn't answer in hopes he'd lose interest he answered his own question.

"Passion."

Yep.

He was crazy, too.

"And when that shit finally explodes all over the place, you'll get it."

"Get what?" I stupidly asked.

"The reason she drives you crazy. The reason why you took one look at her and agreed to help Charlie even though you had no clue what you were agreeing to. I wasn't there, but the way Theo tells it, you were all-in at first sight. However, I was there when you found out I'd seen her in Brazil. I was also there when Zane kicked her out of the office and I was there when you got back and I was there in your living room when Charlie admitted he'd kept Anna a secret from her. And finally, I've been with you and her the last few days. I haven't missed a single reaction you've had to her because there's no way to miss them. You're so wrapped up in her you can't see straight, which means it's going to take you being knocked on your ass for you wake the fuck up and open your eyes. In the meantime you have one objective—keep that trap of yours shut and don't say something stupid you can't take back."

That was the second time he'd given me that warning. The second time he looked sucker-punched while giving it. I knew the story, we all did, but that didn't mean Smith liked talking about it or about *her*. As a matter of fact I'd only ever heard him say her name once. After that he'd referred to her as 'she' or 'her.' Which in my opinion meant he wasn't over what she said to him.

"Brother—"

"We're not talking about *her*."

He spat the word 'her' like it tasted foul.

Nope. Not over her.

"Maybe we should."

The atmosphere in the kitchen changed. I couldn't say it went subzero but it sure as fuck got frosty.

"Sure," he mock-agreed. "As soon as you pull your head out of your ass about Nebraska we'll talk."

With that, he nabbed his plate with two more sand- wiches on it and brushed past me.

"One more thing," I called out. "In Brazil, what was she like?"

The fucker turned and smirked.

"Didn't talk to her. Watched a guard let her into the prison. Just walked right in like she owned the place. The guard peeled off so I followed her. She found her target, moved in behind him, and sliced his throat. Clean and methodical. She didn't make a peep, didn't flinch, didn't delay making her exit. In and out and that was it—she was gone."

Smith didn't say it but he didn't have to. Not only because I knew him well but also because he didn't hide it —he was impressed.

Wet work was a far cry from taking out a target from a distance. It was up close and personal and took a certain disposition to stomach it.

"So, good call making sandwiches. I wouldn't make her anything that requires utensils until after the two of you have worked your shit out."

With another smile he took his plate into the bedroom he'd claimed and shut the door behind him. It took a minute for me to get my shit together enough to move. My contemplation had nothing to do with my teammate's concern for my safety and everything to do with his warning.

Sometimes you have to go with a gut feeling when all your intel is showing you something different.

My gut was telling me not to let her get away.

My gut was telling me I needed an explosion to happen so I could break through.

I just hoped that breakthrough didn't break her.

On that thought, I walked across the poor excuse for a living room to the door.

The door that separated me from the woman who drove me crazy.

I didn't bother knocking.

My excuse—I was pleading insanity.

As soon as the door opened, Nebraska whirled and pinned me with a semi-dirty look.

"Why am I not surprised?" she asked.

"That I couldn't allow your only source of nutritional intake to be a sugar snack?" I quipped. I held out the plate as an offering.

Her gaze dropped to the plate. Mine dropped to her bare legs that unfortunately were not on offer. They were bare because she only wore a t-shirt that barely covered her underwear. And suddenly I really wanted to know if she was wearing another pair of ugly-assed cotton undies or if she'd switched to something...who the hell was I kidding? Ugly or not I didn't give the first fuck about her underwear. They could be lime green with toucans on them and I'd still want to peel them off—with my teeth.

"You made me dinner?"

She no longer sounded combative but instead perplexed. And since she hadn't stopped staring at the plate I'd say perplexed was an understatement.

"Not sure grilled cheese is considered dinner once you're over the age of five, but yeah, I made you something to eat."

Finally her eyes lifted and I wasn't sure how I'd missed it. She wasn't beautiful, she was fucking gorgeous. It wasn't just one of her attributes that made her physically attractive, it was Nebraska as a whole. Mind, body, soul—she was nothing short of stunning.

Nebraska wasn't a woman you won. You had to earn her love and trust. She'd put a man through his paces, she'd make it difficult, she'd fight and slice you to shreds, and take you to task before she found you worthy.

I'd once won a woman, I'd never earned one. I'd never had to work to prove I was good enough. I'd never found a woman who was worth the effort, worth the pain and struggle.

Correction: I'd never found a woman worth the effort *until* Nebraska.

I had a feeling Smith was wrong. There wouldn't be an explosion; but one way or another the woman was going to annihilate me. And the fuck of it was she wouldn't do it on purpose. She'd break me like she was right then with the look of shock on her pretty face—over a sandwich.

"Nebraska—"

"You made me a sandwich?" she whispered.

Yep.

The woman was killing me.

"Baby—"

"I've been a pain in your ass and you made me dinner."

This wasn't about her being a pain in the ass or about dinner.

"Never," she went on whispering.

When she didn't go on I prompted, "Never what?"

She shook her head so hard her hair shook with her movements.

"Nothing."

"Don't do that," I gritted out.

"Do what?"

"Give me something then take it away."

She blinked then asked, "What'd I give you?"

"*You*, Nebraska. You keep giving me bits and pieces of you then you take them away."

Her eyes slowly lowered and her head tipped forward.

Yeah, she was going to destroy me.

And it wouldn't be words that shredded me, it would be the knowledge no one had ever loved this woman the way she deserved.

EIGHTEEN

I couldn't breathe.

I wasn't sure if I was holding my breath or if all the oxygen in the room had magically evaporated.

My head was filled with strange, if not unpleasant thoughts.

A sandwich.

My lungs burned and my heart felt funny because of a sandwich.

That was a lie.

My lungs burned because Easton had stolen my breath.

Don't do that.

Do what?

Give me something then take it away.

What'd I give you?

You, Nebraska. You keep giving me bits and pieces of you then you take them away.

My heart felt funny because I couldn't remember ever feeling...*this*. I couldn't find the right words to describe what *this* was. Mostly because I'd never felt something so contradictory—cared for but unloved.

It was too much. I didn't know what to do with it all. The emotions too big, too scary, too intense. I wanted to run away while simultaneously throwing myself at Easton.

My thoughts were all over the place.

Scattered. Jumbled. Messy.

I didn't know how to fix this. I'd been taught from a very young age how to prioritize my thoughts. Arrange them in logical steps. According to Charlie, order was paramount.

But how was I supposed to organize thoughts that were flitting in and out of my mind—one flew in and darted out, and on its heels another flashed in.

My life no longer made sense.

My emotions were up and down.

My mind all over the place.

One thing was for certain; prolonged exposure to Easton Spears was bad for my mental health.

I felt a hand cup my cheek.

Calloused. Work-rough. Hard.

At the feel of it my eyes shot open.

And there he was, up close and in my personal space. His blue eyes, shades darker than mine, zeroed in then locked onto mine.

It wasn't the sandwich, it was what it represented. It was what his eyes were right then confirming.

Care.

Concern.

Thoughtfulness.

"Hey," he whispered.

I opened my mouth, but when no words formed I clamped it closed, my teeth catching on my bottom lip. His gaze dropped but only for a moment and when I got his eyes back I could only define them as stormy.

Yikes.

A minute. Five. An hour. I didn't know how long we stared at each other. I didn't know why or how it happened, only that it was me who pounced.

Suddenly my lips were on his and I was kissing him.

Easton went stiff.

His hand convulsed on my cheek.

Just as mortification started to set in, his palm slid into my hair, his fingers tangled in my damp strands, his other hand went around my waist, and he *kissed* me.

There was a distinction.

My kiss had been clumsy.

His was anything but clumsy.

It was deliciously demanding.

So delicious I lost what was left of my mind. No thoughts could possibly penetrate. All I could do was *feel*— the way his tongue demanded entry, (which I gladly gave) the way his hand held me exactly where he wanted me, (which, I happily stayed) but mostly I felt his hard body pressed against mine (which I seriously liked).

It didn't take long for this kiss to turn. That turn was for the better because it now included Easton's hand on my ass not only squeezing but pulling me closer, which had the glorious side effect of pressing his erection into my belly. I remembered I had hands and so I put those hands to good use. One snaked around his back and roamed, the other went to his chest and explored.

And that was all it took.

I needed more.

Unfortunately I didn't know how to communicate this. A frustrated groan slipped free when I couldn't maneuver my hand down the back of his pants (stupid belt). Thankfully that was all Easton needed. His hand left my hair and went between us. I felt him working there, then I heard the belt slide through the loops of his cargos. A moment later my hand slid in and I made the wonderful discovery he went commando. The belt move was hot and as much as I would've liked to have watched, I was more than happy to sacrifice the sight to keep his mouth on mine.

I had approximately three seconds to revel in the perfectness of his muscled ass—though in fairness, time meant nothing so I might've had more—when he broke the kiss.

No.

My eyes popped open, and the second they did my pussy spasmed.

Never, *ever*, ever had a man looked at me the way Easton did. Never, *ever*, ever had I seen desperation and desire swirl together into a cocktail of need.

Easton was the most beautiful man I'd ever clapped eyes on. When he was being annoying he was hot (that didn't bode well for me). When he was angry he was hotter (sucks, but that's the truth). But right then, looking at me the way he was after that kiss, the hotness factor ratcheted up straight to stratospheric.

This time I didn't pounce, I attacked.

My hands went to his shirt. I tugged it out of his cargos and yanked it up. Thankfully he helped in this endeavor, pulling it the rest of the way off and tossing it to the side. My shirt was next. He divested me of it, and as soon as it cleared my arms I went at him. My arms went around his shoulders, and when I found purchase, I hoisted myself up. My legs circled his hips and my lips found his.

If the first kiss was demanding and measured, this one was wild. Clearly whatever control Easton had left snapped. With his tongue in my mouth, his hands on my ass, the tips of his fingers gliding over the gusset of my panties, I'd gone back to mindless. I was so into our kiss I whimpered when his mouth left mine.

Then I was whimpering for an altogether different reason when he lifted me higher, dipped his chin, and pulled my nipple between his lips.

"Easton," I groaned.

He released it, moved to the other side, and sucked deep.

I arched my back, giving him more room and groaned again, this time with my hands fisting his hair.

I had no choice but to let go when my back hit the bed and he reared up. From his knees, he listed back again, and was on his feet at the side of the bed, staring down at me. I was uncertain about this. Then when his hands went to the button of his pants I wasn't uncertain anymore.

I was elated.

My hands went to my undies. I hooked my thumbs under the lace, but got no further.

"Stop."

At his command, I stopped.

His eyes roamed my bare breasts, my stomach, down to

the sheer pink lace covering my sex. He did all of this while unbuttoning and unzipping.

I realized then, the issue with being mindless also meant you were mesmerized. And as such you were so into feeling you forgot your other senses. Thankfully part of my brain kicked in just as he pulled his pants over his hips and his dick sprang free. I was equally grateful I didn't miss the perfection that was Easton Spears naked. Not that I had a lot of time to take in his boxed abs, or the light dusting of light brown hair highlighting his pecs, or his beautiful shoulders, or thick thighs before he leaned forward and tore my panties down my legs.

"Been waitin' to do that." I wasn't sure if he meant to say that or if he, too, was mindless because he didn't look at me when he said it. He'd watched my panties skim down my legs. He also didn't look up at me when he dropped to his knees, used my calves to yank me down the length of the bed until my thighs were propped on his shoulders, and especially not when his head disappeared between my legs.

"Oh my god," was what I'd said but only because I didn't have it in me to shout hallelujah.

I'd had one man, many, *many* years ago go down on me. So many years ago I had very little recollection of the event. Not that it was an event as such; it was more of a minor incident, hence why I barely remembered it. But one thing I was absolutely sure of was it was nothing like what Easton was doing.

He went down on me.

I'd never been eaten and that was exactly what Easton was doing. He ate, and licked, and sucked my clit, and ate some more. His head shook between my legs as they trembled. He tongue-fucked me until my breath was hitching more than I was sucking in air.

I was so close to climax I was having an out-of-body experience.

I was right there...

Then his mouth was gone.

"No," I hissed.

Before I could yank his mouth back where I wanted, he came up over me, hooking my leg as he went, then he slammed inside.

My climax hit. My pussy convulsed, my back arched, and pleasure ripped through me. Throughout this my eyes were locked with Easton's. I watched his eyelids flutter like he was the one experiencing the single most powerful orgasm in the history of orgasms.

And he hadn't moved.

He'd filled me full and that was all it had taken.

One thrust.

"Christ," he grunted. I felt his dick twitch inside me and watched another eyelid flutter but this time he looked like he was pained. "Gotta move, baby."

He didn't wait for my reply which was good because I was incapable of speech. Not only hadn't I recovered but his tongue had invaded my mouth. I took his fucking and his kiss—both feral. I finally slid back into consciousness enough to hold on. I lifted my knees high, pressed them tight around his sides while my hands frantically roamed over his back.

He grunted into my mouth, I moaned into his.

My hips surged up.

His drilled down.

Just when I didn't think it could get any better he shifted his weight and moved his hand between us. I felt it glide over my belly, then down farther, and with shocking accuracy his thumb rolled my clit. He added pressure and rolled again.

I had to tear my mouth away so I could cry out as another orgasm powered through me.

Savage. Wild. Out of control.

Take your pick.

It was all of that and more.

It was everything.

The feel of Easton inside me, all of him surrounding me, his pounding thrusts, his labored breaths, the magic he was making between my legs. The sweat coating his back, my skin heated and sensitive.

I was out of my head but fully aware.

Never, *ever*, ever had I felt so much all at once.

I held on the best I could while he fucked me utterly senseless.

"Unlatch, baby."

I had yet to process Easton's command when he pulled back and pulled out. My legs fell open as he came up on his knees. I glanced down and watched with rabid attention that borderlined fanatical memorization as he stroked his cock.

Holy hell.

That attention became avid when he shot off.

My eyes flew to his face, not wanting to miss his come hitting my belly but wanting the full show. As soon as I lifted my gaze our eyes connected. His were fully engulfed in his pleasure but still focused on me.

If I'd had it together I would've understood what those eyes were saying.

Unfortunately I was too lost in my own euphoria to understand anything beyond knowing that was the best sex I'd ever had.

I knew Easton was done when he fell forward, giving me some of his weight but taking most of it on his elbow. He used his other hand to brush my sweaty hair off my face. I wasn't sure why I was perspiring since he'd done all the work but apparently getting fucked nearly dead took it out of you.

"You okay?" he asked.

The way he asked made me grin. It was an earnest albeit silly question since I was lying under him with his climax on my stomach, my heart still pounding in my chest, and lady parts doing a cha-cha after having two off-the-charts-good orgasms.

So I tried, I really tried, not to laugh.

But I failed miserably.

It also took a while for me to get this under control and only when Easton started to roll to the side did I wrap my legs around him and sober up.

I also learned that multiple orgasms gave you loose lips.

"That was awesome."

Easton blinked.

"The best sex of my life. Not that I've had a lot of sex. I've done it a few times, but...wow. I thought sex was over-rated, like it was one of those fishing stories where people exaggerate how big their catch was."

He blinked again.

"Ditto on the going down part. Ho-lee-shit. You're

really good at that. Award-winning good. I get it now. Totally."

No blink this time. Just staring.

"And you're a really great kisser. Best kiss I've ever had."

Nothing from Easton.

Okay, damn, I was screwing this all up.

"Yes, Easton, I'm okay. Are you?"

"No."

It was my turn to blink.

"Not even close."

Mortification set in.

I'd pounced and I'd attacked, not giving any consideration if that was what Easton wanted.

"Baby, get that look off your face." He leaned in closer, which forced me to push my head deeper into the mattress to keep some separation. Easton was having no part of that and I knew it when he slid his hand into my hair and fisted. "I think you get I liked everything you gave me, the evidence of that is soaking into your skin. And I use *like* because if I told you exactly how marking you made me feel, it'd scare the shit out of you. So we'll leave it there for now. I also think you get I was totally into you and everything we were doing, but just in case you missed it I'll confirm."

Well, thank God for all of that. But none of it explained why he wasn't okay. I didn't get a chance to ask because Easton wasn't done.

He dipped closer. "I've *done it* more than a few times, and that, right now wasn't awesome. Wasn't even great. You're fucking gorgeous and if that was all there was of you, straight up that would be enough to get off, but you're a fuckuva lot more than just beautiful. You feel good, you taste good, you've got great tits, you let go and get wild, so with all of that, no way it could be anything less than fucking phenomenal."

Now he looked pissed and I was more confused.

"I don't get it."

"I lost control."

And that was bad?

That was one of my favorite parts. It made me feel sexy and powerful and wanted.

"And?"

"Baby, right now my come is drying on your skin." He paused and shook his head. "Do you get what that means? I fucked you bare, Nebraska."

Oh, shit.

"At this point it's moot but I've never had unprotected sex. We all get checkups every six months. I had one four months ago and haven't had anyone since. I'm safe."

Well, that was very good news even if it was belated, and as he said, moot. The deed was done.

There was silence and it wasn't until his brow lifted that I realized he was waiting for me to share my history.

I drew in a breath, shoved the embarrassment aside, and gave him what he needed.

"It's been six years—"

"Come again?"

My attitude instantly bubbled.

Did he really think I'd lie to him about something important? We were talking STDs here, not WMDs and who was stockpiling what where.

"You don't believe me?" I snapped and gave his chest a shove.

Well, shove was an overstatement. I put pressure on his chest but he didn't budge.

"Get off me," I demanded.

"Six *years*?"

"You're a dick," I told him and attempted to shove him again, this time giving it my all.

"Baby, you just had my dick and you're gonna have it again in about ten minutes so no need for dirty talk just yet."

I decided to roll my eyes to the ceiling.

"How is it possible for a woman like you to go six years without sex?"

That had my eyes rolling back then narrowing.

"And what kind of woman am I, Easton?"

He didn't answer. He just glared down at me with those stupid blue eyes of his that I wanted nothing more than to get lost in.

Charlie was right; love made you stupid and sex was a weapon.

The sharpest weapon of all. And I'd handed it right over to Easton so he could gut me with it.

NINETEEN

It took a lot out of me not to roll off Nebraska, get dressed, find my phone, and call that asshole who raised her so I could warn him I was going to kick him the balls the first chance I got.

With all of my concentration being used up tamping down my desire to kick Charlie's ass, I didn't have enough left in me to guard my response.

"Are you fuckin' shitting me?"

Nebraska jerked.

I understood her reaction. It was just that I didn't give the first fuck.

"Tell me you're shitting me," I demanded when she didn't answer. "My dick's still wet with you and already you're retreating."

"Retreating?"

"Honest to God, you think I'd still be where I am right now after fucking you, or say, fuck you at all if I thought about whatever fucked-up shit that's in your head right now."

Her face twisted in a way that told me she was going to spew more bullshit so I got back in there before she could piss me off.

"I already told you what kind of woman you are. *Gorgeous*. That was what I was asking. How in the hell with how you look, how you carry yourself, your sharp-ass tongue and attitude, have you not been laid in six years? I know it's not because of lack of interest; again, you're fucking beautiful. So explain to me, Nebraska, why?"

Total shut down.

"Oh no, you don't get to retreat, not after that. Not after you gave me that gift. It's mine, baby, and I'm keeping it."

"Get. Off. Me."

"I will as soon as you explain."

"When a woman tells you to get off, you get off."

I didn't think now would be the best time for a joke, so I kept my quip to myself.

"I would if I thought for one second that's what you really wanted."

Her right eye twitched.

Oh yeah. She was pissed.

"So now you're telling me what I want."

"Yep."

"You're very wrong, Easton."

I was very right and I knew it.

"You're shit scared. I terrify you."

"I'm—"

"Terrified," I repeated. "I know why you haven't had a man in your bed for six years; because you do everything in your power not to feel what you just felt. You hide behind your walls. You keep separate and live lonely. You're scared to feel anything. You're doing it now. Whether you purposely misunderstood me or did it subconsciously out of self-preservation, I don't know. I also don't care. Either of those reasons are whacked and I'm not letting that shit slide."

"Are you for real?" she spat.

"Yep. And I'm right." She opened her mouth but I talked over her. "Swear to fuck, baby, you call me a dick, you'll be on your hands and knees taking my dick while I smack your ass."

She clamped her mouth shut.

Christ, she was a pain in the ass.

"Listen closely, baby. I don't know who twisted this shit up in your head, though I can guess. Not everyone is out to fuck you over. Not everyone is out to play you or lie. I get why you'd think that. I get why you'd slide straight to thinking the worst. But hear this, I ain't them."

I felt her body get stiff but I was more interested in the way her eyes flared, the way they changed from glaring to staring.

"Now that we got that straight, tell me, baby. You got birth control covered?"

She nodded.

Her confirmation was a relief. Just not as big of one as it should've been.

"Your dinner's fucked. I'm gonna toss it and make you a new one." She started to shake her head but I didn't give her a chance to argue. "Then we're gonna shower and I'm gonna fuck you again before we get some shuteye. Flight leaves at oh-dark-hundred."

Still shaking her head she said, "I don't care that it's cold, don't make a new one."

"Baby, cold grilled cheese sucks. You gotta eat it when the cheese is still melty. Not to mention it'll be soggy."

"I don't care."

"Well, I do."

"It's not cool to waste food, Easton," she asserted.

No eye twitch, but a snappy tone.

She wasn't pissed but she was determined. Nebraska didn't give a shit about wasting food, or on a whole she probably did; no one with common decency liked to waste food. But this wasn't about food insecurity or world hunger. It was way bigger than that.

You made me a sandwich?

Never...

She hadn't finished what had never happened but I would bet my savings account it had to do with Charlie.

"I get you, Nebraska, but I'm not a fan of you eating a cold, soggy sandwich. So I'll eat that one and make you a new one."

She looked like she wanted to argue but she couldn't without giving away more than she wanted to give.

She wanted to eat that cold sandwich because for some reason it meant something to her. But she wasn't prepared to explain why.

"Fine," she ungraciously gave in.

Total pain in the ass.

"Now kiss me before I roll out."

A startled expression washed over her features.

It was cute as fuck. It was also something I never wanted to see again.

"I don't think—"

"How about for the next twenty-four hours you stop thinking and start feeling? Turn this off." I tapped the side of her head, slid my hand down to her neck, across her throat, shifted to the side so I could reach her chest, and flattened my palm over her heart. "And let this do its thing."

I knew she got me when her heels dug into my calves and her hands still on my chest trembled.

"That's not smart, Easton," she whispered.

"Maybe not but that's what I'm asking you to do. One day. Give it *one* day. If you don't like what you feel, if you don't like what I'm giving, if you can't hack it, I'll find another way."

More fear when she asked, "Find another way?"

"To make you trust me. To prove to you I can keep you safe while we see if there's something here worth exploring. To show you what it's like to have someone give a shit if you've eaten dinner, where you're going, if you'll be safe doing it, and taking your back in a real way if you won't be."

In the short time I'd known Nebraska, I'd seen her take more than her fair share of hits. Life-altering hits that shook the foundation of everything she thought she knew. I'd seen her in pain, devastated, breaking down, dragging herself back together. I'd held her while she cried. I'd heard her moan sweet, I'd tasted her, I'd fucked her. We'd exchanged barbs and argued. I'd seen her scared and I'd thought I'd seen her terrified.

I had not. Not when the stark panic now marring her beautiful was true terror.

"But what if I like it, then what?" she whispered so quietly I had to strain to hear her.

That was the most honest, real question she'd ever asked me.

"Then we see where this goes."

"Then what?"

Fucking hell. She was killing me.

"I'm not trackin', baby."

"What if I like it, then we see where this goes, and you find out you don't like it and leave? Then what?"

I wasn't going to kick Charlie in the balls. I was going to shoot him.

Nebraska would handle the fucker Maddon, and her mother was up for grabs. I wasn't fond of taking out women —neither were any of the men I worked with. Layla had no such qualms and Jasmin would be thrilled at the opportunity to get out of the office and take care of business. Not even a month ago I heard her bitching that the only action Penelope got these days was at the firing range. Yes, Jas named her sidearm Penelope. I thought it was goofy as fuck until I joined her at the range and saw firsthand how close Jas and Penelope were. She'd be thrilled to give Penelope some field time.

"The only honest answer I can give you is, I can't predict the future any more than you can. What I can promise is, you're safe with me. However this works I'll go gentle, you got my word on that. Here's more honesty for you. I don't care that you're beautiful, I don't care that smart mouth of yours turns me on, I don't care that from the moment I saw you I wanted you right where you are— naked under me. If I didn't know this was something I wanted to explore in a real, lasting way, what just happened never would've happened. I didn't fuck you to get off, baby. I've admitted I can be a dick, but I'm not a morally bankrupt asshole who would take advantage of a woman. Not any woman, but especially not you. And I think I've proved that, but it bears repeating—I won't ever use you. Not your body, not your heart, not in any way. All I'm asking for is one day. Let's see how that goes, if you like what you're getting we'll take another day. One day at a time, Nebraska."

She still didn't look convinced.

And with the damage the assholes in her life inflicted mixed with the life she led, I knew it would take more than naked-after-sex talk to convince her to take a chance on me.

So I had no choice but to leave it there and do what I could to show her I wasn't anything like the vultures who raised her. But that would take time and a fuckton of patience and dodging bullets.

Luckily for me, I had the best body armor money could buy—Zane Lewis didn't skimp on ballistic plates. I just hoped they deflected the verbal blows I knew I was going to take.

Out of options, I did the only thing I could do—I dropped down, gave her more weight, and took her mouth. By the time my tongue touched her lips she'd relaxed under me. At the first glide of our tongues she was fully committed. Under her whimpering protests, I kept the kiss slow and sweet.

There was plenty of time to give her what she wanted.

But only after I fed my girl.

I broke the kiss, smiled when she lifted her head off the mattress to chase my mouth, and rolled off her.

"Be back."

I grabbed my pants off the floor, tugged them on, tagged my shirt, and was at the door pulling it over my head when I turned back.

Nebraska had yanked the corner of the coverlet over her naked body.

Shame.

I left the room. The house being as small as it was meant I didn't miss Smith sitting at the two-seater bistro table off the kitchen, nor did I miss his smirk.

He'd heard.

Not a surprise. As I mentioned, the house was small, the walls were also thin. I'd heard both showers go on when Smith and Nebraska got in them and I was making dinner. I'd also heard Nebraska drop something in the shower and her muttered "Ouch." I didn't think she shouted, so yeah, the walls were very thin. Something I would've taken into consideration had Nebraska not kissed me. But as soon as I'd felt her lips on mine all rational thoughts had fled.

"Not a word," I warned.

For once, Smith kept his comments to himself. Though he didn't need to open his mouth. His smile said it all.

"Got anything new?" I asked as I passed him on my way to the kitchen.

"Layla called," he informed me. "She said Zane downplayed the scene at the office. He had fourteen pissed off tier one operators get in his face. Of the men, Garrett was the most pissed. Jasmin was calm, but Layla figures that was only because she has access to certain parts of Lincoln and she reckons she'll have his balls in private. She said it was bad. The only ones not giving Zane shit were Theo, Jonas, and Cash."

I figured that'd be the case. We hadn't been around as long as the rest.

"She confirmed what we already knew. It's good now but it didn't take an hour, it was more like three. During which time she was worried the cops were going to be called until she remembered the conference room is soundproof."

"No shit."

"No shit. She said she contemplated running to the armory and grabbing a pair of ear plugs they were so loud. Once they got in their licks and blew themselves out, Zane explained why he never told anyone about Black Team."

"He was protecting them," I surmised. "If shit went sideways they'd all be in the clear. Plausible deniability. Red, Gold, Blue, and now us, were on the up and up. Clean contracts. Oversight. Black is just that, black. From what I understand they're not mercs, not PMCs, they're straight up assassins."

"You'd be correct."

I had all the fixings for the grilled cheese on the counter and was buttering the bread when Smith continued.

"Nebraska's a part of that."

Something in the way Smith said that, like he was trying to break the news to me gently, gave me pause.

"And?"

"Black's HQ is in Wyoming, brother."

Okay.

I still wasn't tracking.

"And?"

"We're based in Maryland."

What he was saying finally clicked.

"A little premature for that, don't you think, brother?"

"Any other woman, I'd agree. With her, no."

What the fuck?

I set the knife on the counter, turned, and gave Smith my full attention.

"Wanna explain that?"

Obviously Smith did, because he didn't make me wait.

"I don't know her, but I do know I like her. But I do know you."

I wasn't sure I was happy about the direction this was going.

"Are you saying, you think I'd fuck her—"

"You just did," he pointed out the obvious. "But, fuck her over, no. Not intentionally. I know you got shit buried, just like the rest of us. Not like Cash—his issues run far deeper. But that doesn't mean you don't got issues. And you and her have something in common. Something you both need to be aware of before you jump into this. A different woman might be able to hack it. Nebraska, no way."

Suddenly I regretted sharing with Smith.

"What issue do you think I have?"

"Commitment with a track record of scraping off any woman who even thinks she might get in there. It's like you're Mumbley with that shit; you can sniff the thought percolating in a woman's head before she can fully suss it out. I get why you do it and I get you're upfront with women and what they're gonna get from you."

Smith wasn't wrong but he also wasn't right. He was confusing my *issues* with his issue. He was the one who had commitment issues and after *her* I didn't blame the guy.

He'd been burned and bad. My issue was and always had been my job. Being deployed, then working with the CIA, then going dark for ten years didn't leave much opportunity to have a woman in my life. None of us had time for that shit in the last decade—a sacrifice we all knew going under-cover. At the time I didn't view the prospect of never getting married or having a family as a loss. I was unin-terested.

But now, after giving up those ten years and coming home to work at Z Corps and seeing my other teammates with their wives and children, I was seeing it as a loss.

And as far as Cash went, his issues had nothing to do with *him* committing and more to do with a mother who couldn't commit to being a mother. Her lack of commit-ment to the task of caring for her son had led to CPS getting involved and eventually putting him into the system. So really, he didn't have commitment issues, he had abandonment issues with a healthy dose of trauma tossed in there. It would take an act of God Almighty Himself to get Cash to give a woman a chance to get close.

And I saw his point about Nebraska. I couldn't even get her to commit to twenty-four hours.

"You're wrong, Smith. I don't have the issues you think I do. What I had, what we all had, was circumstance. I wasn't willing to entertain the idea of a relationship while I was active duty. It was a hard pass when I joined the Agency. No woman should have to put up with her man being gone as much as we were, and then there were the lies I'd have to tell and I wasn't willing to lie to the woman I loved. So you're right, I scraped off any woman who gave me the vibe she hadn't heeded my warning—fun and nothing more. But you're a hundred percent correct about Nebraska. She's not going to commit until she trusts me, and maybe not even then. So again, where her team is located is more than a little premature."

My friend's stare turned incredulous.

I didn't get it but I would when he said, "You know that shit hurts like a motherfucker."

Her.

With Smith it always circled back to her.

"Can't say that I do. I've had one relationship, if you can call a twenty-year-old idiot stumbling his way around a relationship. But still, she was sweet and loved me and I cared for her so it sucked when I had to end it. It didn't feel all that great but I wasn't crying in my soup. I suspect if all of this with Nebraska turns to shit and she leaves I'll be thinking back on this warning. What I won't do is wonder why I didn't listen because that woman in there deserves to know what it feels like to have someone care about her. *Her.* Not what she can do. Not mold her into what they want. Not use her for their benefit. Genuinely care about her. And if I can give that to her for a day, a week, a month then whatever hurt she lands on me will have been worth it."

I gave Smith a few moments to respond. When he didn't I left him with his thoughts, turned back, and finished making Nebraska a new grilled cheese.

By the time I was done and ready to get back to Nebraska, Smith had something to say.

"Ignore me. I'm the last person who should be dishing out advice."

We seriously needed to put in some effort with him and dig this shit out of him once and for all.

"I know jack-all about relationships," I returned. "But, brother, I know you. And that woman isn't worth it. She's still living in your head. After all these years it's time to evict the bitch and move on from what she did, what she said, and start fucking living. And, Smith, when I say she's not worth it, I mean she's seriously not fucking worth it."

Christ.

It was like a competition between Nebraska and Smith on who could shut down the fastest.

No one had ever accused me of being well-adjusted or open with my feelings but compared to these two I was living free and open.

"Brace, Smith, your time's coming."

That got me nothing. Not that I thought it would. Unlike Nebraska, he didn't have a tic or a tell. Smith Everette was stone cold.

I didn't waste the effort or my breath.

I had a woman to feed.

After that I was going to attempt to take my time and show her exactly what she'd been missing out on the last six years. Though the way she ignited, the slow in the scenario might be difficult to pull off.

That wouldn't solve a single one of her problems but at least she'd fall asleep next to me after I wrung out as many orgasms as I could from her.

In other words, she'd go to sleep with a smile and I wasn't sure if that was something she'd ever done.

TWENTY

It was a damn good thing I'd quit-fired my job.

I was o...v...e...r...*over* traveling.

Connecticut to Maryland. Maryland to Florida. Florida to Egypt and that wasn't counting my layover. Gallivanting around Egypt only to fly back to Maryland again, not including the layover. Not the first time I'd done something similar but I was happy it would be my last. Well, not my last—I still needed to find Maddon and solve that problem —but the end was near.

I thought maybe I'd feel some sort of way about hanging up my mediator coat but the only thing I felt was relief. I wanted quiet. I needed quiet.

Greece, here I come.

I was daydreaming about what my new life was going to be like and what color tassels I was going to get for my beach cruiser bicycle when I felt the bed compress next to me.

Easton.

We'd been back in Maryland three days and for three

nights he'd slept next to me and three mornings I'd woken up next to him.

Three days I'd struggled.

Three days I'd been terrified but had done nothing to stop him. Not from getting into bed with me, not from fucking me, not from asking me questions or him telling me about his life.

I needed to but I knew I wasn't going to.

What I won't do is wonder why I didn't listen, because that woman in there deserves to know what it feels like to have someone care about her. Her. Not what she can do. Not mold her into what they want. Not use her for their benefit. Genuinely care about her. And if I can give that to her for a day, a week, a month, then whatever hurt she lands on me will have been worth it.

What could I say, the walls in the Luxor house had been thin. I hadn't listened to Smith and Easton's conversation on purpose but I didn't, say, go into the bathroom and get into the shower in an attempt to drown out the conversation. I was me, the mediator. Old habits die hard and I'd been taught knowledge was power.

Unfortunately in this case knowledge might be my downfall.

If I could go back to being ignorant, in this case I would.

For three days I couldn't stop thinking about what Easton had told Smith. It was selective in the sense I'd also heard what Smith had said about Black being based in Wyoming and Silver in Maryland. Not that location was an issue since I was moving to Greece. But I was ignoring the one statement in that whole conversation that, if not locked away in my brain and marked 'do not enter!' could be cataclysmic: *and then there were the lies I'd have to tell and I wasn't willing to lie to the woman I loved.*

I'd spent my whole life being lied to, then as an adult learning how to master lying. I wasn't sure if I'd know what honesty looked like if it came with a label and smacked me in the face.

At this point in my life, I didn't think I was capable of telling the truth—period.

"Whatcha thinking about, baby?" Easton asked as he pushed one arm under my shoulders and used his other hand to grab my elbow to roll me into him.

This he'd done every night when he'd gotten back from taking care of the condom. After that first time, he'd used protection. And there had been seven times, not including the first.

That night in Luxor he'd come back with my grilled cheese and we sat on the bed eating—him the old, cold one, me the fresh, warm one. When we were done, he'd done exactly what he'd promised—fucked me within an inch of my life, then we showered, and he didn't leave my room.

The first night back in Maryland he took his time, fucked me breathless but not into a coma. He waited until day two to do that. Morning sex, slow and lazy. Nighttime sex, fast and wild. Same with day three. Only this afternoon he'd added a lunchtime quickie which included him eating me for dessert and fucking me bent over in the kitchen since Smith had gone into the office and we had the house all to ourselves. The house being one of Zane's safehouses, though it was no longer safe in the sense it had been used twice before so it was going on the market. He was selling it, and in the process of purchasing a new one. Incidentally I was staying in the house Bridget had stayed in when she was waiting to testify and under witness protection.

I rested my cheek on his bare chest then proceeded to be stupid.

It couldn't be said I wasn't fully participating in my downfall. I totally was. Every night I snuggled into Easton like I had the right, like he was mine, and I was keeping him.

My stupidity led me to placing my hand on his abs. My after-sex coma was starting to set in, which was what I blamed the rest on.

"I was thinking about when I move to Greece I want to buy a bike. It's going to be the most girly bike on the island. I'm thinking white frame and hot pink basket on the front to carry groceries and hot, sparkly pink tassels. Though I might settle on a wicker basket because those are pretty, too."

"Come again?"

"If I can't find an island that's outlawed cars, and admittedly, I don't know if that's a thing but I hope it is because I think it would be awesome living somewhere where there are no cars. But if I can't find that, I just won't buy one."

"No, baby, back up. You're moving to Greece?"

"Yep. Right after I slit Maddon's throat."

I hadn't been paying attention so I couldn't be sure when it happened exactly but Easton's body had gone solid.

My desire to kill Maddon wasn't a secret nor was my skill to get the job done.

"You know I've—"

"When were you planning on telling me you're moving to Greece?"

Um...

"Or were you just planning on up and disappearing?"

That sounded more like an accusation than a question.

My temper simmered just under the boiling over point.

"I didn't know my future living arrangements were your business," I snapped.

"Christ," he growled.

I wasn't a fan of the irritated growl, which was a thousand times different than the sexy, turned-on growl he did when I was getting close to climax and he was coaxing it out of me.

One never failed to make me detonate, the other I could do without.

I'll let you guess which was which.

"Christ, what?"

"*Christ,* we're starting back at square one. We've had three days, I thought we were making at least a little progress. Now I see we haven't inched out of the starting box yet."

What the hell was he going on about?

"I think you get I'm into you," he unhappily snarled.

Oh, shit.

Nope.

I didn't want to talk about this. I'd been able to avoid all talk about anything that remotely touched on me and him for three days. Not that we had much time to talk about anything other than Maddon. We'd (and that included Smith) gone through everything I had on the man, and that was extensive, so it had taken a long time. We'd (again with Smith) talked out scenarios and motives. We'd had copious calls with Layla and Kira and one with Zane. Today, Smith had gone into the office, tomorrow, we all would. The only reason I'd hung back was because Zane was being cautious and wanted a few days of footage outside of the office to make sure no one was doing drive-bys looking for me. After all, there was a bounty out on me. Not that I thought Maddon would have that executed while I was in the US. It would be too risky. Outside the US, especially in Asia, the Middle East, or Africa, it would be easy. Maddon was a risk-taker but a calculated one.

Unfortunately it seemed like my good fortune had run out.

"Easton—"

"No, Nebraska. Just *no*."

Warning...Boiling point!

I pushed off Easton's chest. He swiftly yanked me back to where I was.

"You're not doing that either."

What happened when a nuclear reactor overheated? Whatever that reaction was, I was close to it. Dangerously close to a full meltdown.

"Easton—"

"Nope," he denied. "Before you retreat and shut down, think."

Oh, I was thinking all right—of ways I could kill him in his sleep.

"What am I thinking about other than how big of a dick you are?"

Easton's arm went super tight around me. He shifted me higher, bringing me closer to his face.

It was dark in the bedroom, as in pitch black, so I couldn't see him—not at all. But I didn't need to see him; I couldn't miss the waves of hostility rolling off him.

"Warned you what was gonna happen the next time you called me a dick. Three good days, baby. Three nights where I got you to moan sweet for me, get so fucking wild I got claw marks on my back to prove how into it you are. Three nights I go to sleep with you cuddling into me. Not next to me, Nebraska, cuddled *close*. Holding on. I thought you were coming to the understanding not only am I into you but you're coming to mean something to me. So I'll ask you again: when were you going to tell me you were moving to Greece?"

I didn't know how he did it in the dark, but somehow, his fingers found my lips and stopped me from answering right away.

"But before you answer, remember as soon as the last of your answer comes out of that pretty mouth of yours, you're on your knees and you'll be taking my *big* dick and you'll be doing that with *my* marks on *your* ass."

Perhaps a smart woman would've taken Easton's threat, rolled out of bed, and flipped him the bird on her way out the door. As noted, I was stupidly participating in this game. As such my pussy spasmed at the reminder.

Since I was neither smart, nor was I going to roll out of bed without a fight, I let my temper off the chain and shoveled shit right back.

"I wasn't going to tell you. Seeing as I don't feel I need to explain my travel plans with the man I'm fucking."

Mistake.

Huge.

So big, days later I would still be ruminating how big of a mistake calling Easton "the man I was fucking" was. It was worse, way worse, whole nother universe worse than calling him a dick.

The first thing that happened was his mouth slammed down onto mine. Foolishly I opened, then more foolishness happened when I moaned as the heat of his kiss seared through me.

What could I say? Easton was that good of a kisser.

Moaning turned into groaning when his hand went up my shirt. He expertly found my breast then just as expertly rolled my nipple until I started panting.

Easton was the best; a master at all things my body, and he'd touched and tasted and teased enough to know exactly what my response meant.

He tore his mouth from mine and irately asked, "Does that feel like fucking?"

I was in an Easton-induced fog so I couldn't answer. Not that I had time before he rolled up, taking me with him. He yanked my shirt up and tossed it away before I was once again on my back, and he was tearing my undies down my legs. This all happened within seconds.

The next thing I knew he'd hauled me up and twisted me. I was on my hands and knees, and his hands were on my ass.

"You got a sweet ass, baby. It's gonna look even sweeter with my handprint."

I braced for a smack that never came. This meant I was unprepared when his hand went between my legs.

"Drenched."

He sounded pleased, which in turn made my breasts heavy and my nipples pebble.

Two thick fingers slid through my excitement. Not one to start slow (except for morning sex which was slow and lazy start to finish) Easton set the pace he intended to keep. That meant his intrusion was about building my climax as quickly as possible.

I was well on my way when I whimpered, "Easton."

I lost his fingers when he curled over me. His mouth went to my ear when he growled in the way that I super-duper liked, "Does that feel like fucking?"

Again I was too far gone to answer.

But if I hadn't been, the answer would've been no.

"What about this, baby?" he asked as he rubbed the head of his dick through my wet and used it to circle my clit. "Does this feel like fucking?"

It didn't, it felt glorious.

"Honey," I moaned.

He slammed inside me. As he was prone to do, Easton wasted no time making his point.

Deep. Wild. Rough.

I slid straight to mindlessness.

The world vanished.

It was me and Easton.

It was Easton covering me. The scent of him. The safety of his arms. The feel of his dick. My body heating and getting hotter by the second. My breasts. My pussy convulsing. My clit throbbing.

Just me and him.

Just that.

Us.

"What about now, baby, does this feel like *just* fucking?"

I didn't know what this was beyond an otherworldly connection I was too terrified to think about, much less admit.

I shook my head and reared back, needing more.

"Answer me, and I'll give you what you need."

Of course he knew what I needed. It was him who'd shown me. He was the one and only person who I'd ever felt safe enough with to take what I needed.

"No."

"Goddamn right," he snarled.

His hand glided from my hip to my belly then straight between my legs, and he hit his target. Instead of his brilliant fingers rolling, he pinched.

My neck craned back and I let out my shocked mewl.

"Can you take more?"

I could take anything from Easton.

"Yes," I hissed my encouragement even though I didn't know what *more* was.

His chest left my back. His fingers pinched and pulled at my clit then gave a smack to my ass. The sting made me jump in surprise before it morphed into something else and I moaned through the pleasure as it swept over me.

"Fuck yeah," he groaned and slowed his thrusts. "More?"

"Yes."

Another slap, this one harder.

The surprise was absent but the heat spread faster. It pooled in my belly, it coated my skin, it left me needing.

Wanting. So close to the edge of ecstasy I was willing to beg to get more.

"More."

He didn't give me more, at least not another swat.

His drives became harder but slower. His fingers between my legs no longer pinching but toying. He was driving me crazy. Out-of-my-mind insanely crazy. So much so I dropped my top half to the bed, reached down, slapped his hand out of the way, and found my clit. Without his expertise it wasn't the same. I was reaching, trying to get myself there.

"Easton."

It was a plea. I was almost there but I couldn't do it. I needed him.

"Tip your ass just a little more, baby."

I tipped.

My reward was a sharp, stinging slap to my ass.

I flew apart.

Broke into a million pieces and floated off into oblivion.

All I could feel was *us*.

Me and Easton.

When I came back to myself his lips were gently brushing over where he spanked me. I stayed perfectly still, too afraid if I moved he'd stop.

"You good?"

"Yeah." I smiled.

I was positive it was a drunken smile and not just because my "yeah" was slurred. I felt sloshed, like that time Stella plied me with wine to get her intel.

Easton's lips left my behind and skimmed up my back, pausing only to press a few small kisses here and there.

Then he twisted to his side, taking me with him so my back was to his front, and he molded himself around me.

Nice.

It was then I felt it, or actually didn't feel what I thought I'd feel against my butt when he pulled me tight.

"What about..."

Nope. I couldn't ask. Not even after all he'd done to me, that now included him spanking me, could I find a way past my embarrassment to ask if he was going to finish.

"What about what?" he asked softly.

When I still didn't answer he gave me a squeeze.

How was it, I could sit down with mob bosses and negotiate territory knowing that each and every person in the room was armed and dangerous and I could end up riddled full of bullets at one wrong move, but I couldn't ask why he was cuddling with me and no longer hard?

Instead of verbalizing my question I wiggled my ass into his groin.

"Greedy," he murmured into my hair.

"Greedy?"

"Baby, I had a sweet orgasm not even an hour ago and pulled three from you. Just rode you hard, pulled another out of you, which I have to say was way fucking sweeter than the first three if the way your pussy was clutching at my dick is anything to go by, or the way you were leaking down my balls. Just came harder than I've ever come in my life. You want more, I'm happy to oblige, but I'm gonna need a few minutes to rally."

Ohmigod.

He thought I wanted more.

"It wasn't three, it was two," I shared.

Though it possibly wasn't the truth. I either had three or one of them was just really long.

"Baby, it was three. You don't think I can feel you when you come?"

Wait.

What?

"You can feel it?"

I felt him start to shake.

Was he laughing?

"Yeah, I can feel it."

"Are you laughing?"

"Shit yeah."

And he was. Not only was his body shaking, his voice was vibrating with hilarity, and it had now become audible.

I wasn't sure how I felt about this.

Oh, wait, I did know.

"I don't think I like you laughing at me."

Suddenly I was rolled onto my back and Easton was mostly on top of me.

"I'm not laughing *at* you."

All humor was gone. He sounded as serious as a heart attack.

"I would never laugh at you, not for any reason, but especially when we're in this bed. I told you, you're safe with me and I fucking mean that."

I knew he meant that. He'd spent three days tirelessly— one could even say, diligently—proving I was safe with him.

"Okay," I whispered.

"I think it's cute as hell, you have no clue I can feel it when you orgasm."

"How would I know that?"

"You can't feel it when you play with yourself?"

Heat hit my cheeks, spread to my chest, then proceeded to singe my insides.

Thank God it was dark in the room.

"Baby?" he prompted.

"I've...never...I don't...I mean I've tried but I can't. So I don't."

"You don't what?"

Gawd. Embarrassing.

"Can we please not talk about this or say anything and just go to sleep?"

"Why don't you want to talk about this?"

"Do I need a reason?"

"I've been inside you," he murmured softly. "I've had my tongue in your pussy. I've kissed and licked almost every inch of you."

This was all true. But I didn't see what that had to do with anything.

"So? Some stuff is private."

"Not between us."

He dipped his face and somehow, like the superhero I was starting to believe he was, his lips hit mine on the first try.

"You're lying there with my mark on your ass, my come up your cunt, and I got more nail marks on my back than I can count. Yesterday I had you on your knees in the shower, my dick in your mouth, while you let me fuck your face and you swallowed me. Tell me, baby, with all of that, what's private when it comes to us?"

Us.

"You're crass, Easton Spears."

"And you're deflecting, Nebraska Michaels."

I hated that he had a ready comeback for everything.

"Fine. No, I don't play with myself. I tried, but I couldn't do it. It was worse than sex because I couldn't even get to the buildup part that at least feels okayish even if it doesn't culminate to the good stuff."

"The good stuff?"

"Climax."

As soon as I spat the word Easton went stiff but he immediately relaxed and gave me another lip touch.

"No other way to explain this to you without being crass, baby, so buckle up for real talk."

I didn't think I wanted real talk. I wanted real quiet and bedtime.

Easton didn't give me the chance to tell him this or to buckle up before he launched in.

"You are unbelievably fucking tight. When you're close you get tighter and wetter. But fuck, baby, when you come you squeeze my dick so tight I gotta fight the urge to join you, you feel so fucking good. Does that answer your question?"

"Um...yes."

"You sure?"

"Positive."

He kissed my forehead then rolled, bringing us back to me on his chest, cuddling in.

"Now, back to the beginning. You having a question I now get you were too embarrassed to ask."

"You're like a dog with a bone."

"No, what I'm like is a man who has a woman in his bed who he cares about and wants her to understand she can ask or say anything without embarrassment. I'm also a man who just learned his woman never had an orgasm, self-induced or otherwise...that is, until me. I'm feeling pretty fucking happy about that even if it makes me a dick. So to make up for being an asshole I'm feeling the need to give her another one. So, if you'll hurry up and ask what you were too embarrassed to ask, I'd like to get down to business giving my girl the good stuff."

A man who has a woman in his bed who he cares about.

His woman.

My girl.

The good stuff.

I clenched my thighs.

Damn, I was greedy.

"I don't have any other questions," I blurted out, uncaring if I sounded eager.

Easton was really good at the good stuff.

And other stuff besides.

If I didn't smarten up quick, I'd do the unthinkable and start to fall in love with a man who was far too good for me.

"I did all the work the last two goes. I want you on top this time."

I could do that.

Totally.

TWENTY-ONE

With the morning I had, I should've known shit was going to go awry.

It had started off perfect, too perfect.

Something I'd learned since I started waking up next to Nebraska—first thing in the morning she was sweet.

Drowsy, cuddly, and sweet.

Now that I took full advantage of—giving her soft and slow in the morning, taking my time, giving her intimacy while at the same time giving it to myself. Quiet, easy, closeness. Things I reckoned she'd never had. Things I didn't allow myself to take with the life I'd led and the suggestion of what that kind of closeness would imply.

But Nebraska was different.

I wanted the closeness and all that it implied. I wanted the quiet, easy times when it was about losing myself in the moment. It was about touch and feel. It was about using my body, hands, and lips to deliver a message. It was about affection—something else that Nebraska had never experienced.

Early morning was when her guard was down. By the time she got a cup of coffee in her, she slipped right back into who she'd been taught to be. The walls came up and the mask was firmly in place. She stayed that way until I got her alone and in bed again.

Night and day.

Around Smith she was all-business. Period. A few of her fake smiles, but even those were rare.

So, yeah, I should've known she was going to close up tight the second we were back up in the office. I'd fucked up and was unprepared, but even if I would've planned accordingly I still would've vastly miscalculated her response.

It had started in the Escalade. The closer we got to the office the worse it got. As soon as the elevator doors closed us into the lift she looked like she was going to come out of her skin.

I caught Smith's eye. His gaze flicked to Nebraska standing between and just in front of us, then back to me.

He didn't miss it.

Not that you could.

Whatever was eating at her occupied the air around her.

The doors opened and Nebraska hustled out. Before she could turn toward the hall to the conference room I nabbed her hand. Her reaction was over the top. Not only did she startle to the point her body jerked, she also attempted to yank her hand free.

"We'll be right in," I told Smith. I tightened my grip and damn near dragged her to my office.

Without further protest she followed.

This was my first warning shit was not right. Nebraska had no issue voicing her opinion.

As soon as we cleared the threshold of my office I released her hand and shut the door.

"What's wrong?"

"Nothing."

She was looking me dead in the eye but she was totally vacant.

What the fuck?

"Straight up, baby, I'm not stupid. If your body language and silence wasn't obvious, which, I hate to break it to you, you're not hiding there's something wrong. You using woman-code for 'back the fuck up, I'm gonna throat punch you' would've done it."

Her eyes got squinty.

But no right eye twitch.

Again, what the fuck?

"For your information, Mr. Smarty Pants, the woman-code word for 'back the fuck up before you get throat punched' is 'you're right'. Which means 'you're wrong, but we're over it', and the next step is physical violence. Nothing means nothing."

Mr. Smarty Pants.

If she didn't look like she was ready to have a breakdown I would've laughed.

"If nothing's wrong then why do you look..." I trailed off, not knowing what she looked like.

Scared.

Nervous.

"Are you worried about meeting with the team?" I finished.

That got me the universal woman stare that clearly stated I wasn't the sharpest tool in the shed.

Contradictorily, she said, "No."

I didn't believe her but I knew better than to call her out.

"Then what's wrong?"

"I told you, nothing. But if you don't like that answer we can try this one...none of your business."

"Thought I explained that shit last night."

"What shit?"

It took a lot to remember the woman standing in front of me had never had anyone in her life give a shit about her. So much so it was a struggle to lock down my temper. I was applying for sainthood if I managed to check my anger. If any other woman thought she could take me on this ride and throw attitude like Nebraska did, I'd jump the fuck off and she'd see the back of me.

Overly argumentative women were a total turnoff. Bullshit games and drama were not my thing. At least they never had been, until Nebraska's prickly ass walked into her father's study and I got an eyeful. Now it seemed I had a taste for drama and attitude.

"I'm not going to let you retreat."

"Nothing's wrong."

"Bullshit."

Her right eye twitched. Now we were getting somewhere.

"God, you're such a—"

"Careful, baby. I didn't check but I'd venture to say you still got my handprint on your ass."

"Careful, *honey*. That might work while you have my

head muddled and I'm naked but I promise—you try that shit while I'm pissed and fully dressed, you'll learn the true definition of getting your balls busted."

I hadn't been entirely correct in my assessment. Not only did I now have a taste for drama and attitude, I totally got off on the way Nebraska delivered it.

"Head muddled?" I asked through a smile.

"I think I want to shoot you now."

Fuck yeah, totally got off on her throwing attitude.

"What's wrong?"

"Nothing."

"Bullshit. Tell me what's wrong."

"I'm worried about Charlie!" she shouted.

Well, fuck.

"I haven't talked to him since...well, you know. And no one's mentioned him."

Not since she found out he'd kept a really fucking big secret from her.

"So ask Kira for a—"

"I can't ask Kira about Charlie."

"Why the hell not?"

Belatedly she glanced around my office. There wasn't anything special about the room I tried my very best to spend as little time in as I could. Unlike the others, I hadn't added a single personal item to the space. The cream walls were bare. The desk had a closed laptop sitting on it and nothing else. A high-back leather chair that I had to admit was comfortable as fuck, but still I loathed my ass being in it. And two chairs on the opposite side of the desk.

Nothing else.

"Is this *your* office?" she asked.

I knew she was deflecting but something in her tone made me answer, "Yep."

Her eyes moved around the room again, going as far as craning her neck to look behind her.

"You've worked here awhile," she rightly pointed out.

"Yep."

"Have you not moved your stuff in?"

Stuff?

I had no idea where she was going with this and we had a meeting to get to.

"We got people waiting on us—"

"Why haven't you decorated your office?"

We didn't have time to talk about the state of my office. But since this topic seemed to mean something to her I gave her what she wanted in hopes we could get back to Charlie and why she felt she couldn't ask Kira for an update.

"I come in here only when I have to. Get work done then get the hell out. I'm not a behind-a-desk kind of guy."

Her gaze came back to me.

"I can see that. But still, where's your stuff?"

"What stuff?"

"You know, pictures of family. Awards. Cool snapshots of you and your buds in multi-cam strapped with gear. A plant. I don't know, posters of hot chicks on Harleys or bathing suit models on the hoods of hot rods. *Stuff.*"

I didn't find it pertinent to the conversation to tell her I'd never had a poster—not hot chicks, not bathing suit models, not of a band, nothing. Growing up, my mother would lose her mind if I tacked something up in my room. A half-naked woman would've sent her into cardiac arrest. My father wouldn't have said anything one way or another about it. He deferred to his wife and followed the same rules of the house that I did.

"I see my family every day. Why the hell would I need pictures of them? As for the rest, I don't need to display awards. I earned 'em, don't need to show that shit off like a douche who wants whoever walks in to know how important he thinks he is. I don't need a plant in here because I'm never in here and I'd kill it. And I'm forty-five."

"I know how old you are, Easton, but I don't understand what your age has to do with anything."

Of course she knew how old I was and not from me telling her. She had a full workup on my entire team.

"Right. So seeing as I'm a grown-ass man, bikini posters wouldn't be douchey, they'd communicate to whoever walked in that I had a small dick and couldn't get past it, never learned how to use the pinky dick those posters would say I had. We both know that's not the truth. And straight up, posters are just lame."

"You see your family every day?"

"Yep."

"But they live in Alaska," she carefully told me something I was very aware of.

Another tidbit of information her dossier would reveal. A month after I joined the Navy, my parents up and moved to Anchorage. They hadn't told their son before he left for basic that his father had taken a new job and the move was imminent. They hadn't written me a letter to tell me about the move. No, not my parents; they moved, didn't give me a new address, and I only found out when I completed Battle Stations and was allowed a phone call home. During which time, I also found out with my father's new job being so far away they wouldn't be coming to my Pass-In-Review.

"My *family* is in the conference room waiting for us."

"Easton," she whispered.

I felt the burn of her pity. The sympathy-laced whisper that was so unwelcomed I forgot who she was and what she'd gone through.

"Don't."

My warning was met with her jerking her shoulders back.

I knew she was gearing up to snap back, something I wasn't in the right frame of mind or mood to deal with. So I swung us back to why we were in my office in the first place.

"Why don't you want to ask Kira about Charlie?"

That goddamned right eye twitched right before she stepped closer.

Not a good idea.

I stepped back.

"Ah," she drew out the word, interjecting a fuckton of snark into it. "I see how it is. You give some bullshit speech about how nothing's private between us, you push *me* to tell *you* all sorts of stuff I don't want to tell you, but when the tables are turned you get to change the topic. And I'll point out, *you* changed it back to something *I* don't want to talk about. But you won't give me the option not to talk about it. How about this, Easton? How would you like it if I told you *I* wasn't going to let *you* retreat?"

She'd emphasized a bunch of yous, mes, and I's. Adding to that, she'd squared up with her hand up, finger out, and was jabbing it into me as she spoke.

"Not a fan of the finger, Nebraska."

"Well, I'm not a fan of being pushed. Nor am I a fan of being bossed around. Nor am I a fan as you so crassly put it, of the man who I'm banging closing down and acting like an asshole because I expressed emotion at his pain."

The man she was banging.

That sounded all sorts of wrong coming out of her pretty mouth.

"They're not worth the emotion," I rumbled.

"They might not be, but you are."

But you are.

You are.

Her hand dropped, went to her hip, and she proceeded to rip me to shreds.

"You know," she stated, softening her voice. "I never go into a situation without all the intel I can get my hands on. So, you know that I know you joined the Navy right after you graduated high school. I know your parents moved from the house you were raised in to Alaska shortly after. I couldn't find any records of you ever visiting them in Anchorage, though that only means you didn't fly there. I could have no way of knowing why or what that meant but I know enough to know whatever the reasons are, they're not good. That's all I know. I didn't dig deeper."

It wouldn't have mattered if she did, there was nothing there for her to find. No abuse. No neglect. Nothing. Just a whole lot of nothing.

"Though you took a yearly trip to South Dakota. The only family you had there was your grandfather. Once he passed you handled his estate and stopped going."

Once my pop died, there was no reason to go back to South Dakota.

"You don't have to tell me why. You don't have to explain your parents. But what you have to do is remember it was you who asked me to trust you. If you can't—"

"You're right."

Her eyes narrowed.

"I don't have a vagina, baby, so when I say you're right what I'm saying is you're right. I asked you to trust me. And you're right to call me on my shit. I don't talk about my parents because there's nothing to talk about. They fed, clothed, and housed me. The end. My childhood was unremarkable. No story. No trauma. No lies. No dysfunction. Just nothing. When I left for the Navy that didn't change. I just no longer slept under their roof and they were no longer responsible to feed me. But that shit actually stopped when I was fifteen and got a job. By the time I was sixteen and one of them no longer needed to cart me around, I spent as much time away from the house as I could. They had no issue with this. Hell, I'm not even sure if they knew I was gone."

"I caution to say this, but that's dysfunction, honey."

I shrugged, not knowing if it was dysfunction or simply two selfish people who never should've had a child.

"What I know is, it was fucked growing up not having anyone give a shit about you. You can slap whatever label on it but that's the truth of it. So, again, my family is in the conference room. Smith, Jonas, Cash, and Garrett, those are my brothers. Theo slipped in when Garrett left. Kira and Layla joined the team and they have my heart. Zane and the rest have become family, too."

"Is that why you didn't fake your death like Theo did?"

Jesus fuck, the woman was thorough.

"Yep. No need. I didn't have a family like Theo did who would miss him. As you know, Cash didn't either."

Suddenly her features went soft and the tension left her body. A look I'd only seen first thing in the morning, when she was still sleepy and hadn't climbed behind her walls.

"I don't want to ask Kira to look into what Charlie's doing because I don't want anyone to think I'm weak."

Christ.

No prompting, no fighting, no coaxing.

"Why the hell would anyone think you're weak for asking about your father?"

"He lied to me my whole life."

"He kept a secret," I corrected, unsure why I was defending the asshole.

"That's the same thing."

"If you live in black and white, sure. But we don't, and people like us understand the varying degrees of gray."

The tension she'd lost in her shoulders came back tenfold. Clearly I was doing myself no favors pointing out what we both knew to be true.

"You think it's okay he kept that from me? My mother—"

"No, I'm not saying that at all. You know I think it's fucked. I think he should've told you a long time ago. What I'm saying is I don't know why he didn't tell you and neither do you. Zane gave you good wisdom, Nebraska; family isn't perfect and what was meant to protect can hurt. Charlie hurt you but the piece you don't have is the most important one—the why. Straight up his reasons might not be good enough for you. But at least you'll know and move accordingly. But mostly what I'm saying is no one in that room is going to think you're weak for loving your father. You can't turn off love just because you're hurt and angry. It doesn't work that way, baby."

"Do you still love your parents after—"

"Yes. It's a distant love, but yes, it's still there. That doesn't mean I want anything to do with them but I can't deny I love them. And maybe that's all you're left with—a distant, nostalgic love that's rooted in gratefulness. My parents didn't give me much but I didn't have it bad."

She didn't look convinced and I couldn't blame her.

"Our situations are very different," I started to explain but got no further.

"Not by much," she contradicted. "We were both fed, clothed, and housed but neither of us got the important stuff."

I felt my chest compress and my throat felt like someone had wrapped a hand around it and was choking me.

"Zane was right," she went on softly. "I grew up being trained, not loved or cared for. I knew that already. I just didn't understand until I met you, all that I was missing."

I could take no more.

"We need to get to the conference room," I announced.

Hurt saturated her eyes before she covered it up with attitude.

"You're right," she hissed.

Fuck, her girly growl was cute.

I smiled at that, knowing her definition of that statement.

"I am, baby. After you gave me that, I have two options; fuck you on my desk to show you how much what you just gave me means to me or get your ass out of my office into the conference room so we can get this shit over with so I can get you home and fuck you in our bed. I'm good with either of those but I'm thinking you'd appreciate the office not hearing you when I get you to moan sweet for me."

Her eyes narrowed.

"I don't moan sweet for you."

"Right again; you moan sweet for me in the mornings. At night you pant, whimper, and groan. I'm thinking right now with how I'm feeling, the enormity of it, you're not gonna be moaning sweet. I'm gonna get you wild and you're gonna scream for me."

"Easton—"

"Honest to God, Nebraska. You finally gave me you. We need to get the fuck out of this office or I won't be responsible for what comes next."

Unfortunately she didn't hightail her ass to the door. She stared at me with no small amount of panic.

"I promised I'd go gentle. I'm not going back on that but I'm not fuckin' around with this anymore. You said it straight out—until me, you didn't understand what you were missing. Which means I got in there. There's no going back, and if you try, swear to fuck, Nebraska, I won't let you."

I watched with spellbound fascination as Nebraska struggled with her emotions. The battle might've been internal but she looked bloody and beaten by the time her lids drifted closed.

"I won't go down easy." Her whisper was tinged with regret.

"That's not lost on me."

"I'm gonna make you want to leave."

I stayed silent and let her finish.

"I'm gonna lie and hide and push you away."

I waited for her to continue and when she didn't I asked, "Is that all?"

Her eyes popped open.

"Isn't that enough?"

Any other woman, it would've been more than enough to get me gone.

"Trust. Me."

Another epic battle ensued. During which she held my gaze. I knew I won when she started sucking in breaths deep enough to make her heave.

"Easton—"

"Trust. Me."

"I—"

"Nebraska, *trust me.*"

"Okay," she breathed.

Two syllables that were nothing more than a whisper. One word that floated across the space and slammed into my chest.

Fucking finally.

"Okay," I repeated.

I knew this wouldn't be the last time I had to beg her to trust me.

I knew she was going to backslide.

I knew she was going to fight like the hounds of hell were nipping at her heels to get me to leave her.

It was time to show Nebraska Michaels all that she'd been missing. And if that didn't work, I'd play dirty. It didn't matter to me how I won, just that I was going to win by any means necessary.

TWENTY-TWO

"Hey, KK, do you have anything on Charlie?" Easton asked as soon as we walked into the conference room.

Between going over my files with Smith and Easton, I'd been thinking a lot, and one of the things I'd given a lot of consideration to was how I could be level-headed, calm, and collected while at work but I couldn't hold my temper with Easton. That led me into trying to remember if there was anyone else in my life whom I'd lost my temper with. The answer was no. I gave that some thought, too. Unfortunately I'd yet to come up with a reason why it was only Easton who got under my skin.

And right then while I was waiting for my head to explode at his question—the first thing he asked as we walked into the conference room after Smith watched Easton drag me to his office, something I was positive he shared—I gave up trying to figure out the reason and accepted that I had no control over my attitude or mouth when it came to him.

I also found I didn't have it in me to check that attitude in front of an audience.

"Easton," I hissed.

His hand pressed against my lower back. Without missing a beat, he gave me a tiny shove forward.

I dug the heels of my Vans into the shiny wood floor and tipped my head up and to the side.

"Seriously?"

Easton's lips curved up.

"Seriously," he calmly returned.

"Maybe—"

Easton's hand shot up, curled around the side of my neck. He lowered his face closer to mine.

"Trust me."

The knot that had formed in my stomach pulled tighter.

Trust him.

He engaged his thumb. It slid over the underside of my jaw, and his eyes grew intense. There it was, the reason I'd agreed to trust him. It was crazy. It made no sense but there it was, the sincerity, the honesty, the significance of his request was not lost on him. He knew what he was asking. He knew what it would mean for me to trust him—the gravity of it.

Trusting him would make me vulnerable.

Weak.

I was exactly what Easton had accused me of being—terrified. My first instinct was to close down, armor up, and cloak myself in the facade I'd used to keep myself safe.

The Dove.

She didn't let anyone close. She didn't have emotions.

The realization struck with such brutal force it was a miracle I kept my feet. With Easton, there was no Dove. There never had been. When he was around I couldn't find her.

"Baby," he muttered and gave my neck a squeeze.

"Well, that took less time than I thought."

My gaze went to Zane sitting at the head of the table. A weird sense of déjà vu hit me. At the same time, I heard Cash chuckle and when I glanced his way he was seated in the same chair he was in the last time I was in there. Actually, everyone was in the same positions around the table as last time.

I was totally vulnerable. Out there and exposed.

I tried to pull away from Easton, but was frustratingly halted.

"Ignore him."

"What'd I miss?" Lincoln asked from behind me.

"Either Easton slipped something into her water or he's better than I thought," Zane responded and I felt myself stiffen.

"Already? Damn, Cash was right," Lincoln muttered.

Easton sighed and lowered his forehead to my temple. The closeness did nothing to alleviate the unease, the prickly feeling at the back of my neck that warned me to run.

"Let them burn themselves out, baby."

"Cash is king," Cash whooped.

I jerked back. Easton's head lifted but didn't go far. His eyes came to mine and started roaming. I didn't know what he saw because I didn't know what I was feeling beyond extreme confusion and terror which was quickly morphing into anger.

Why in the hell had I thought it was a good idea to come into the office? Of course Zane would get in his digs, of course he'd taunt and insult me now that he had me where—

"Nebraska," Easton called. "Stop."

"You stop," I snapped and yanked free.

Easton's hand shot out, hooked me around the waist, and tugged me to his chest.

"They're teasin', baby."

"Stop yanking me around."

"They're teasing both of us," he continued like I hadn't spoken. "They'll get bored in five minutes and we'll move on."

"Better make it ten," Jonas interjected. "Linc and Cash have been making bets. So far Linc owes Cash a c-note. Depending on the state of play, he might be into Cash for five."

I heard a rumbled growl come from Easton. His gaze skidded to the side and he spat, "Are you fucking kidding me?"

"Don't look at me. I wasn't stupid enough to bet against you. Just giving you a heads up."

Easton's gaze shifted back to me.

Blue eyes sparking fire.

He was pissed. Not at me, on my behalf.

He knew I was uncomfortable and didn't like it.

He knew.

He knew.

He knew.

He knew and didn't like it.

Easton's fury calmed me. It settled my mind and centered my thoughts.

How weird was that!

It was because of that I lifted my hand, pressed my palm to his cheek.

"Standdown, killer, it's all good."

"Neb—"

"It's all good," I repeated.

"Fuck," Linc rumbled. "I'll hit the ATM later."

I didn't know exactly what that meant, or how much money Lincoln now owed Cash, but I didn't care.

As in I really didn't care.

I didn't care Easton's team had made bets.

I didn't care the first thing Zane had said was a wisecrack.

I didn't care that I felt open and exposed in a room full of powerful men and equally formidable women.

If one of them made the wrong move, said the wrong thing, he'd have my back. These were his people. His family. But I knew with absolute certainty he would not allow them to harm me. Not like Charlie, not like Maddon. Easton's brand of protection would be blanketed in truth and honesty.

"What's happening?" I heard someone whisper, but since it was a soft murmur I couldn't make out who asked. If I had to guess I'd say Cash, but maybe Smith.

"That's what's called acceptance," Zane grumbled, not

sounding happy. "This is progressing too quickly. I'm losing control of the situation."

"Did you ever have control?" Layla remarked.

I didn't take my eyes off Easton.

"Who's accepting what?" Cash asked.

"This is what happens when a man and a woman—"

"Zane," Easton grunted.

Yep. He'd let them tease but he wouldn't let anyone take it too far.

I couldn't stop my smile.

"Brother, I get why your head's in the gutter after four days of bang-chitty-bang-bang but I was going to explain to our friend Cash here, this is what happens when a man hands his balls to a woman."

Easton rolled his eyes.

I felt that tight ball in my stomach loosen.

It was crazy, insane even, it made no sense. I was standing in the room I was in, with the people I was with, in Easton's arms, on full display for all of them to judge. Wide open. Fully exposed. No armor. No Dove.

And I'd never felt safer in all my life.

Was this what real trust felt like?

Was this what real protection was?

Before I could suss out if I was right, Easton proved my thoughts true.

"You've got thirty seconds left with this shit."

"But we haven't gotten to the good stuff," Kira complained. "And I don't know her well enough yet to tell her to cap it before she lets you tap it. I need more time. I'm new at this. I haven't found a good rhyming word to go with uterus."

Um...

What?

"Murderous," Smith offered.

"That doesn't work." Kira scoffed. "No one's murderous for the uterus."

I felt Easton start to shake and since I was staring right at him I saw the humor light his handsome face. As strange as this situation was, I had to admit that was funny. Obviously the room thought so, too, because it filled with laughter.

No, not just any laughter. It filled with the laughter of a family who was teasing and joking.

Something else I'd never experienced.

"Check it, my protégé. You don't wait until you know them to hand them shit. You just do it. It's more fun that way."

"Women don't work that way, Dimples."

Did Kira just call Zane Lewis, the Viper King, *Dimples?*

Holy hell.

I pinched my lips to stop the giggle from erupting.

A giggle.

From me.

I'd entered the Twilight Zone.

"I can't just tell her if she doesn't want to do the term, don't take his sperm. She won't be receptive."

This time I couldn't hold it back. I busted out laughing. My body shook with it. My eyes watered. And for the first time in my life I understood the meaning of a belly laugh. My muscles clenched tight as the hilarity of her comment overtook my body.

As the laughter receded, the look on Easton's face registered.

His smile said it all but the light shining in his eyes told the tale.

I'd made the right decision trusting him.

This was indeed what protection felt like.

TWENTY-THREE

Jesus fuck.

That right there—Nebraska in my arms, open, free, belting out laughter—was what made it worth it. All of it. The promise of all that she was. I'd take the fear, the walls, the barbs, and the attitude if it meant getting *this*. The real Nebraska Michaels. The soft and sweet she protected with a tough, hard, razor-sharp exterior. I'd work my ass off to get more of this. I'd fight to get her to the place I needed her to be to give us a shot. A real shot, at a real future. To a place where she'd learn she didn't need to protect herself alone, not from anyone. I'd see to that. I'd be her shield, leaving her free to be her. The Dove. Nebraska. Whoever she wanted to be, she'd be safe to be just that. And that included her being the daughter of a man who didn't do right by her, yet she still loved him. That included me cushioning the blow when Badger found her mother so she could be free to feel however she wanted to feel.

"I feel like a proud daddy," Zane belted out, pulling me from my thoughts.

"Daddy Zane," Jonas put in.

"Big Daddy," Zane corrected.

Christ.

This was going to deteriorate, and quickly.

"For the love of all things holy, please stop talking," Layla started. "No one wants the deets on your kink."

"Speak for yourself," Cash put in. "I might want to give Big Daddy Cash a go."

"And with that, we're done," I announced.

"Is this normal?" Nebraska asked.

I ignored the pang of anger she'd never had a family that gave you shit, ribbed, joked, and annoyed you in the spirit of love and camaraderie. The bond that made the shit they dished out about care, not malice.

It was difficult, but I locked it down and answered, "No, nothing about them is normal. But you'll learn to roll with it. You'll learn that if they didn't like you or give a shit when we walked in, it would've been all business. It might be whacked, but this is their way of showing you you're one of us."

"By betting and talking about my uterus?" she asked with wide eyes.

"And his sperm," Smith added.

"You'll get used to it." Theo shocked the shit out of me by stating. "It might take a month or two or maybe a year but after a while you learn to sit back and let them act like idiots and eventually we get to work."

Nebraska blinked at 'a month or two or maybe a year'. She was getting it. No one thought her presence was short term.

"Speaking of work, I'm not paying you all to sit around

with your thumbs up your bungholes," Zane proclaimed. "Mini Me, update."

"Says the one who started it," Smith rightly argued.

"This is a do as I say, not as I do situation," Zane asserted.

"It always is," Linc muttered.

"Yo! You two over there, do I need to call in an extraction team to surgically separate you or are you ready to get to work? I'm not paying you to make googly eyes at each other. Bad enough I'm footing the bill for the love shack the two of you are making good use of."

Nebraska's head snapped to the side. The force of it swung her ponytail and jerked my body.

"I quit-fired, remember?" she declared, full of fire.

"What's quit-fired?" Layla asked.

She turned slightly to look at Layla when she explained, "I quit. Zane didn't let me because he said he fired me. I took the termination only because I want the exit package he's paying me for years of service and pain and suffering. But to keep my pride intact I'm claiming the resignation."

"Gotcha," Layla mumbled through a smile.

"Pain and suffering?" Zane tossed out. "Woman, the only pain and suffering that's been dished out is the pain you inflicted on your enemies. Though I have had to suffer through hours of Dutch bitching at me to be nice to you. I'm not a fan of being told what to do. Ten out of ten do not recommend. And I'm not paying severance on years of service I didn't know were being served. Take that shit up with your boss. Thankfully, that's not me."

"Oh, so now you're admitting you're *not* the boss of me," she quipped.

I didn't miss the triumph in her voice.

"Sit, Dove, and I'll explain the chain of command to you." Zane swept his hand to the many open chairs but didn't wait for either of us to take one before he continued. "Silver Team. Layla, team leader. Kira, her intel specialist. Theo, her point. Black Team. Dutch, the boss. Bishop is team leader. Badger is... how do I say this?...clean up. You, his fixer." Zane paused, pointed to himself, and announced. "Me the big boss."

Bishop was a name I'd never heard mentioned before but I didn't get the chance to ask who the hell he was when Nebraska shoved shit right back at Zane.

"I'm confused," she said in a way that said she wasn't confused but instead she'd slid straight into her attitude and wasn't going to let Zane off the hook. "Are you Big Boss, Dimples, Big Daddy, or Viper King?"

At that Zane smiled outright, both dimples compressed, and I could swear Nebraska jolted.

"Here we go. The dimples come out and it's woman down until she remembers he's a sarcastic prick," Linc grumbled. "Been this way our whole lives."

Nebraska recovered quickly and turned her eyes to Lincoln.

"Right, like you had any issues with the ladies."

Jesus.

It was a good thing Jasmin wasn't in the room to hear Nebraska say that.

Linc shot her a smile and wink.

I shot him a filthy look that in no way he could misinterpret.

"Easy, brother..." He let that hang.

"Are we going to have a dick-measuring contest or are we getting to work?" Layla asked in an attempt to get the meeting back on track.

Though it was a faulty play with Cash in the room.

"I'm all for—"

"No, you're not," I cut him off and dropped my arm around Nebraska to pull out a chair for her. "Sit, baby, or this will go on all afternoon."

"I thought you said they'd burn themselves out," she murmured while taking her seat.

"I was wrong. I forgot, with Cash here this can go on all day."

"I'd take offense to that if I didn't know that was your way of saying I'm witty as fuck."

He wasn't wrong, he was witty as fuck and normally I'd participate and give him more ammunition to keep going, but he could get raunchy—or raunch*ier*. It was best to keep Cash leashed in mixed company.

Thankfully Kira followed Layla's suggestion and got down to business.

"To answer your first question," she started, looking up from her laptop. Her gaze went to Nebraska. "Dutch spoke to Charlie before he sent Badger out after Pigeon. He urged Charlie to make use of a safehouse. Charlie refused but did agree to report in to me. The last message I received from him was this morning expressing his intense dislike of having a cyber babysitter, as he calls it, and demanded a status update on you."

I glanced over at Nebraska struggling to find her emotional cloak to shield herself from exposing the relief she felt that her father was doing okay.

"Thanks," she pushed out.

"Not to be a dick," Cash started and I braced.

"Cash—"

He ignored my warning and spoke over me. "People love who they love. I know there's a saying—love's only a light switch away, but that only pertains to men who take ugly chicks to their bed. Other than that you can't just flip it on and off."

Jesus.

Fuck me.

"Dude," Smith grumbled and shook his head.

"What? I'm not lying. She's sitting there like we're going to judge her for worrying about her father. What the fuck is that about?"

One thing that could be said about Cash Phillips—he said shit straight. The good, the bad, the inappropriate. He'd give the shirt off his back to a stranger and take a bullet for any one of us. His loyalty and love went to the extreme. He made an artform out of shit talk. He used humor to mask his pain. He had more demons than anyone I knew and that might include Zane. But when it came down to it, Cash was always the one to give it outright and he was rarely wrong with what he was saying whether you wanted to hear it or not.

So, he wasn't wrong about turning love on and off, something I'd already conveyed to Nebraska, something she needed to hear again and again until that shit settled deep and sunk in.

"You're right," Nebraska croaked.

As soon as she uttered the phrase I shifted closer to catch her in case this was one of those times when 'you're right' meant Cash was going to get a kick to his balls. Not that I was worried she'd damage his ability to reproduce, seeing as he'd cured himself of that.

She paused to clear her throat and began again. "You're right. I am sitting here thinking you'll judge me even though Easton told me you wouldn't. But it's not because I don't believe Easton. It's because my whole life I was programmed to think a certain way."

"What way is that?" Smith asked.

By all accounts Smith looked like he was lazing back in his chair, forearms resting on the padded armrest, hands dangling off the end. But knowing him the way I did, he was anything but relaxed. At a moment's notice he'd be ready for battle. And by the way he was staring at Nebraska, I knew the battle he'd be willing to fight was the war within Nebraska. The one she was struggling to win.

Family.

The good kind.

The kind that was selfless.

The kind you could count on.

Always.

"That everyone is against me. That the only way to survive is to outmaneuver—tactics will win over skill. That harmless means helpless and helpless gets you dead. I was taught in order to accomplish a task I had to be willing to inflict harm. That emotions are a weakness and love will break you. That I need to be a problem solver and when a solution wasn't available to create one. That powerful men can sense the slightest hesitation. That women are much more dangerous than men. That—"

"Jesus, fuck me," Zane growled. "You know the fucked part is none of that is wrong. As jacked as it is sitting here listening to you spew that shit, knowing neither of the men in your life had in him to complete those lessons they weren't wrong in what they taught you. Harmless is helpless. Emotions are a weakness. You never go into battle when the anger's fresh. That shit gets you killed. Love can break you but that goes hand-in-hand with betrayal and loyalty and learning who's worthy of those emotions—not avoiding them all together. Something that neither of them could teach you, but more importantly, taught you to avoid. Because once you felt it, really felt it down to your soul, they'd lose control of you. You'd figure out what true loyalty looked like, you'd feel safety and protection in a way you'd never felt. And once you had that, they'd lose their puppet. And I say they but I really mean Maddon. Charlie was too deep in his guilt to stop what was happening to you. Which was a weakness. Though, I'll repeat, I don't blame him for backing Anna's play."

I lifted my hand, slid it under the heavy fall of hair she'd secured in a band, and curled my fingers around the back of her neck. She tipped her head to the side and gave me her attention.

The woman looked totally lost.

Cast adrift.

That shit ate at my gut like nothing ever had.

"He's not wrong," I told her.

"But—"

"Not everything they taught you was wrong." I gave the

back of her neck a squeeze. "You're strong, smart, brave, and skilled—all of those things they trained you to be. It's just time for you to learn something new, something different. And that starts here in this room. No one is against you. No one is out to get you. Every person in here respects you. No one is judging you or looking down on you. The takeaway from that is everyone has your back and if you let them they'll help get you through."

I saw her eyes flare so I knew it was coming.

"It's not that easy," she groused, full of attitude.

"Didn't say it would be. And nothing that's worth it is easy."

She knew I was right but with Nebraska I learned she could argue about anything.

Shockingly she nodded and turned back to face the table.

"I'm worried Charlie turned down going to a safehouse. My father's stubborn but he's not stupid. He knows the safest thing for him to do is disappear. If not for his safety, for mine. He's a liability, the only thing that can be used against me. If Maddon gets to Charlie he knows I'll do whatever he wants to ensure my father's safe return. I have to call my dad."

Her assessment was spot on, like always. But something struck me. I'd never heard Nebraska call Charlie 'dad.' He was father or Charlie. Nothing else.

"You wanna do that now or wait for privacy?" Kira asked.

Nebraska glanced back at me with a small, secret smile that made my dick twitch and my gut clutch.

Christ.

She'd once again been run through the gauntlet yet still had it in her to give—something that on the outside looked small but really it meant everything.

Every-*fucking*-thing.

One step closer to where I needed her to be.

I watched determination leak in as she called up that steel backbone I knew she had.

"I'll call him now," she said, not taking her eyes off me.

Right or wrong, I didn't think, I just leaned over, pressed a hard kiss on her mouth, and straightened before she could mouth off, or worse, punch me in the balls. Unlike Cash, I had plans to make future babies.

"Call him, KK," I ordered.

Without giving Nebraska time to overthink, Kira connected the call immediately, demonstrating why we called her Kid Genius. Not only was she a whiz with her computer she also had a deep understanding of what happens when you analyze and dissect situations until you're paralyzed with indecision.

"I'm still in my study, Mrs. Cain." Charlie's deep voice filled the room.

Kira had said the man wasn't happy about having a cyber babysitter and she hadn't exaggerated. The guy sounded pissed.

Next to me Nebraska sat statue-still. Not a breath. Not a blink. Nothing.

Fucking shit. This was not a good idea.

I shook my head at Kira, hoping she'd catch my hint and make up some bullshit excuse why she was calling. Kira returned my gesture and did the exact opposite of what I wanted her to do.

"You're on speaker with the team."

"Whose team, yours or my daughter's?"

Nebraska jolted at the question.

"I'm at the office with Silver," Nebraska answered, then looked at Kira. "This line is secure, correct?"

"Of course." KK scoffed.

Nebraska launched straight to the point.

"I need you to go to the safehouse Dutch offered."

"Nebraska—"

"Maddon's feeling the pressure. He's off script. I didn't anticipate him moving so quickly which means he's desperate. He won't be able to get to Amani so he'll target you. Two birds—he takes you and he has me. He knows you're the only way to me."

"Am I?" Charlie asked, sounding like he genuinely wanted the answer.

No. The man *needed* the answer and he needed it to be in the affirmative.

Nebraska didn't take the bait.

Cold as ice she went on. "This shouldn't take more than a few weeks. Now that I'm back in the States he can't use his GB team and that hit he put out on me won't stand. It's one thing to take me out OCONUS but he won't risk it now. Silver has me covered and if I need I can call Bishop and he'll send backup. You're the only loose end and I need you covered."

I figured it wasn't the right time to tell her the use of acronyms was a turn-on and her Ice Queen was sexy as hell as long as it wasn't aimed in my direction.

"You mean Easton Spears has you covered." There was

a thread of concern in his tone but not aggression, which meant Nebraska's next response was over the top.

"Yes, Father, *Easton* has me covered," she seethed. "And in case you care, Smith's had his back while he's seen to me."

"I knew he'd—"

"Take care of me," she spat back as she leaned into the table.

I glanced around the room, taking in varying expressions of concern on my teammates' faces. Except Zane. He was smiling. Linc was staring at the table in front of him with a frown and deep lines between his eyebrows.

"Why don't we discuss this in private?" Charlie suggested.

That was the wrong thing to ask. Nebraska's reaction was to reach over, take my hand, lace our fingers, and test the limits of her strength. I was fucking thrilled she'd reached out to me for comfort. I was not happy she looked like she was ready to go ballistic.

It was not the freeze-out that worried me. She had a loose hold of her emotions and I couldn't blame her, but when she was done with her father and came back to herself I didn't want her embarrassed or ashamed for doing it in front of the team. The feeling would be irrational, but she'd repeatedly said emotions were weak. I hadn't had enough time to convince her the opposite was true; showing your emotions was a sign of strength and courage. Any asshole could mask how they felt. It took a fuckton of bravery to be true to yourself and honest with your reactions.

"There is nothing I need to say to you that requires privacy."

"Well, there are things I need to tell you," he returned sharply. "And I'd prefer to say them without an audience."

"And I would've preferred to have a father who hadn't lied to me for twenty years but here we are, neither of us getting what we wanted."

The room went still. That was, still with the exception of Nebraska's chest heaving with fast, choppy breaths.

Fuck this.

I twisted my hand free, pushed her chair away from the table, scooted mine back, plucked her out of hers, and planted her on my lap. Once she was settled I grabbed her hand and relaced our fingers. If she was going to have to endure another hit that was going to leave her hurt and upset she was taking it while in my lap so I could see to her.

"Slow. Breathe," I mouthed.

She nodded and slowed her breathing.

"Again," I whispered.

Another shallow breath.

Unfortunately Charlie chimed back, and did it nasty.

"Do not think for one second you understand the truth. I don't know what they've been filling your head with, but—"

"What I understand is my mother is alive and you knew. What I understand, because it is seared into my brain, is that I went to a funeral and mourned a woman who is *not* dead. I know I spent twenty years with you and you never told me. I know that Maddon knew and never told me. But now I know why Maddon withheld that information. He was biding his time waiting until just the right moment to impart that news to cause maximum damage. And what I know is when he told me, that damage he caused wasn't maximum—it was earth shattering. Want to know who was there to hold me together? Not you, my father. Easton. Want to know what *they've* been filling my head with? They've been trying to convince me you had good reason to lie to me. They've been trying to explain to me that sometimes a lie is meant to protect and not harm."

Some of the pain slid from her features, morphing into glittering shards of blue ice. Her right eye barely twitched. If I hadn't been staring right at her I would've missed it. I wasn't sure if this meant she was slightly pissed or if this was a level of pissed I hadn't seen yet.

I'd learn it was the latter.

"Dmitri Zenin." The name vibrated from her chest. "You kept that from me, too. A flighty bitch who didn't want to keep her daughter and a mob—"

"Watch your mouth, young lady, you're talking about the woman I love!" Charlie exploded. "You have no idea how hard it was for her to leave you. You can't fathom what she went through to keep you safe. You think she wanted to leave you? She had no option once she heard Zenith was looking for her. If he found her, he found you and she would die before she let him get his hands on you. And yes, you're right, I didn't tell you. I was in an impossible situation between the only two women I've ever loved. I promised to keep her secret. I vowed to protect you."

Nebraska's eyes had widened. She obviously didn't know the depth of Charlie's feelings for Anna.

"Love breaks you," she whispered.

"Goddamn right it does. I loved her enough to let her

go. And I did that knowing there would never be anyone else. That's how much I loved her. I had you, her secret, and the knowledge that to protect you both I had to betray you. Anna told you your father died in a car accident. I didn't correct that story because I couldn't, though truth be told, even if I could've, I would've taken that to my grave. That man doesn't deserve to look at you much less claim you. You're my daughter. I love you. Not Zenith. Not Anna. Me."

Nebraska's eyes were shining with unshed tears. Her chest was rising and falling at a rapid pace. Her face was pale and the freeze-out had ended. There was nothing but pain coating her entire being.

No more.

She was done.

I entered the conversation. "Give Nebraska what she needs and get to a safehouse."

"I'm perfectly—"

"That wasn't a suggestion," I cut him off. "Get your ass to a safehouse or a team will be there in a few hours to escort you."

"Mr. Spears—"

"Jesus Christ!" I exploded. "Give her what she needs."

"I'll call Dutch," he relented.

The line disconnected. Either Kira cut the call before he could say something more to piss me off or slice Nebraska, or Charlie hung up.

"Baby," I called.

"Hm?"

"Need you to focus on me for a second."

She blinked and I watched a tear escape down her cheek.

I quickly swiped it away then left my hand cupping her face.

"I need you to tell me what you need from me right now."

"I don't know," she whispered.

Fuck.

Fuck.

Fuck.

"He loves you," Zane announced. "Not Easton, your father. Or maybe Easton does, too. I don't know, these assholes drop like flies."

My eyes shifted to my boss. "Read the room."

"I did, the vibe sucked ass. Bottom line takeaway is that Charlie Michaels gave up the woman he loved to keep Nebraska safe. He did it knowing he'd never get that woman back and one day he'd lose Nebraska, too. And that is the very fucking definition of being a father. Sacrifice. The rest, the details, those don't mean shit. I'm a man who loves his children and his wife. Of those three I couldn't tell you who I love more and that's the God's honest truth. That man was fucked from the beginning in a no-win situation. Now, Maddon, that fucker will be handled accordingly."

"Zane's right, honey. That's the bottom line I have to hold onto right now. I need to see this through with Maddon, then we'll deal with the emotional fallout. I just don't have it in me right now."

I was going to give her that play but only because my

heart was thumping in my chest so hard I was courting a broken rib.

We.

We'll deal.

Us.

Fuck yeah, I'd give this to her knowing when the time came she'd let me help her through the rest.

"Whatever you need."

"Whatever I need," she whispered.

"Speaking of Maddon," Theo interjected. "Garrett made some calls."

Nebraska shifted to get off my lap. My first instinct was to keep her where she was, where I wanted her, where I could keep her close and make sure she was good. But this wasn't about me, it was about her and what she needed. While a drama was in progress and she was under fire she'd let me comfort her. While business was being discussed, no way.

Once she was back in her chair the change happened.

She didn't slip back into the woman she was the first time she was in this room. She wasn't in full freeze-out mode, but neither was she who she was with just me, or me and Smith.

She wasn't Dove.

She wasn't my Nebraska.

She was somewhere in the middle.

That was good enough for now. In time she'd get used to the rest of the team and relax.

"Did he get anything?" she asked.

Theo's gaze glided down the table and his attention

went to her. It was no secret he didn't like Charlie Michaels. At one time that dislike extended to Nebraska. It hadn't mattered to him that neither of them had posed an actual threat to his woman. Charlie had made Bridget feel unsafe and that was enough for Theo. Seeing as I was now where he was I couldn't blame him. Viable or perceived—a threat was a threat and that wouldn't stand. Not a threat to Nebraska physically or mentally. So, shit yeah, I understood Theo. I just hoped he could get past it with Nebraska.

"He's got nothing other than what we knew. Maddon spun up a GB team, spent thirty-six hours in Egypt before the team went back to Yemen, and he flew back to the US."

Nebraska nodded. I had her in profile but still I saw it— her mind was in hyperdrive, her body still, but her eyes darted around the table.

"Need to let us in on what you're thinking, darlin'," Jonas noted.

Something all of us had to relearn after working alone for ten years. Teamwork. It had taken a minute for us to fall back into the swing of it, remembering to rely on your team to help you work through your thoughts and strategize. Something I wasn't sure Nebraska had any experience with.

"Maddon doesn't waste time or an opportunity. The phone call I had with him prior to coming to Maryland, I had a feeling he knew something was amiss. I'd caught on, or was close. Charlie assured me Maddon was just being impatient. Obviously I was right. My approach was his suggestion. At the time, I thought his play was to jerk Zane's chain and corner him into having to reveal Black—"

"How does Maddon know about Black?" Theo stopped her to ask.

A question I hadn't thought about.

Nebraska blew out a breath and shifted in her chair before her gaze went to Zane.

"I should've told Dutch Maddon had figured it out. I didn't and part of why I didn't was at Maddon and Charlie's counsel and the other reason, I admit, I wanted that information in my back pocket in case Dutch screwed me over. But, as the years slid by and I got to know Dutch I should've told him sooner." She took another breath and went on, ignoring Zane's glare. "Maddon had always suspected Zane was behind Black Team. He knew the connection to Dutch. He knew Badger had done some work with Zane in the early days with Red Team. He didn't have proof until..." She paused again and frowned, looking more uncomfortable by the second.

"Until what?" Theo pushed.

"Ghost Town," Zane ground out.

"Ghost Town," Nebraska confirmed but didn't explain.

My boss's demeanor changed. Not his normal warning shit was about to red-line. It was a look of disgust with a healthy dose of ominous.

"The only job I personally saw to."

"What was the job?" I asked.

Zane didn't hesitate.

"Gangs are rampant in Cape Town. There were neighborhoods emergency vehicles couldn't enter without a police escort. There were other neighborhoods the police wouldn't enter."

Zane was giving us a history lesson we were all very

aware of. I'd spent time in South Africa. I'd witnessed the beauty of Cape Town with my own eyes, contrary to that I'd seen the devastation. The slums, the no-go areas that reeked of devastation and despair. Evil that overshadowed the good people who couldn't escape.

"The job was personal. Badger had a friend, the only one from his childhood he'd kept in contact with. This friend's daughter went with a church group to George on a mission. The area's safe, high quality of life, friendly to foreigners. Bad luck, the girl got nabbed. This friend calls Badger, he goes all out tracking his friend's daughter. He finds her but he can't go in alone. Dutch calls, he's spinning up, taking Bishop with him, but he needs me. Red had just gotten back from an op, they're on R&R, Blue is out in the middle of the North Pacific on a cargo ship. Brooks, Kyle, Thad, and Max are in Washington playing babysitter. No one to miss me, so I roll out. Five days later the girl's back with her family and I'm home, no one the wiser I was gone."

"Except Maddon, he saw you there," Nebraska put in. "I've spent time thinking about this. Why Maddon was all for me taking Dutch's offer, meaning I'd have less time to give to him. He pushed hard, said it'd make him feel better if I had men like Dutch and Badger at my back. At the time I figured he thought me working with Dutch meant he'd have access, specifically to Badger. But now, I'm seeing the long game. Me in with Black connected me to Zane. When the time came, he needed leverage. He needed Zane in a corner having to expose his secret, he needed me to be the tool he used to push that, and he held my mother's secret close, waiting to use it when he needed. Dutch never trusted Maddon, but Dutch doesn't trust many people so that wasn't surprising. But he still kept Maddon on a string, did jobs for him. I'm seeing that clear now, too. He wanted Maddon close to watch him, especially after I told him Maddon knew you were involved."

That last statement had Zane's eyes getting flinty.

Flinty was never a good look on Zane.

"Dutch and I already had words about that when he told me you've been collecting a paycheck."

Nebraska didn't know or didn't care that when Zane got steely, it was time to back off.

"Anyway, the point of all of that was to say, Maddon knew I was in Egypt to warn Amani. I'm sure of it. His appearance was nothing more than a setup since he'd know Amani would take precautions and he'd never get to him. He used my meeting as a way to send false information to the CIA. I'm sure he knew Charlie would plead my case and get Zane to send someone to back me up. Charlie's smart but predictable. With Zane now involved Maddon had everything he needed to set his play in motion. But Maddon didn't come straight back to the US after we left, something we didn't hide. Maddon doesn't waste time. He has a woman there; I'm thinking he stopped and had a visit."

"You think he stayed in Egypt to get laid?" Cash tossed out.

"This woman has money and connections. She's a widow. A Brit who married a wealthy Egyptian and stayed in Egypt after his death. I've never been able to get a lock on what she does for him, just that he visits her. Not frequently but regularly. If he's on that side of the world he makes time for her."

"What's her name?" Kira asked with her laptop already open.

"Patricia Sawiris, formerly Summorville. She was married to Yasseen Sawiris. His family owns the largest distribution company of construction equipment in Egypt. Her family is also wealthy but the Sawiris money trumps the Summorvilles."

"I'm on it."

And when Kira was on something it could only be described as rabid. She'd have everything there was to find on Patricia Sawiris within twenty-four hours and she wouldn't sleep a wink while she hunted for intel. This would drive her husband Cooper around the bend, but he'd stay up all night with her making sure she augmented her caffeine consumption with food and water.

"Do we have anything else on this fuckwit? I'm not feeling warm and fuzzy he's out there planning a terrorist attack."

Nebraska held Zane's stare.

My gut tightened and I braced.

That look said I wasn't going to like what was coming next.

"Maddon sold a blank sale of goods. A theory. A theory that would easily cripple the US but the last I knew he hadn't handed over the innards. Without those plans and connections the Chinese just have an outline."

"The Chinese don't need more than an outline. Haven't you heard they're the king of the reverse engineer?" Zane's tone was full of heavy sarcasm.

"You don't say," Nebraska returned in kind and my lips twitched. "That's why I need to head out and hit up a few contacts."

There it was.

It wasn't that I didn't like what she had to say—I fucking *hated* it. Before I could get a lock on it—not that I tried very hard because that shit would've been a wasted effort—I let it rip.

"That's not happening."

Lightning quick, Nebraska's head swung to the side. Her blue eyes danced with fire when those pretty lips opened and spewed venom.

"What's not happening now or *ever* is you telling me what I will and won't be doing. No one, not *anyone*, tells me how to do my job. Period."

"Guess, I was hasty in collecting on my win," Cash muttered.

"You're taking Easton with you," Zane decreed.

That was something but not enough.

"That's not—"

Zane didn't let her finish.

"Jesus fu..." He abruptly stopped, his eyes swinging to the door. "Fudgeycakes." He hilariously if not disturbingly finished.

All eyes went to the door.

Ivy was standing there with a baby bundled up in her arms, Eric, Robbie, and Asher at her side. A smirk playing at her lips, eyes dancing with humor, Zane's wife was a knockout. She also kept Zane on a short leash. A leash he'd chained around his own neck and happily handed her the lead. I figured his wife was the only person who could make

Zane come to heel and curtail his use of profanity in front of their children and his nephews.

"Sorry to interrupt," she said, humor lacing her tone. "Linc, Jasmin had to run out to meet an informant on a case so she left the boys with me. I'm headed home and taking them with me. Also, Badger called. He's been trying your cell but you're not answering. I told him you were in the middle of something. He asked me to interrupt and tell you he has a lock on the target."

I heard Nebraska draw in a sharp breath. The rest of the occupants in the room stayed seated but became alert. Save Linc and Zane; they stood and shuffled toward the door.

"Get Cujo and Chewy to the car and get back up here," Zane ordered.

"I'm gonna punch you in the junk if you don't stop calling my boys those stupid names," Linc groused.

"I can go back to semen demons," Zane magnanimously offered.

I didn't catch Lincoln's response but I did hear Cash ask, "Are we not going to discuss fudgeycakes?"

I wasn't, not right then. I filed that away to give my boss shit about when he annoyed me, and turned to Nebraska.

"Hey."

She continued to stare at the table.

"Baby, look at me."

"I can't."

"Nebraska—"

"I can't," she hissed. "If I do, I'll fall apart. Please, just give me this."

This being allowing her to lock her emotions away.

I hated it but I had no choice.

"Anything you need."

There was a beat of silence before she whispered, "Anything I need."

Maybe. Hopefully. Possibly she was finally fucking getting it.

TWENTY-FOUR

I was numb. Totally and completely.

It felt like I was outside my body watching from a distance. Like it wasn't my life or my mother that was being discussed.

Badger found Anna.

Found her thirty miles from my current location. Which had me thinking—how many other times in the twenty years had my mother been close without me knowing it? Had I passed her on the street?

You have no idea how hard it was for her to leave you.

You think she wanted to leave you?

I promised to keep her secret.

I vowed to protect you.

And Charlie, had he seen her?

The woman I love.

I was in an impossible situation between the only two women I've ever loved.

Charlie loved Anna.

That explained why in all the years I'd lived with him I'd never seen him with a woman.

I couldn't process the rest and not because I didn't want to face it. I truly didn't have the mental capacity. I'd listened to Zane, I'd listened to Easton. I now understood what they were trying to explain about family and how something wrong could really be right depending on the motives.

But I was all out of headspace. I couldn't think about my phone call with Charlie or what he revealed without having a breakdown. What shocked me was Easton hadn't pushed, he'd given me what I'd asked for even though I knew it was killing him to watch me shut down. I wasn't stupid. I knew it was nothing more than a reprieve, but it meant a lot to me that he respected me—which translated into him trusting me to know what I needed, which made me trust him.

That meant that part of my out-of-body experience I was in the process of having, included admitting that even though I wasn't processing the knowledge, I did trust Easton. Further, I cared about him. I wasn't fool enough to believe that sex equaled love but there was also respect, admiration, and an inkling of adoration. Maybe the first blushes of love. I couldn't know because I'd never loved anyone. But the way he'd kept his promise of going gentle, and the way he took care of me, the way he stuck with me when I had a shit attitude, and the way he stayed even though he knew I was terrified and could run at any moment, made it difficult not to start to fall in love with him.

There was a lot going on around me in the conference

room of Z Corps. A lot of talk. A lot of planning. All of it had to do with me, yet I was sitting there next to Easton not paying a lick of attention. And I could do that, because I trusted Easton. I could lock myself away and know all the way down to my soul that he and his team would handle the situation.

How had that happened?

I trusted Dutch and Badger and even Charlie (though now Charlie only had a smidgen of trust) but I would never zone out and let them talk about me. I'd suck it up, lock it down, and participate.

But the moment I heard Badger say he'd found Anna and she was in Maryland, my heart had begun to break. And when he announced he had a location but he hadn't made contact, thus he couldn't confirm she was alone in the house she'd been staying at for days, my broken heart shattered.

She was close.

Had been for days.

That meant she knew where I was, knew the jig was up, yet she hadn't attempted to make contact. There was no other reason she'd be thirty miles away. None.

That hurt.

Like a lot. So much, I couldn't deal. So I left Easton to it and blanked my mind.

I felt a hand on my thigh, knew it was Easton's but didn't move. His hand squeezed and I blocked it out.

"Nebraska," he called. "Need you to focus a minute, yeah?"

I shook my head.

"Just for a second."

I gave him my eyes and he didn't delay. "We're headed out. If this is something you want in on, you need to be up to speed and focused. You coming or staying here?"

Was I coming?

I'd fully checked out and he was giving me the option to check back in and be a part of whatever they were planning.

If I hadn't already confessed albeit mentally that I had feelings for him and those feelings were leaning on the side of loving him, snapping me out of my stupor to give me that option would've forced me to evaluate my feelings.

I hadn't given a single person in the room any evidence to suggest I wouldn't be a liability, yet Easton still had faith in me.

Oh yeah, I was getting a strange feeling in my belly. It wasn't terrifying—it was *ter-ri-fy-ing* with the emphasis on the *ing*. Meaning that terrified feeling was ongoing and only getting stronger.

"Dove?" Badger's voice came through Zane's cell phone on the table.

"I'm here," I answered.

That was, I was there physically. Mentally, I was closed for business.

"Sit this one out," he suggested, though his tone said what his words didn't, and that was he was ordering me to sit this one out.

"That's not your call," Easton returned, his tone also conveying what his words didn't say, and that was *back the fuck up*.

"Actually, it is. Like it or not she's still a part of Black. And with this I make the call. She's sitting this out."

I felt the vibration of hostility rolling off of Easton and filling the room. If I could feel it, his brothers could. This was not the way these two teams needed to be introduced. Not to mention, Easton was a badass but Badger was stone-cold. Not only would nothing good come of these two going head-to-head, it would end in bloodshed. The kind that lands you on a slab in the morgue.

"Actually, Zane fired me," I told Badger, not caring I was throwing Zane under the bus and not giving the whole story. Badger wasn't the kind of man who'd appreciate my thoughts on quit-fired and severance packages anyway. "So it's not your call and it's never been your call. I move where I need to move. And I want in."

"I'll be having words with Viper when this is done about what the fuck's up with him firing you. But for now, I'm telling you, you coming isn't smart."

"Maybe not, but this is my life and—"

"That right there is why this isn't smart. Give us a chance to contain the situation and get a feel where Anna's head's at. She's in the right place, we'll bring her to you."

It hit me then. Badger wasn't shutting me out; he was trying to protect me from Anna.

I was torn. I wanted in, but my head was fucked up. My concentration could slip and I could put the team in danger.

I glanced at Easton, needing direction. He instantly read my dilemma and went to work giving me what I needed to put my mind at ease.

"Whatever you need, you'll get. You took another hit today from Charlie. A big one. Badger finding Anna tipped you. You're not where you need to be to kick in a door or clear a room. You having a weapon in your hand is a hard no. Saying that you need to be there, I'll have your back. But straight up, I'd feel better if you waited here for me to bring her to you. Badger's right. It'll give us a chance to feel her out. But just saying, even if she's not where I think she needs to be to sit across from you, I'll cuff her, duct tape her mouth shut, and still bring her in so you can lay eyes on her."

That was what I needed.

"Promise? No matter what, you bring her to me?" I pushed.

"Swear on my life, baby."

Whatever you need, you'll get.

He said that a lot, or some variation of it.

"Okay. I'll wait here."

"Kira, you're here with Nebraska," Zane ordered.

"Duh. Someone's gotta be here to arrange bail money and dental services whenever you leave the office."

Zane smiled at Kira, showing off a white, toothy grin that was so wide it depressed his dimples.

I was momentarily dazzled. Not that I'd ever admit that to anyone, not even under torture, but Zane Lewis was hot. Scary-hot but hot nonetheless, and when those dimples came out, he lost the scary and sexy inched in.

"You're drooling, baby."

I pulled out of my stupor and blinked at Easton.

"Huh?"

Easton didn't elaborate, at least not verbally. His lips twitching said something—I just wasn't sure what. And him leaning over, pressing a kiss to my mouth, also said something but I didn't understand that either.

It wasn't until I heard Badger's cantankerous grunt, then his equally rough voice say, "Christ, those fucking dimples. Are there any women who are immune?" did I finally get it.

Easton caught me staring.

I shot him an unhappy look that not only did nothing, it totally deflected off of him like he was coated in Nebraska-attitude-proof Teflon.

I knew it deflected because he smiled.

"You're a dick," I muttered.

"I'm gonna let that one slide, but just saying, baby—"

"Nah-uh, nope, don't finish that," Kira cut in. "You have places to be and people to see. You should get on that."

I'd heard good things about Kira. I'd respected her long before I met her. With her history, she could've crumbled. Hell, she should've crumbled but she didn't. She stood strong and survived. But watching her with the team, she impressed me. She'd had to have steel in that spine of hers not to let these men walk all over her.

That went for Layla as well as the team's leader. I had firsthand knowledge of the work Patheon had done and I knew she was the woman behind it all. I'd also heard the story of her digging through the rubble of a building that had collapsed with Zane and Kevin inside, not knowing if they were dead or alive. She did this for hours with her bare hands until they were bloody and raw and she had to be sedated.

She was the type of woman other women aspired to be. That was, if the woman was going for strong, brave, and badass.

"Let's roll," Layla ordered.

Everyone got up to do her bidding, Zane included. That was, everyone but Easton. He stayed seated and turned my chair to face him.

"You good?"

No, I was absolutely not good.

But I wouldn't tell him that.

"Yeah."

"Liar," he whispered and leaned in close. "But I swear to fuck you will be."

Since he was close he sealed his promise with a kiss.

Not like the closed-mouth ones he'd given me in front of his team. Not like the wet and deep ones he gave me that made me wild. Not like the soft and sweet ones I got first thing in the morning.

This one was new.

Different.

A vow in the form of a really great kiss that took the top spot for the best kiss of my life.

TWENTY-FIVE

"So...Black."

I glanced up from the report Kira had printed out on Patricia Sawiris. It was cursory; most of what she'd found I already knew, but there were a few tidbits in there I hadn't uncovered, which made me wonder why I'd never asked Dutch to get someone to dig deeper.

"What about it?" I asked.

"What's it like?"

This felt strange. First, being able to talk about my team, and second, sitting in Kira's office with her like we were old pals. And that was exactly how she'd made me feel. Without hesitation she'd invited me back to her office instead of working in the conference room—a place she never would've allowed me to enter a week ago. Unlike Easton's office, hers was decorated—her life in the form of pictures all over the walls. Her and her parents. Her and her brother Finn. All of them together. Her and Cooper. Snapshots of the guys goofing off, playing with Nerf guns in the middle of the office. Cooper and his brother. Tons and tons of pictures. Personal photos she wouldn't share with me unless she was trying to make me feel comfortable.

"The team's much different than what you have here."

She closed the lid to her laptop to give me her full attention before she asked, "How so?"

I followed her lead and put the stack of papers I had in my hands on her desk.

"We're more like Patheon than Silver Team. We work mostly alone or at least I do. I go in first, try to negotiate a deal. Most of the time that works and from there the situation's monitored. If I can't swing a deal, then I sit down with Dutch, give him the details. From there, he and Badger work out the rest. My part's over and the team moves out."

"The team of assassins." There was no judgment or disgust in her tone.

It was a statement. A factual statement but still I gave my two-cents.

"More like peacekeepers. If a deal can't be made, one side has to be taken out to stop a war from breaking out and more innocent people dying. But we don't step in until it becomes obvious the conflict has become uncontrollable by local law enforcement, that's when we contain the situation."

"Zane said there's another mediator," she pried.

"There is. Two more actually. There are certain cultures that wouldn't appreciate a woman calling men to the table." Kira's nose scrunched in clear distaste. It was cute and made her look younger than her years. "There are also jobs I won't do."

"Like what?"

Hostage negotiations.

I glanced at the picture of her brother proudly displayed next to her wedding picture. Her brother who had been beheaded live on the internet. Her brother who'd still be alive if it wasn't for greed and treason.

Did it always come down to money and power?

I didn't have to think too hard about the answer—yes, it always came down to money. And money bought you power.

What a sick and twisted world we live in.

"I'm sorry if I'm being nosy. I'm just still in shock Zane has the whole other team no one knew about."

Why I felt the need to defend the sarcastic asshole I didn't know. It might've had something to do with seeing a different side of him. I knew of Viper, everyone did. But I didn't know Zane, the man. His loyalty was legendary, his years in service were still talked about and passed down like fables. If you were smart you knew to keep your distance and never tangle with one of his teams. But I had no idea under all of that was a man who loved deeply. His wife, his children, his brother, and his teams. Loved them in a way I didn't know was possible. He wouldn't die for one of them. He'd burn cities, he'd kill, he'd harm, he'd mark his soul straight to hell if it meant protecting them.

It dawned on me that was why his loyalty was returned tenfold. That was why I'd defend him, not only to Kira but to anyone who posed a threat to Z Corps.

"He was protecting everyone. Nothing about Black Team is legal. There are no government contracts. There's bad and really bad. Evil and vile. If we go down, he didn't want that to touch any of you."

"I get it. I'm just shocked. Nothing's kept a secret around here for long. These boys gossip like old biddies and nothing is sacred. They flap their lips and you never know what they're going to say. Zane keeping this a secret for so long is...impressive. But he's Zane so I guess not."

That said it all.

Zane was Zane and I was fairly convinced he could do anything.

"Dutch reminds me of Zane. Quieter, not as dickish, but they're a lot alike."

"Does he pass out condoms to his men, too?"

Her question was so crazy, so off the wall, I reared back in my chair in surprise.

"Condoms?"

"Yeah, that's what that was about when you came in. Zane's always up in everyone's business giving wisdom."

"And this wisdom's about birth control?"

"Mostly." She smiled. "I was told when I started working here his love language was asshole. But it's not. His love language is handing his people shit so they understand they're family. I still think he should just try saying I love you, but apparently he's stingy with those words and the only people who hear them are Ivy, Rose, and Eric."

I kind of loved that. I bet Ivy did, too, knowing she and her kids were the only ones who got that. It made it special. Zane didn't toss out sentiments willy-nilly.

I still didn't understand why Kira had brought up sperm in our meeting though, and since I was new at this girl-talk thing I wasn't about to ask.

Instead I answered, "No, Dutch doesn't pass out

condoms. Or if he does, not in front of me and I'm happy to report he's never offered me spermicide or a cervical cap."

There was a beat of silence before Kira busted out laughing. More weirdness happened when I smiled, liking that I could make her laugh.

Stella was my only girlfriend and our relationship was complicated. Sure, we'd laughed together but never in a room full of personal effects. I knew what I knew about the woman because I'd investigated her. She knew what she knew about me because she'd done the same. We ran in the same circles, we had work in common. But never would she open up to me and be herself.

Two *real* people having a *real* conversation.

I was Dove. She was Lore.

Always.

"That would be awkward," Kira said, still laughing. "Though truth be told, if I would've thought of it before you came in I might've tossed one on the table. Next time."

Um.

I didn't want a contraceptive device thrown at me in the conference room. Not even if that was Kira's way of making friends.

"That's a hard no for me."

"Not you." She laughed. "I mean the next chick that gets dragged in here by one of the boys. Oh, and I'm gonna need your help. Zane's always got these quips, you know, like 'wrap it before you tap it.' 'Cover your stump before you hump.' All I came up with was, don't take his sperm if you don't want to do the term and I used that with you. There are three more men. I need to come up with more."

So, Zane had a sense of humor. It would seem Kira did as well. Me, not so much.

"I'm not funny, KK. I don't...shit, I'm sorry, that was rude. I mean, Kira, I'm not funny so I don't think I'll be any help."

Kira's brows pulled together and her chin tipped the side.

"What was rude?"

"Me calling you KK."

She added a deep frown to her already pinched brows and said, "Rude?"

Shit, now I was making a bigger mess of this.

What was it about these people that threw me off my game?

I was a goddamn mediator. My job was to *talk* and persuade. I was damn good at it but as soon as I got around Easton I lost my temper. My very first team meeting I had a breakdown. I couldn't speak to anyone in this office without sounding like an idiot.

What the hell was wrong with me?

"You look like you're taking a bad trip down to Shitsville," she pointed out.

Great.

Now I couldn't even mask my feelings.

It was a good thing I'd quit-fired because I'd officially lost my edge.

"I don't know how to do this," I blurted out. "It's like all you people have voodoo. You know, three months ago I sat at a table with a mob boss who's missing three fingers and some wannabe twit who's encroaching on territory that's not his. But he's so gung-ho and stupid ambitious he doesn't heed warnings. Big Boss decides to teach him a lesson and there's a drive-by shooting in a neighborhood. The house Baby Boss lives in with his family is hit but so are four other houses and there were kids playing basketball in the driveway of the house across the street. Those kids saw that shit. Those other houses were occupied and someone could've died. I had zero hesitation calling a meeting. Not a single moment of dithering during negotiations. Two mob bosses, no problem. But sitting in a nice, cozy office, safe and sound, I can't think straight. I'm screwing this up because I don't know how to do it. No one trained me how to be a friend. No one taught me how to be normal."

Since I was on a roll, spilling my guts, I continued.

"And Easton. What's up with *that*? I barely know him and I'm falling in love. Am I delusional? I must be. I've gone totally insane. I found out my whole life was a lie and what do I do? Fall in *like* with some guy. That's the first step, right? You fall in like?"

"Yeah, that's the first step," she confirmed.

"Right, okay. But before that, like the day before that, he's annoying as shit and I'm calling him a dick. A lot. I told him he was a dick repeatedly and I was liberal with my assholes, too."

Kira smirked and suppressed a chuckle.

"Gross, not like that. I mean, not gross if you like butt stuff, but I wasn't liberal with *my* asshole. I was calling him an asshole left and right."

Kira's hand came up, palm facing me, and she was shaking her head.

"Please...please...stop." A laugh burst from her with such force she bucked. "Oh. My. God. Dead. I'm dying," she hooted. "Liberal with your asshole. I'm stealing that. Not your asshole—Easton can keep that—but I'm telling this story."

My back shot straight.

What had I done?

Who was she going to tell?

"Okay, Nebraska, here it is for you," she said when her laughing stopped. "First, badass you worked that deal with those bosses. Next is, we don't have voodoo. You can't be badass Dove around us because you're not Dove to us. You're Nebraska."

She stopped and made a show of waving. "Hi, I'm Kira or KK or Kid Genius, or as Zane calls me, Mini Me. Feel free to call me any or all of my nicknames or make up one of your own. That's what friends do. It's not rude to call a friend a nickname. It's what friends do. Next, you calling Easton a dick, I've called him a douche nozzle dozens of times when he's annoyed me. I call Smith Smithsonian a bunch because he hates it and he can be annoying, too. Jonas is mostly cool and chill so I've only called him a fuckwit a few times. And Cash, I've given up. You can call him anything and he'll embrace it and turn it and that's more annoying than the original thing he did. And don't let the Dimple King fool you; he's still a demon and I call him that to his face. Right or wrong it's just what we do around here. It's a way to blow off steam, it's the way we joke, it's family."

"The last time I called Easton a dick he spanked me." As soon as I blurted that out I covered my mouth so my order was muffled. "Forget I said that."

"Sure. I'll forget if you promise to call me KK."

"I'll call you the Queen of the Universe if you never tell that to a soul."

She sobered immediately.

"Here's a lesson for you. There is a difference between a good story that's embarrassing but hilarious and a secret between sisters. I'll share the asshole story because it's funny. What you confide in me, whether it's a slip or intentional, never, and I mean *never*, leaves my lips."

I was back to screwing this up.

"I didn't mean to offend you."

"You didn't, honey, but that part's important. So please tell me you get me."

I rubbed my sweaty palms on my jeans and ignored the detail that they were sweating at all. The last time that had happened was the first time Charlie had taken me with him on a job. He'd reamed my behind for giving away I was nervous. After that I never did it again. That wasn't to say I hadn't felt the nerves. I just did better at hiding it.

"I get you."

"Okay. So, next. Love's crazy, Nebraska. It sneaks up on you and slaps you in the face."

"That sounds painful."

"Says the girl who likes to get her bum spanked. You liked it, right? I didn't see Easton with a busted face so..."

I felt the side of my mouth curl up before I giggled.
Me.

I giggled. Not a laugh. Not a chuckle. A girly giggle that even shocked Kira.

"Um, yeah."

"Right on."

Was this really happening? Was I seriously talking

about Easton spanking me and liking it with a stranger?

Twilight Zone!

"People say that love comes from the heart. It doesn't; you feel it in your soul. That's when you know it's real. A day, five, a month, six years, it doesn't matter. When it hits, it hits. You don't control it, it controls you. When your soul knows, it knows. It's that simple and that hard. You want to fight it and that's the painful part. You don't want to believe in it, and that's the annoying part. You don't want to trust it, and that's frustrating. You want to pump the brakes and hit the accelerator at the same time, and that's the confusing part. Bottom line is, you can't control when love hits or how or with who. Your soul knows and bam, suddenly you love a man who you've been calling a dick and have only known for a few days."

Maybe I wasn't so crazy—love was.

But still I said, "You're smart."

She shrugged and smiled.

"They don't call me Kid Genius for nothing, girl. Stick with me and you'll have this friendship thing down, too."

Friendship.

She was offering to be my friend and teach me how to be one.

She also thought I'd be around for her to teach me.

Lying in bed with Easton, Greece had lost its appeal.

But right then in Kira's office after Easton once again proved he was the man I needed him to be, and Kira offering to be my friend, Greece was officially scratched off the list of places I wanted to live and Annapolis was moved to the top.

"You're on," I accepted.

And saying that, I didn't think I was crazy or insane.

I was finally getting smart.

"Patricia Sawiris," she announced, switching back to work. "Stick with me on this. I need to talk it out."

Her wanting to talk something out with me felt crazy good.

I grabbed the stack of papers, nabbed a pen, and sat back in the chair, noting Zane sported for comfy office furniture.

"Hit me."

"Warning, this might be convoluted and I haven't had time to cross reference."

"Okay."

I flipped the papers over so I had a blank sheet ready to take notes. Kira opened her laptop and she was back to all business. One minute joking and teasing and handing out wisdom, the next total focus on work. Joking, teasing, ribbing each other at the start of a meeting then business. I didn't joke when I sat in a meeting. I didn't tease the criminals who sat across from me and I certainly didn't share how much I liked to be spanked. Though that was a new revelation, but still, I'd never tell Big Boss Mobster I was falling in love, and part of why I talked about it now was because with Easton, I knew I was safe to be me. I didn't have to keep my composure and pretend I didn't have emotions. I could be me, any way I wanted to be. Say, do, behave, react how I wanted.

Kira was right.

My soul knew what it needed.

And it found it.

Found Easton.

TWENTY-SIX

"Long time, Pidge," Zane drawled.

The woman on the couch with her knees bent, feet tucked on the cushion, glass of wine in her hand, smiled.

She hadn't made a single move to get up or put her wine down when we entered.

And Christ, Zane was right; it was like looking at Nebraska in twenty years. The sight was far from bad. Anna was in her fifties and a knockout. Her daughter's smile was better, or maybe it was only when she was smiling at me with her eyes lit after I said or did something she liked. Anna's grin was cocky, chalked full of attitude. Something else mother had passed down to her daughter.

"Well, if it isn't my old pal, Viper."

"You're losing your touch, woman," Zane noted and dipped his chin to indicate her lounging on the couch instead of moving to her gun on the coffee table in front of her.

"Saw Badger at the coffee shop yesterday morning. Figured you would come knocking."

I glanced over at Badger who was staring at Anna but seemed to be looking straight through her. Totally devoid of any expression. The dude was huge—a tall, built, wall of muscle. He'd be hard to miss but still, if he didn't want to be seen, he wouldn't be. Which meant he wanted Anna to know he was there.

"And if I was coming in here to shoot you?" Zane pushed.

Anna shrugged.

"Then it was my time and what better way to go out than by the hand of the infamous Viper. Besides, you wouldn't shoot an old friend, would you?"

"Of course I would."

Her smile widened. This one looked genuine, like she found Zane amusing.

"Don't be a dick."

Dick.

Jesus.

Like mother, like daughter.

Anna dragged her gaze around the room, pausing on me. Those pool-blue eyes sized me up. I could see Zane falling for that—those soft eyes, pretty face, the desire to protect that beauty.

"All this for little me?" she quipped.

Theo, Smith, Cash, Jonas, and I were spread out around the living room. None of us had holstered our weapons. Add in Zane and Badger and the show of force was mighty. If we'd wanted to take her out, she'd be lounging on the couch in a pool of blood. And we wouldn't have had to enter the house to make that happen. The curtains were open. She hadn't been hiding, and neither did we when we walked in the front door after Badger reported she was alone.

Why make shit more difficult when you could turn a handle and walk right in?

"Get up, Pidge, we got shit to do," Zane informed her.

"What kind of shit would that be?"

"The kind that means after long last, you're meeting with your daughter."

All the color drained from Anna's face. Gone was the bravado and attitude. She might've been a good actress. Back in the day she might've been able to turn on the charm and play the damsel in distress to screw Zane, but no one was that good. No one could fake that kind of fear.

"Zane—"

"It's done. It's over. It's time, Anna. You gotta daughter who's mourned you for twenty years. That ends for her today."

Anna's gaze came directly to me. Eyes pleading. Panic evident.

"You don't want to do this," Anna said, shaking her head.

"Do what?"

"You need to protect her from me."

Acid leaked into my gut as her threat registered.

"You obviously don't know your daughter or you wouldn't make that threat. She'll chew you up and spit you out before I could lift a finger. Now get your ass up and let's go."

"You don't understand—"

"What I understand is, I promised my woman I'd be bringing her mother in so she could see for herself you're alive. What you should also know—I promised to do that even if I had to cuff you and tape your mouth shut. She has some things she'd like to say to you that I suspect don't require a response, so that tape will remain in place until Viper or Badger decides what to do with you."

"Trust me, she's better off not knowing," Anna whispered.

"Woman, I don't trust you. But Nebraska trusts me so what'll it be? Cuffs and tape or are you gonna come with us and give my woman what she needs?"

I didn't miss the flinch when I said Nebraska's name.

"I had a man love me like that once."

"Yeah, you had a kid who loved you like that, too. Yet you still left them."

Anna surged to her feet, wine sloshing over the bowl, before she side-armed the glass and it shattered on the floor. Not a person in the room moved with her outburst.

"Don't you stand there and pass judgment on me, asshole." Anna's face twisted up in pain and anger. "You cannot imagine what it took for me to leave them. *Both* of them, but especially my daughter. You cannot for one fucking second understand the pain. The guilt I've lived with. I prayed for death. Wished for it. Without them, without her, I had nothing. I *am* nothing. You want to give her what she needs, you'll keep me far away from her so she can live the rest of her life without being tarnished by me. She'll forgive Charlie. He's a good man. They're a family. They don't need me fucking that up."

There was no denying Anna's pain suffocated the room; it was stifling, the magnitude of it. I felt for her—felt each of her words hit me square in the chest, felt her guilt like it was my own. But her pain and suffering weren't my problem—Nebraska's was.

"You sure about that?" I asked.

"Positive."

She didn't sound positive. She sounded broken.

"She's so much like you it's uncanny. Gives a new spin on nature versus nurture. Or maybe she had enough time with you to get both. You're fucking terrified, and instead of saying that, you're hiding behind attitude and defiance. She tried that with me, too. Called her on it and put a stop to that shit. So check it, Anna, this is how this is going to go. You're coming with us to meet your daughter. When you get there you're gonna drop Pigeon and be Anna. And when you sit across from my girl you're gonna remember she's Nebraska, not Dove, and you're gonna do that remembering she loves you. You leaving tore her apart and as much as it fucks me to admit I can't do something for her, you're the only one who can piece that back together. So you're doing it or you wishing for death all those years will become a reality. You feel me?"

Anna's gaze sliced to Zane. The anger slid out, leaving guilt and shame behind.

"He's just like you."

I wasn't sure if that was an accusation, an insult, or a statement. I also didn't give a fuck. I wanted this to be over so I could get Anna to Nebraska. I wanted that to happen quickly so I could get to work helping my woman deal with the aftermath of another hit.

I was done with this shit. Not only Anna and Charlie. I was done with Maddon hanging out there while we waited for him to strike. I wanted this over for Nebraska so she could move on and I could get busy convincing her Greece was no longer an option and Maryland was where she wanted to be.

"They all are," Zane returned. "You think I'd hire some fuckwit to have my back?"

"I'll go if you promise—"

"Lady, you're in no position to ask for jackshit," Smith spoke up.

"I think he'll make this one," Anna contradicted. "Promise you'll fix whatever I break."

She was right, I'd make that promise. But not for her, for her daughter.

I didn't tell her that.

"Let's go."

With a graceful sweep, she tagged her Sig off the table and shoved it into the back of her jeans. Zane met her at the front door. She tipped her head back and studied him for a moment.

"I never apologized," she murmured.

"Nope."

"If I did that now would it buy me your word you won't shoot me in the back?"

"You know me better than that, Pidge. On both fronts— empty apologies mean shit to me and I have enough respect to look you in the eyes when I shoot you."

"And that's why I don't let him out of the office," Layla groused. "You can't go around shooting people in the face, boss."

"Says who?"

"Says the United States justice system."

"Never heard of it."

Zane and Layla flanked Anna down the walkway to the curb. The rest of the team filed out, leaving me to take up the rear with Badger a few steps behind me. I was man enough to admit this position gave me a shiver. I didn't know the man; he was a monster, and by all accounts not a man you wanted to tangle with. So, yeah, Badger behind me—I wasn't a fan.

"You got this?" I heard him rumble.

"Yep."

"Good, then I'm gone."

I looked over my shoulder to see him peeling off through the grass. I watched as he disappeared around the corner of the house.

And just like that, Badger was vapor.

I WAS QUESTIONING MY SANITY, watching Nebraska fidget in the elevator.

"Hand," I demanded.

Nebraska glanced at my offering before she lifted her hand and placed it in mine.

"I won't leave your side."

"I know."

She knew.

No pause. No prevarication.

"You're in control, baby. Don't forget that."

"I know."

"You can leave whenever you want. We'll come back, grab our shit, and go home."

She jerked my hand and squeezed.

"Honey, I *know*."

Honey.

Christ. She'd said it before, both full of sarcasm and when she was being sweet. But right then it hit different.

"You seem calm," I noted.

Too calm. She was seeing her not-so-dead mother for the first time in two decades. She'd already had a rough morning and locked herself inside her head.

"That's because I am."

"Nebraska—"

"Are you going to leave my side?"

"Fuck no."

"Then there you go. Why I'm calm."

Jesus, fuck me.

I yanked her hand, pulled her to my chest, slid my other hand from her neck up to her cheek, and tilted her head back so I could catch her eyes.

Christ, so fucking pretty.

No question, I was falling, and fast.

I know.

It was just that right then I wasn't sure there was much further to fall.

And she should know that.

With a brush of my lips, followed by a touch of my tongue, her lips parted with a mewl. A sweet invitation made sweeter when she pressed closer and swept her tongue against mine. With bad timing, the elevator stopped and the door opened.

When we broke apart Cash was standing there grinning like an idiot.

So it wasn't bad timing, it was the worst timing.

My friend opened his mouth but Nebraska got there first.

"I recently learned you're impervious to name-calling. As much fun as I think it would be to test that, I'm in a hurry. So if you make a wisecrack I'll be forced to use physical violence."

"KK has a big mouth," he grunted.

"No, she was sharing with a sister the best way to stop you from being annoying."

Sister?

How long were we gone?

Cash's gaze snapped to mine, his eyes dancing with humor, which was never a good thing. He declared, "With her in tight with KK, you're fucked."

He wasn't wrong. And if I was lucky I'd never get unfucked.

"You mind letting us out of the elevator so we can get this over with?"

Cash stepped to the side, humor fading, brotherhood seeping in.

"I'll be right outside the door. If you need me, holler."

Hand-in-hand, we followed Cash down the basement corridor. He stopped at the end in front of the room we'd put Anna in. An interrogation room might not have been the coziest place for a mother-daughter reunion but there was zero chance Anna was making it upstairs into the office.

"Ready?" I asked.

My gorgeous girl looked up at me, blew out a breath, and nodded.

I opened the door, entered first, keeping Nebraska behind me.

I didn't need to see Nebraska to know when it happened. I didn't need to hear the swift intake of oxygen that whistled past her teeth. I didn't need to feel her hand in mine squeeze so tightly I courted broken bones, to know the exact moment when she saw her mother.

The air charged, the static crackled, the room sizzled.

I slowly shifted to look at Nebraska.

Grief and pain and longing, stark on her face.

Both women were frozen, suspended in a place that I would never fully understand. I was teetering on the edge of regret for allowing this to happen so soon. I should've taken time with Nebraska upstairs, prepared her, made sure she was where she needed to be before taking her to Anna. Instead, I was so hellbent on keeping my promise I hadn't stopped to think of the repercussions.

"I'm...I'm..." Anna broke the silence. "I'm so sorry."

Nebraska startled.

Anna unraveled.

"I should've taken you with me. When your father found me, I should've packed you up and ran. But I was terrified he'd find me and you'd be with me. The day I called Charlie and told him what I was going to do, I knew I'd regret it for the rest of my life. I knew there'd be no going back. He begged me not to do it. He promised he'd take care of it. But I was so scared, so sure that if Dmitri found me he'd take you, I couldn't chance it. I had to keep you safe. *I had to!* Charlie loved us. Even before you went to live with him he loved you like crazy, loved you because you were mine. I knew he'd never let anything happen to you. I knew you were safer with me gone."

Anna paused, looked to her feet, and shook her head. Nebraska leaned closer, tucked herself under my arm, and wrapped an arm around my stomach. When Anna's eyes lifted they locked on her daughter. With another shake of her head she finished.

"I was too weak to see past my fear. Too weak to believe Charlie would make us safe and keep us together. I was terrified of losing you to Dmitri so I lost you a different way. A way I could control. If I couldn't have you I needed to know you were safe and loved and taken care of and not with a monster. I don't regret loving you enough to walk away to protect you. But I will never forgive myself for being so weak I didn't stay and fight for you."

Nebraska pressed closer, her cheek firm against my chest, her arms wrapped tightly, holding on for dear life. I did the only thing I could do and stood strong, giving her what she needed while she fought a battle I couldn't fight for her. I wanted to. I wanted to shuffle her out of the room, get her to safety, but that option was not available to me.

"Why didn't you come back?" Nebraska's question was nothing more than a whisper.

But Anna heard.

"I did. So many times. So weak I couldn't stay away even though I knew every time I got close I was bringing danger with me. Watching you graduate high school and not be the one you ran to and hugged after you got your diploma *killed*."

The brokenness in Anna's tone was testament to the truth behind her words. She sounded wounded.

"Seeing you graduate college, so beautiful, so happy, tossing your cap into the air, laughing with your friends after, and not being the one who you were smiling at was worse than a thousand knives to my heart. But I didn't earn that, Charlie did. I was an outsider watching my daughter, like a crazed stalker catching glimpses of you when I could. Getting close enough to hear your voice, close enough to touch you, but too terrified to show myself."

"What?"

"I'm *weak*, Nebraska. I should've taken you with me or I should've taken out Dmitri sooner. But he was in too deep, his death would've been avenged. They wouldn't have stopped until they found me. They would've taken you and I couldn't ever let that happen."

The *they* was the Russian Mob. And Anna wasn't wrong. They would've hunted down Dmitri's killer and they wouldn't have stopped until they found her. If Nebraska was with Anna, they'd either kill her or take her, the second of those options worse. A beautiful young girl... I couldn't bring myself to even think of the horror that would've become Nebraska's life without feeling murderous.

But something struck me.

"Sooner?" I interrupted to ask.

"With Maddon making his plays I knew he'd go to Dmitri. I couldn't let that happen."

Fuck me.

Fuck me.

Fuck me.

"Are you telling me we're gonna have the Bratva breathin' down our necks?" I growled.

Nebraska might no longer be young but she was gorgeous and the daughter of someone who they would consider an enemy. We could build a fortress around her and fortify it with an army and still have trouble keeping those motherfuckers from getting Nebraska.

"No. I made a deal."

She made a deal.

What the fuck!

"For the love of Christ tell me you're not standing in this office with my woman telling me you made a fucking deal with the Russian fucking Mob. In other words, putting her life in danger."

Anna's demeanor changed. The room cooled, the air wasn't quite so thick even though Nebraska was still burrowed close.

Are you going to leave my side?

Then there you go. Why I'm calm.

She hadn't lied. With me at her side she was calm.

The vibe in the room was all Anna.

The shock and longing—Nebraska.

The ugly regret and guilt—Anna.

"I know I didn't do one thing to guide you to it, and God knows I didn't earn the right to say it, but that doesn't mean I'm any less happy that you found it."

"Found what?" Nebraska asked.

"Your strength. Him. Being brave enough to give your trust to the man who holds your heart. To lean on him. To believe in him. To be strong even when you're terrified. So I didn't earn it, but, baby girl, that doesn't mean I'm not all kinds of happy you have a man who's willing to do anything to protect you."

I wasn't sure I was at the point I cared that Anna obviously approved of me being at Nebraska's side. However, I was pleased as fuck she gave her daughter something straight up good. But more, I was happy Nebraska got that from her mother. If nothing else, she'd always know her mother admired her strength.

So it sucked I had to break the moment, but the threat of an impending attack took precedence.

"What kind of deal did you make?"

"The kind that gave a very powerful man information he wanted in exchange for cutting a soldier loose."

"There is no such information when it comes to the Bratva. Bond is bond to them. Nothing breaks that. Period. The end."

"Bonds break quick when you watch a porno starring your enforcer and your wife."

Yep.

That would do it.

"You're positive there will be no blowback?"

"Absolutely not, seeing as I wasn't the one who put a bullet in him. Unfortunately, that honor went to Dmitri's boss, though he was kind enough to let me watch."

Suddenly it dawned on me that we were speaking about Nebraska's biological father and her back-from-the-dead mother killing him—she didn't pull the trigger but the man died by her actions.

"Baby?"

"I'm fine."

Shit on a shingle.

"Is that a fine as in you're okay knowing your father's

dead or is that a fine as in I need to take you home and talk this shit out?"

Nebraska pulled her cheek off my shoulder, tipped her head back, and gave me a small grin.

"My father's alive, honey. Zenith was never my father. And the world is a better place with him no longer in it."

She looked like she was telling the truth.

"You sure?"

Her grin became a smile.

"Positive. Can I have a little while longer with my mom or do we need to get back upstairs?"

I wasn't sure why she was asking me when she was in control.

But still I answered, "Anything you need."

"Anything I need," she whispered.

I heard Anna's sob rend the air but I didn't stop staring at Nebraska, and that was because she didn't stop staring at me.

I was right, I'd hit rock bottom.

There was no further to fall.

TWENTY-SEVEN

This was strange.

Very, very strange.

And if I allowed myself to feel the fullness of it I'd probably burst into tears.

The strange being Easton in the kitchen wearing an apron with a silverback gorilla on it surrounded by the words *Silverback Rule The Jungle With 6 Centimeters.* This given to him by Bridget Keller. After everyone in the room—everyone being Theo, Smith, Jonas, Cash, Cooper, Kira, and of course Bridget and Easton—finished roaring with the rowdiest laughter I'd ever heard, Easton pulled Bridget in for a hug. The hug ended with a gut punch from Bridget after Easton called her Birdie Bird.

None of this I understood.

The other strange was that the team plus Kira's husband, minus Layla and her husband (they had dinner plans with friends so they couldn't make it), were over for dinner.

At the safehouse.

This was *strange.*

Yet it wasn't strange because I understood what was happening. Everyone was checking on Easton after a shit day. And me. They'd made it clear they were there to make sure after I'd spoken to my father and spent hours with a woman who had faked her death, leaving me motherless, that I was okay.

I wasn't.

But everyone being there went a long way getting me there.

And Easton, he'd get me where I needed to be. I knew he would. He'd repeatedly told me he'd give me anything I needed and I believed him.

Fully and totally.

Kira was right; my soul recognized something my brain didn't. And my heart was faulty and couldn't be trusted. I'd shut that muscle down twenty years ago. It would need a lot of work polishing the rust off before I could trust it. But my soul...now that I trusted.

And my soul knew Easton Spears was mine.

I didn't need him to protect me or to complete me or any of those other storybook romance tales. He settled the noise, he steadied me. He didn't make me strong but he did strengthen me. He made me feel like I was on solid ground, totally free to be Nebraska Michaels. No rules. No lessons. No training. No Dove.

Just me.

I never realized how disconnected I'd been. I'd been living a double life, the two sides always at war. It was exhausting. I didn't want that anymore. A week ago, that terrified me. If I wasn't Dove, if I gave her up, then who was

I? My identity was so wrapped up in who other people wanted me to be, I'd never considered I had a choice in the matter.

"Need a refill?" Bridget asked, bringing the bottle of red wine to the table.

I was told to sit and drink and commune with the women. Yes, Easton said commune when he ordered me to stay put after I tried to help him in the kitchen.

"I'm good," Kira answered from my side.

She, too, had been told to take a load off and relax, those being Cooper's instructions to his wife.

It was sweet. I felt lazy sitting there watching the men in the kitchen but I liked that they took care of their women. And the view didn't suck either.

"How much money do you think we'd make if we videoed that?" I stopped to jerk my head toward the kitchen. "Six hot guys in the kitchen."

"A lot more if we could talk them into being shirtless." Kira snickered.

"I heard that," Cooper called back.

"I'm down," Cash put in.

"Is there anything you're *not* game to do?" Jonas asked.

There was a stretch of silence but not long before Cash reported, "Nope."

"Let's not test that theory," Theo bit out.

"Dude, I don't know what your problem is, you're the one with the nine-inch pecker, Mr. Long John Silver."

I sputtered. I tried to swallow my wine. But I couldn't do it. It sprayed out all over the table while I choked on the wine that was already in my throat while at the same time busting a gut I was laughing so hard.

"That was my reaction, too, sis." Cash chuckled. "Who knew Theo was packing that kind of sausage."

"Sorry," I muttered and helped Bridget mop up my mess with my napkin.

She glanced up from the wine I'd spit out and smiled.

"Nothing to be sorry about, but I gotta ask—"

"Baby, careful. You open this door and they'll pounce," Theo warned.

Bridget smiled wider, making it brighter, adding a spark in her eyes that screamed trouble.

And with this group trouble could mean anything.

"Payback." Was her weird response. "I warned him one day I'd be sitting at a table with his woman and there'd be payback. The time has arrived."

I heard Easton's laugh. Funny how I wasn't looking into the kitchen and I still knew it was his.

"Told you, Birdie, I'm secure in my manhood. I can admit I don't need a sling to carry my nine-inch package around. It might be small, but he is mighty."

Small?

What in the world was he talking about?

"Six centimeters is not mighty, Silverback!" she shouted back. "That's not even cocktail-wiener sized."

The room once again filled with laughter that made my insides vibrate—or maybe it was my laughter that did that. I couldn't be sure and it didn't matter—laughter was laughter, hearing it, feeling it, it was all the same. It felt good and nourished the soul.

"Are you talking about Easton's dick?" I blurted out.

More laughter, this time only from the men.

"His claim is that it's teeny-tiny," Bridget informed me.

"Well, he lied. It's huge."

Bridget sputtered and through her laughter yelled, "I want my present back, you liar!"

"YOU DOING OKAY?"

I cuddled closer, my belly full of the tacos Easton had made. The bottle of wine the girls and I polished off was making me sleepy. But I roused at his question—the third time he'd asked it since we'd been home but the first time since he'd put me to bed. I'd melted into him—not due to the drowsiness. What woke me was the care behind the question.

I didn't bother hiding or evading. Not that Easton would've allowed that. He'd find a way to pull the truth from me, but I didn't want to evade.

"She went to my graduations."

"Yeah, baby," he murmured softly, his voice thick with understanding.

"She called every birthday," I went on, telling him stuff he knew since he hadn't left my side the whole time I'd talked with my mother.

And by that I mean, he didn't leave my actual side—he stayed close, holding my hand or wrapping his arm around my shoulder. This after he'd stood strong while I burrowed into him, the pain of seeing my mother so great it sliced through me. And Easton took the anguish and gave me something beautiful in return—protection, peace, safety, concern. I knew with him by my side, if it had been too much, if the hurt cut too deep, if Anna had said anything that caused so much as a flinch from me, Easton would've unapologetically whisked me away.

Easton remained quiet, but his hand on my hip gave me a squeeze.

I blew out a breath and gave him what he was after.

"I don't know what I'm feeling. That's not me prevaricating, I truly don't know. On one hand it makes it worse knowing she called, she went to my graduations, she'd sought me out and found me at restaurants and sat close without me knowing. But somehow it makes it a little better knowing she cared, and in the only way she felt she could she keep me close. Knowing all of that means I know Charlie lied about more than her being dead. But I'm starting to come to the understanding he did what he felt he had to do. I don't agree with his decisions but I can't deny he might've been right to keep her secret. It might've made it harder if I knew she was alive but I couldn't see her. And I definitely would've looked for her. So really there's no *might have*. He was just plain right keeping the truth from me. And I don't know what to do with *that*."

"Makes sense."

I nodded against his chest, marveling in the way we fit. From the first morning I'd woken up to him that had been the case. The fit had nothing to do with the way we physically fit together, though I loved that we did. It was what the physical closeness said that made the fit so perfect. Two people who had been cast adrift finding each other. Never experiencing true, deep, abiding love from the people who brought us into this world—though evidence was suggesting I did have that from my mother even if that love came with pain. She'd left to keep me safe. Charlie did love me in his own way, but it wasn't enough. I figured with all that we had and didn't have we'd recognize the bounty of having it now. At least I did, and from all that Easton had given me, I believed he understood how we fit and knew how special it was.

"You didn't leave Anna with much when you left," he noted.

He was correct. I didn't close the door on a future but neither did I welcome mommy home after two decades with declarations of inviting her into my life.

"I only make promises I know for a fact I can keep, and I'm not sure how I feel right now and I'm not sure if I'll know what I want in a week or a month. I just don't know. Maybe tomorrow I'll feel differently and I'll call her and ask her what she wants for the future. Maybe that call won't happen for years. What I am sure about is that call is mine to make and I'll make it when I'm ready. I've spent too much of my life doing things to make others happy or proud or doing them to earn the love and respect from people who I shouldn't have had to do that for. I was trained into who I became, not guided with care and love."

Easton lay there quietly.

Just his fingertips gently sweeping over my hip, down my thigh as far as he could reach, then back up. Giving me sweet. Giving me quiet. Giving me calm. All of this after a shitty day that had broken me but didn't destroy me. Easton had made sure of that, and he continued when he announced to everyone it was time to leave when he saw me stifle a yawn. He continued when he guided me to our room after we'd said our goodbyes then told me to get ready for bed while he helped Smith lock up. He came back just as I was coming out of the bathroom, and continued taking care of me, giving me what I needed when he pulled back the bedclothes, helped me in, tucked me in, then went to get ready for bed himself. When he came back out, he hit the lights, got in next to me, and curled me into his side, commencing in giving me more.

This.

No sex. No kissing. No groping. No wild.

Sweet. Quiet. Calm.

I couldn't say for certain but I was pretty sure there wasn't another man on the planet who was as perfect as Easton. However, I was certain there was no one else who was perfect for me.

And he should know that.

"I'm falling for you," I whispered.

"Good," he softly returned and kissed the top of my head. "It would suck standing down here all by myself and you not nearing the edge so I could catch you."

Did he...

Did that mean...

He kept his mouth where it was, when he continued to give me *everything*.

"When you're ready, I'll catch you, baby. You got my promise on that."

Trust me.

You got my promise.

I closed my eyes, held on tight, and jumped.

The fall wasn't far.

But lying there in Easton's arms, he fulfilled his promise to catch me.

TWENTY-EIGHT

"Zane needs to move the office to a warehouse."

I glanced up from the mess I'd made on Easton's desk, which included colored Post-it notes I'd borrowed from Kira, to Lincoln standing in the doorway.

"Or you can just take over Easton's office since he's never in here." He paused again, smiled—no dimples like his brother's but still sinful. "Bet if he shared it with you he'd be in here more."

I had no idea what he was talking about other than he was correct; for the last three days I had taken over Easton's office. His desk now had papers strewn all over it. The wall to my left had sticky notes that to the untrained eye (meaning anyone but mine) would look haphazard. And I'd asked Cash to bring in a rolling whiteboard.

There was a method to my madness.

Sticky notes on the wall: stuff to research.

Sticky notes on the desk: Patricia's husband's associates before he died.

Whiteboard: Maddon's movements.

Easton had not cared I'd commandeered his office.

Maybe Lincoln did.

"I could move to the conference room," I offered.

His smile fled and his green eyes narrowed.

It made him no less handsome in a badass sort of way that *screamed* he wasn't pleased.

"Seriously? You got 'move to the conference room' from what I said?"

"Well, your brother having to pick up and move shop would be a pain in the ass and cost a whack. I'm taking up an office that's meant to be used by one of his employees. So..."

I let that hang and Lincoln Parker pounced.

"And you're not an employee? Have you checked your bank balance today? Paychecks hit last night. I think you'll find you're no exception. What I meant was, the team's growing. Has been growing since Patheon became Silver and we got KK and Layla. I was joking but I'm not wrong. My brother's grown out of this space but his sentimental ass doesn't want to admit it. This is where Red started. This was the start of him building his family. This is the home he gave me when I came back. So he won't give it up. But again, I was joking. Though not about Easton never being in here. He's allergic to paperwork and hates sitting behind a desk."

I knew about the desk part. The last three days during the team briefs in the conference room he'd stood, leaning against the wall. Close to me, but not sitting. That saying, the other times before when we'd been in there, he sat next to me because he was giving me that—Easton within reaching distance in case I needed him.

"I was fired—"

My change of subject was cut off.

"Do you know how many people Zane's fired over the years? Everyone. That's his way of saying, job well done."

That was crazy.

"He's crazy."

"Not going to get any arguments from me. I wish I could tell you my brother was a complicated man but he's not. What you see is what you get. But when you understand what you're getting is when you see who he truly is."

In my opinion that was complicated.

But I didn't get a chance to inform Lincoln of that.

Without leaving the doorway, he somehow managed to make it feel like his presence was invading the space as his gaze turned intense.

"All of this. Everything you see. Everything you've heard. The reputation he works hard to keep, is to give us something to hold onto. He built this to make a home. He'll lie and tell you he did it because we grew up dirt poor and he never wanted to feel that kind of poverty again. He'll come up with ten more bullshit reasons why he's built Z Corps to what it is and they'll be totally false. He built this for *you*. For me. For my wife. For Leo, Colin, Jax, Garrett, Brooks, Kyle, Thad. Max, Gabe, Owen, Kevin, Myles, Coop. For Drew, Eric, Declan, and Theo. For Easton, Smith, Jonas, Cash, Kira, and Layla. All of this for us. For us to have a family. There's no firing family, Nebraska. Drew left us to give his wife something she hadn't had a lot of while he was serving— his time. Eric died protecting this family. Declan left and took Autumn with him because after the life they endured they fucking deserved nothing touching the peace he was going to give her. Those three left but didn't leave the family. All of that to say this—you need an office, if you're good taking Easton's, have it. If you want something different, speak up and it's yours. But don't ever mistake family looking after family as anything but that."

Whoa.

I think that was the most I'd heard Lincoln say at one time. At least to me. And it was to chastise me for not taking my place in the family.

That felt so good I had to take a moment to savor the feel of it as it soothed some of the fresh wounds my parents had inflicted.

When the balm settled, I gave back the only way I knew would mean something to a man like Lincoln.

The truth.

That didn't mean I didn't infuse a healthy dose of smartass.

"Easton's office works for me. But it might not work for him when I paint the walls and bring in a plant. And his desk is fine but not near big enough so I hope Zane's office furniture budget is generous. With the mental torment I'll have to suffer through, I plan on breaking the bank. So heads up with that. And since I'm new to this whole family thing you can expect me to screw up here and again. You're going to have to deal with that, then deal with my attitude after since I'm not well-versed when it comes to graciously accepting anything that remotely shows kindness and consideration for my wellbeing."

"We'll see to that," he told me and I felt my breath

catch. "But I suspect Easton will get in there before any of the rest have a chance."

"You're being kind, again," I noted.

"Get used to it."

"I'm not sure that's possible seeing as I've been told too many stories about the infamous Ghost."

Lincoln's mouth quirked and that was so far from the Ghost stories I'd heard about the man it wasn't funny. The one story that never changed was, the man didn't smile. The rest of the tales varied, some more brutal than others. But it was widely known Lincoln Ghost Parker was dead inside. And dead men didn't smile.

I'd seen him with his sons and his wife so I knew that was bullshit.

But I now understood the difference—what you gave the world and what you gave your family. It was possible to be two different people and still be whole.

Ghost was proof of that.

So was Viper.

So maybe that could be me, too.

We both had to get back to work, but before we did I had one last thing to tell Lincoln.

"I'm sorry about Eric Wheeler. I never met him. But I didn't have to, to know he was a good man."

"He was the best of us."

With that, Lincoln turned and left.

I pushed aside thoughts of a good man gone too soon. His protection and sacrifice the ultimate act of love. He died so his brothers could live.

That was the family Zane had built.

That was now my family.

GOTCHA, *asshole*.

It was right there in front of my face the whole fucking time and I'd missed it.

I snatched my cell off the desk and texted Easton to ask him to get everyone into the conference room. Then I shuffled the papers into a stack, pulled some sticky notes off the desk, and ran out of Easton's...my...*our* office, not caring I looked like a crazy person. Garrett's huge glass enclosure in the middle of the main space was clouded so I knew he was working on something that was more sensitive than the normal sensitive stuff Z Corps worked with, and made it into the conference room just as Kira was walking in.

"You look—"

I interrupted her to say, "You're a genius."

"Well... I am called Kid Genius and not for nothing, but what did I do?"

"You found what I'd missed for years."

"What'd you miss?" Jonas asked as he entered the room with the rest of the team on his heels.

"I don't know how I didn't put it together," I blurted out. "It was all right there in front of me."

"Baby, what was?"

I looked at Easton, tossed the reports on the table, and tapped the stack.

"The connection. Maddon and Patricia."

The men took their seats, Lincoln, Zane, and Layla coming in last, and when everyone was settled I filled them in.

"Kira dug into Patricia," I started. "But more importantly, she looked into her husband Yasseen Sawiris's associates. His business is distribution of large construction equipment. I followed up on the contracts Kira got. He did a lot of business with a land developer. On the outside it looked legit. This developer did a lot of projects around Cairo. Not unusual, there's always construction going on. But the contracts didn't add up. I cross referenced the dates and looked up what buildings were being built or renovated. About fifty percent of those contracts to rent equipment were bogus. I went on to other construction companies and found the same thing."

I pushed the folders to the middle of the table but no one made a move to take them. Not even Easton who was sitting, yes sitting, with his full attention on me, and damn that felt good.

"That could be anything from money laundering, buying protection, basic corruption. But there was a name listed on one of the corporations that was familiar. Austin Wentworth. Wealthy Brit. Not unheard of for there to be foreign investors. When I looked into him, I realized why that name was familiar. Years ago Charlie and I were discussing wine, namely my palate for cheap wine, and he told me a story about him and Maddon being in Italy and staying at a villa Wentworth owned and his wine collection. Charlie told me Wentworth had a cellar that was worth millions and collected rare bottles of Changyu. Changyu is a Chinese wine manufactured in Yantai. Those bottles were gifts. Why would a Brit who invested in real estate development in Cairo, Nairobi, and Durban, all in Africa, come to be on the receiving end of very expensive, rare Chinese wine that is not exported, and bottled exclusively for state dinners?"

I didn't let anyone answer. I was too jazzed at what I'd found.

I took a breath and forged ahead.

"I'll tell you why. Bolin Chen, Wentworth's university roommate. I looked into Chen. His brother Jun De Chen works for the Ministry of State Security. And there's Maddon's connection. I've tracked the locations of Wentworth and Maddon's meetings, and get this—Wentworth is scheduled to arrive in DC in three days."

"Holy shit," Theo muttered, reaching for the files.

"I don't have the access or I would've emailed—"

"Crap, sister, I forgot to give you your credentials." Kira grabbed a pad of paper and a pen off the table and started scribbling. "Username and temporary password. When you log in you can change it."

I had a username and password.

Me.

I had a username and password to access Z Corps' computer system. Their highly encrypted, unhackable system.

The pad went sailing across the wood surface. I barely pulled myself out of my stupor to stop the pad before it went off the edge.

I looked down at the pad. In Kira's very girl handwriting was proof I was trusted.

No, that I was family.

Password: IloveEastonSpears4ever

My eyes flicked to Kira.

Her smirk said enough but she added, "Don't take the

semen, if you're in season" was the best welcome to the family any of them could give me.

Crazy, I know.

"Still needs work, Mini-Me." Zane chuckled.

"Listen up, *Dimples*. This is harder than you think when you don't have internet memes to guide you."

"You should start with vagina and see what rhymes with that."

"China," I tossed out on a shrug.

"That sucked, you're fired," Zane announced. "Read up on Nebraska's intel. I want a mission plan by..." He stopped and looked over at Layla then restarted, "Layla wants a mission plan by ten A.M. tomorrow morning, then Silver's rolling out."

"What he said." Layla rolled her eyes. "And great work, Nebraska."

Damn.

That felt good coming from Layla.

But the pride that was shining in Easton's eyes felt better.

TWENTY-NINE

"This could get messy, Dove." Cash winked at me as we trekked through the woods behind Wentworth's mansion.

The Zillow listing called it a magnificent single-family residence. I suppose you could call it that if a single family needed eight-thousand square feet, five bedrooms, hand-carved railings from Mexico, Venetian chandeliers hand-made in Italy, six fireplaces, a glass conservatory, an elevator, and a rooftop terrace. Yes, all of this from a real estate listing along with the floorplan including measurements on the home and surrounding garden. The only thing the listing didn't give up was the gate code.

People really needed to be more careful.

And the woods Cash and I were now carefully navigating to gain entrance to the property from the rear was easily seen with Google Maps and measured using Google Earth.

Easy-peasy-lemon-squeezy.

Google Maps also provided the helpful information that both houses that flanked the rear had pools. So yesterday I donned a polo proudly announcing I worked for Aqua Pools and visited both houses to offer pool services while scoping out the best way to enter the woods unseen. Both owners invited me in. Both walked me through their homes to the backyard. All of this captured on a tiny camera disguised as a button.

Bam.

I had what I needed.

While I was doing that, Smith and Jonas were across the street from the mansion doing the same thing only offering landscaping services. Easton had parked one street over with Cash should we need backup. Layla and Kira were in the Airbnb we'd rented a few miles away watching our feeds. Lincoln and Zane had still been in Annapolis, only making the trip to Lorton, Virginia, last night.

"Messy how?" I asked, stepping over a branch.

"Zane's in play. Messy could mean anything."

Truth.

"Lucky for me I'm not squeamish."

Cash chuckled.

Silence ensued and I used it as an opportunity to run through the op. I wasn't used to working with a team. When I breached a location, I did it solo with the intent to take out my target and get out. Do that quickly and quietly and unseen. I'd never been on an op with the intent to capture.

Theo and Easton would breach the front. Smith and Jonas would come in through the conservatory and Lincoln and Zane on the opposite side that had access doors to the basement. They'd come up putting them smack dab in the middle with a full view of the house. I didn't like their point of entry and made that known. Zane noted my misgivings but didn't budge. I figured the man knew better than me so I didn't push.

Cash and I were entering through a side door into what the floorplan called a breakfast room that flowed into the kitchen that opened to a hall with an office, double doors to the dining room, a powder room, and at the end, the door to the basement. That opened to the huge family room to the right, living room to the left, the conservatory off the living room. I went through the floorplan one more time in my head, making sure I wasn't forgetting anything, when Cash broke the silence.

"Would you take offense if I said you look totally hot all kitted out in Kevlar with a piece strapped to your thigh?"

"She might not but her man would." Came through my earpiece.

"Right. Yeah. Forget I mentioned it."

I glanced over to see his shit-eating grin.

"Shit stirrer," I muttered.

He tossed me another wink and we walked.

Finally the house came into view, as did the Potomac. The home was magnificent, the view better.

"Everyone lied," Cash mumbled softly. "Crime pays."

That would seem to be the case. The mansion was worth over eight million and it was one of seven properties Wentworth owned.

I drew my Glock from my holster, or I should say my borrowed Glock. I preferred a Smith & Wesson, but I'd taken what I was given with a smile. A hundred and twenty-four grain Winchester FMJ has the same velocity exiting the barrel of a Glock as it does a Smith & Wesson.

Not that I wasn't hoping I'd have to discharge my weapon, but shit happened.

"There's movement in the front," Easton called in. "Sheers are drawn, I have no visual. Two silhouettes."

Maddon and Wentworth.

The cameras Smith had planted yesterday on the trees facing the entrance to Wentworth's property had caught the two men—Maddon and Wentworth coming in a few hours before and pulling into the garage. Nothing after that.

"Six, are you in place?"

Again that was Easton, and Six was Cash.

"Negative. Two minutes."

"Get the lead out." That was Zane.

I waited for a snappy comeback from Cash. None came. So he could be serious when he needed to be.

"Stay behind me and stick to the shadows."

"Not my—"

"Do not make a move unless I do," he cut me off.

"Copy."

"She can follow directions."

Because I was me and I couldn't verbally inform Cash I wasn't fond of his sarcasm. I pinched his ass. Not a friendly gesture—I pinched and did it *hard*.

Startled eyes swung my way. Then a ghost of a smile.

"Not the time to get frisky, Dove."

"Don't be a dick."

I heard a growl come through the comms.

I knew that growl.

Playtime was over.

I jerked my chin, moved behind Cash, and together we

navigated the backyard like we'd done this dance a thousand times. I followed his steps to the terrace, became his shadow climbing the steps, and when he picked the lock my back was to his, scanning the yard, covering him.

"Cash is king."

"Copy." That was Zane.

I guess that meant we went in.

I turned back around and that was when nerves kicked in.

Cash was relying on me to have his back. I couldn't fuck this up. I had to stay sharp and keep my head.

No different than any other time.

Heel, toe. Stay on the outside edge.

I calmed my breath and followed Cash.

It was my job to shut the door.

I depressed the handle, slowly closed the door, and gently let the handle up. It felt like it took ten minutes to execute the task.

No sound.

Cash moved, I followed, and then it happened.

Cash halted mid-stride.

The sound unmistakable.

Tick. Thump.

Another one, the sound of the action, the thump of a bullet making impact. Accompanied by what sounded like a chair scraping on the floor.

"Shots fired," Cash called in. "Suppressed. East side."

"Don't be a hero, dumbass," Maddon calmly advised.

Shit. We needed Wentworth alive.

Cash started moving again. I moved right behind him.

Zane called in; he and Lincoln were in the basement.

Theo had the front door unlocked and they were waiting for our call saying we'd made it to the end of the hall before they came in through the foyer. Smith and Jonas would be last in. Their point of entry all windows.

We were almost at the end. I knew Cash was going to squawk the radio any second. Within a few minutes this would be over.

Maddon and Wentworth would be in custody.

Easy day.

A floorboard creaked under Cash's foot. There was just enough time for him to mutter a curse before a shot rang out. Cash's shoulder jerked back on impact. One hand pointing his gun in the direction of the living room, the other hand firmly on my chest, he shoved me and returned fire at the same time.

"Cover."

I stepped back and crouched in the doorway of the powder room, gun up and ready.

Cash retreated behind the dining room wall and I lost sight of him.

"Silver, switch to ten," Zane grunted.

I had no idea what that meant and before I could ask what ten was, I caught sight of the front door slowly opening. Easton slipped in first, Smith behind him, both of them riding the wall, coming down the foyer toward me, not bothering to close the door. Body tight, face like thunder, and seriously hacked off. He shook his head and held up his right hand. His left curled around the grip of his .45.

Bad timing, but I couldn't stop the shiver that ran over me.

My man was hot in full gear.

"Dove. Perfect timing doll. Come out and say hello to ol' Charlie Buck."

My insides froze.

He was lying.

Charlie promised he was going to call Dutch.

I didn't follow up.

I stared at Easton.

Another shake of his head.

Did he have eyes on Maddon? Could he see?

Suddenly there was a groan that sounded like someone's soul was leaving their body, it was so pain-filled.

"Say hello to your daughter."

Easton's eyes locked on mine, begging me not to move.

"Speak, Charles, or I'll shoot you in the head while Nebraska cowers in the hall."

Slowly, Easton's eyes left mine. The hand he was using to demand me to stay in the bathroom dropped, cupped the bottom of the grip, and he silently waited.

Waited.

What the hell were they waiting for?

Tick. Thump.

"Run, Nebraska," Charlie groaned.

I didn't run.

I came out of my crouch, fire blazing through me.

"Don't move," Easton growled.

Tick. Thump.

"I can do this all day. But Charlie can't. Come out, say hello, and let's sit down and have a talk. What do you say, Dove? Are you ready to negotiate for your father's life?"

Fuck taking him in. I was going to kill Maddon Judd.

I took a step out into the hall but got no further.

"Trust. Me."

My eyes shot to Easton. He was inching forward, Smith at his back. Neither of them looking at me.

Trust me.

Trust Easton.

Charlie.

Easton.

My mind whirled. *Trust him.* Every muscle burned as I locked my body. It was painful not to rush to Charlie. The need to get to my father so overwhelming, bile was inching its way up my throat.

Trust him.

I stepped back.

"Go." I watched the word form in Easton's mouth but didn't hear it.

Cash darted from the dining room, grabbed my hand on the fly, and ran, towing me behind him.

One. Two. Three shots. None suppressed. Not from Maddon's gun.

We were out of the house in seconds.

"Cash."

"They got it." Then he said, "En route to exfil."

I didn't hear that through my earpiece.

"Copy," Cash said again.

The team was talking but I couldn't hear.

"What's going on?" I panted, now running full speed through the woods.

"We're leaving cleanup to them."

"What are they cleaning up?"

"Likely Maddon's brains."

It took me a few seconds of breathing heavy to ask, "What about my dad?"

"Keep running, Dove."

Dove.

My heart sank.

Then it shattered.

THIRTY

Nebraska had been quiet the last eighteen or so hours. Six of those spent in the hospital waiting room while her father was in surgery. Charlie took seven rounds. None of them meant to kill. Maddon was torturing him. He'd had Charlie two days and had started that torture by beating him to shit and giving him his first three bullet holes. Maddon patched him up to keep him breathing. Tossed him in the trunk of Wentworth's car and drove him out to the mansion.

We didn't have eyes in the house or garage so we didn't see them get Charlie out of the car or drag him into the living room, tie him to a chair, and tape his mouth shut.

Our fuckup—we didn't follow up with Dutch to see if Charlie had made contact. A fuckup that nearly cost Nebraska's father his life.

But that wasn't the only reason she'd been in her head and not giving much away. Lincoln and Zane had found Anna in the basement. Not a hostage, the crazy woman was there to save Charlie. To say her mother being there had fucked with her head was an understatement. To say she was pissed we'd changed our frequency so she couldn't hear Zane tell the rest of us the new play, a huge understatement.

Upon learning that, it was the only time since her father had been loaded up in an ambulance that she unleashed her attitude. She made her displeasure known by threatening to dismember Zane's favorite part of his body. She yelled at Cash for getting shot and using only alcohol, Neosporin, and some gauze to treat his wound. Truth be told, it was a graze. It would burn like a motherfucker but there was no need for medical attention. Then she turned on me and yelled some more, for depriving her of the kill shot. When she burned herself out, she dissolved into tears, pointed at Zane, called him a dick, and stormed out of the waiting room.

I'd followed her out and watched her pace the hallway until I'd had enough.

When I pulled her into my arms she nuzzled right in. I gave her a few more minutes then asked if she was ready to go back in. When she nodded I took her back to the team. We all sat there until the doctor came in to tell Nebraska Charlie had made it through surgery but couldn't have visitors until the next day.

Throughout our time at the hospital Anna was noticeably absent. I didn't see her at the house, but Zane told me she'd taken off as soon as Maddon was down and he gave her word Charlie was breathing. All Zane said about that was, "Pigeon does what Pigeon does."

This did not make me happy. Should the time come that Nebraska decided she wanted to have a relationship with the woman, having some flighty bitch who doesn't have staying power didn't fill me with glee.

Now we were back to see Charlie, and Nebraska was standing statue-still in the doorway.

Fuck.

Before we came, I'd warned her about the state her father was in. His face was a mess. Bullet holes in his thighs, shoulders, and arms. I should've done a better job.

The guy had a long road to recovery. One that might lead his daughter up to Connecticut to take care of him.

Something else that didn't make me happy.

I never claimed I wasn't a selfish bastard.

When Nebraska didn't move, I pulled her back to my chest, and shifted her to the side.

Anna.

Christ.

The woman was sitting on the bed next to Charlie holding one of his hands in both of hers and she was silently crying. Charlie's eyes were open, two slits that would make it difficult to focus, but the man was trying his hardest.

Anna's gaze moved to the door. Charlie's didn't stray from his woman. I didn't know if that was because the pain was so great he couldn't or if he was too afraid to take his eyes off Anna so she didn't disappear.

"Come in," Anna softly offered.

Nebraska didn't move.

Fuck.

This was a bad idea. Too soon. Too much.

"Baby, look at me."

She took her time dragging her attention from her parents then giving it to me.

Parents.

Charlie and Anna together in the same room.

I had no way of knowing Anna would show. From what Zane had said about the woman I'd thought she was long gone. But still, I should've checked the room first. The problem with that was, Nebraska might've been quiet and in her head for the last eighteen hours, but that didn't mean she'd turned docile. Evidence of that was we were standing in the doorway of her father's hospital room instead of still in my bed resting like I'd begged her to do. More evidence she hadn't turned meek and agreeable was this morning she'd flat out refused to let me make us breakfast. She stomped around my kitchen, opening and closing cupboards until she found what she needed while I sat at the bar sipping coffee watching her. Good news with that was, she made excellent omelets. Even if they were made while she bitched my fridge was empty and I needed to go to the grocery store. I didn't think it was smart to remind her I hadn't been home in over a week. All of that to say, I couldn't have talked her into waiting in the waiting room while I checked on Charlie first if I'd tried.

When Nebraska wanted something, she got it. The end.

"I'm okay," she whispered.

"You're not."

Blue eyes narrowed.

Pool-blue eyes that at first sight had me intrigued, then they'd held me captive, now I was ensnared. So totally captivated I would've thought I was insane if I didn't know she was it for me. She was the one I'd give up everything for. I got it now why men left the military, why they cut their time at the Agency short—all the deployments, workups, time away from your family. I never got it. I'd thought those men just didn't have it in them to stick, or they'd caved to their women bitching. I'd been wrong. If I'd had Nebraska way back when I was still in the Navy, I would've finished my contract and been out. If I'd been with her while I was with the Agency, I would've left. The woman she was, she wouldn't have bitched but I would've quit to be home with her.

I'd never have to make that choice and that was only a small part of what made her perfect for me. Nebraska Michaels was my equal in every way. But still, if she wanted me to quit, stay home and be a house husband raising our kids so she could continue doing the job, I'd give her just that.

Her hand lifted, cupped the side of my neck, then she engaged her finger and I knew she was tracing the vertical tattoo that started behind my ear and ended right about my shoulder blade. She'd never done that before. Once I'd felt her kiss it, but never had she gently glided her fingertip over it.

"Loyalty." A soft, sweet, whispered word. "Taking care of me."

"Always."

"I'm okay because I know even if I'm not you'll be there later to make sure I am."

Damn fucking right I would be.

I didn't say that.

She dropped her hand and turned back to her parents and walked into the room.

As Nebraska.

No Dove in sight.

"Hey," she called out when she got closer. "Has the doctor been in yet?"

I stood next to Nebraska at her father's bedside holding her hand while Anna ran down Charlie's injuries. I was right; he had a long row to hoe until he was fully covered.

"I'm going back to Connecticut with Charlie," Anna announced.

Nebraska's hand flexed.

"I'll be there at least a couple of months while he recovers," she went on.

At that Nebraska's hand squeezed.

"With Maddon... *gone* and Dmitri no longer a problem I'm free... we're all free. I'm not hiding anymore."

The tightness of Nebraska's grasp became bone crushing.

"I'm not asking. I don't have the right. But if the time comes and you want to call me, I hope you will."

"I'll call."

Anna didn't miss the gift Nebraska gave her, nor did she squander it or push.

All she did was smile.

It was real and it changed everything about her.

Like her daughter, Anna could say a thousand words, none of them voiced, all of them conveyed with their eyes.

She'd missed her daughter. She wanted to heal the breach, and if Nebraska gave the barest hint she was open to connecting she'd be all over making that happen.

I hoped Anna had it in her to do that in a way that was healthy for Nebraska. Though as jacked as the situation had been, as fucked as it was that Anna had left her, the lies and secrets that came after all fucked-up in their own way. Anna loved her daughter. Loved her enough to leave her to protect her. So, bottom line with that was she was a good mother and I didn't have anything to worry about.

"Sweetheart." Charlie's brittle voice drew Nebraska's gaze to him.

The guy sounded like hell, and not only because he was hopped up on pain meds and had tubes and wires coming out from under his hospital gown.

"I'm sorry," he croaked. "So damn sorry."

Nebraska untangled her hand from mine, stepped closer to the bed, and reached out to gently touch his forearm. The forearm touch was out of necessity—with Anna holding his hand, the other having an IV sticking out of it, there was nowhere else to touch the man that wasn't bandaged or bruised.

"We'll talk later," she gently returned, injecting enough emotion into her statement to let Charlie know she meant that.

"Sweet—"

"Dad, you were right. There was never a right time to tell me. If you would've, I wouldn't have been able to stop myself from finding her. If I'd known about Zenith, I would've put us all in danger by watching him. You were right, with all of it. I get it now. Family protects family even if what they're protecting you from is yourself."

"I lied to you."

"Dad—"

"I lied and didn't do right by you, so caught up in my grief of losing your mother. I lied about everything. I never wanted you to feel the sorrow of losing what I'd lost so I told you lies. I made you believe love was weak. I told you..." Charlie trailed off, his words slurring more and more but fighting it to make amends with his daughter.

He loved her, too. He was just shit at showing it the way she'd needed.

"Sleep, Dad."

"Love's not..."

"I know, Easton showed me. But before him, you did. I just didn't know how strong love made you until recently."

I'm falling for you.

Christ.

I know, Easton showed me.

Christ almighty, that felt good. So fucking good her words heated my skin, penetrated my flesh, and dug so deep I'd never in my whole fucking life forget the feel of it.

I was pulled back into the room when I heard Nebraska say, "We'll be back later to check on him."

I glanced at Charlie—his head lolled to the side, totally knocked out—to Anna who was smiling not at her daughter, at me. This one soft and sweet, the kind I got from Nebraska first thing in the morning.

I dipped my chin, slid an arm around Nebraska's shoulders, pressed a kiss at her temple, and didn't move back when I asked, "Ready?"

Obviously she wasn't ready when she asked, "Do you want us to bring you lunch?"

Anna didn't bother attempting to hide her shock or her gratitude when she answered, "I'd love that."

"Any requests?"

"I eat anything. Just no—"

"Onions or pickles, I remember," Nebraska finished for her.

Anna returned her daughter's earlier gift. Anna's was in the form of tears, unchecked, nothing hidden, nothing but wide-open honesty.

In that moment she was nearly as beautiful as her daughter, giving my woman what she needed to start healing.

"I THOUGHT I SUSPENDED YOU," Zane said as he rounded the corner in time to watch us step out of the elevator. "Without pay."

He'd done no such thing, but that didn't stop him from making shit up to push buttons.

Unfortunately for my boss, he'd underestimated Nebraska.

Her play was brilliant.

I wished I'd known what she was going to do before she did it so I could've pulled my phone out and recorded it.

The stomping in Zane's direction was a good diversion. He didn't see her hug coming. That meant he was shocked stupid and had no ready defense when she rolled up on her toes and kissed his cheek.

"Thank you." She further shocked him by saying. "And don't worry, your secret's safe with me."

"What secret? I have no more secrets since your shit outted my only one."

Jesus, the man was a pain in the ass.

"All those stories. Fabled tales of the big, bad, scary Viper King. Lies. You're a marshmallow."

"A what?"

"Admittedly, the marshmallow you are is charred on the outside but that only makes the inside gooey. Who knew if you could stomach the burnt bits, when you got to the middle it was soft and warm? I see you, Zane Lewis. You. Not Viper. Not Dimples. Not Big Boss Daddy large and in charge of his kingdom. The man you really are. The man all of us need you to be."

"You're fired," he grunted.

"Thank you," she whispered. "Thank you for showing me the truth. Without that lesson I would've lived behind my walls. I would've closed myself off more. I would've run and missed out on the best thing that ever happened to me."

"Working for me?" He smirked.

"Easton."

I absorbed her silken blow, the second of the day, wondering if there'd ever come a time when I wouldn't feel the hit of her sweetness. I didn't have to wonder for long. I vowed there would never come a time when I didn't feel the beauty she gave me. There'd never come a time I didn't stop and let it seep in and feed my soul.

Zane remained silent when he kissed her forehead. But when he pulled back he couldn't stop the "Zane" from spewing out.

"You ever call me gooey again, I'm docking your pay and donating it to the prophylactic fund. That shit's running low. Good thing your shit didn't dip in or there'd be nothing left for Smith, Jonas, and Cash. And I have a bad feeling Cash is going to run that shit dry."

"What's the prophylactic fund?" she asked but didn't wait for an answer. "Oh wait, Kira told me you generously supply birth control to your men. Smart. The testosterone in this building is off the charts. No telling how many mini commandos you'd have running around. But just to say they're all big boys—"

"Big boys who think with their—"

"Daddy!" Eric squealed and ran full speed across the office.

"You were saying?" Nebraska drawled.

"I was saying you were fired, but you just won't leave."

"Nope. You're stuck with me now."

She was killing me with this new, open Nebraska.

I fucking loved it. But if she didn't put a lid on it I'd have to spend half my day in the office I was sharing with her to show her just how much I fucking loved it.

Not that I'd mind spending time in my office if it meant I had my woman bent over my desk.

Speaking of...

"We have work to do," I declared, and reclaimed my woman by hooking her around the waist.

"I bet you do." Zane chuckled as he swung his son up into his arms.

We were nearing the door when she said, "For someone who's allergic to paperwork and doesn't like being in his office, you sure are in a hurry."

I shuffled Nebraska in, shut the door, spun her around, and pulled her to my chest.

"We're not doing paperwork."

Her eyes flashed with understanding.

"They'll hear."

"They won't."

"Baby, they won't."

"Easton—"

"Trust. Me."

Her body melted closer, her hands shoved under my tee, and her nails skimmed up my back. I didn't delay showing my woman what her love and trust meant to me. I did it with her bent over our desk, her jeans and red lacy panties around her ankles. With one hand up her shirt playing with her nipple, the other between her legs toying with her clit. When her climax was hovering, I released her nipple, fisted her hair, bent in deeper so I could take her mouth. I swallowed her moans.

She returned the favor and muffled mine.

THIRTY-ONE

I was in the conference room grabbing a file I'd left after the team briefing when my cell vibrated in my back pocket. I pulled it from my jeans and looked at the screen.

I was smiling when I answered, "Hey, Dutch."

"I've lost you to Silver."

He wasn't wrong.

In the two weeks since my father had been shot, I'd redecorated—or I should say decorated—Easton's office, making it officially our office. I liked working at Headquarters, which was how I thought of the Annapolis office since the cat was out of the bag so to speak and everyone knew of Black's existence and about The Ranch.

"I'm still on call when you need me."

"No, Dove. It's time."

"Dutch—"

"I want you free and clear. No more shadows."

I stared at the table, unseeing.

I'd had two weeks of constant reminders. Two weeks of building friendships that didn't need building as such. The foundation was already there, rooted in family. It was the trust and loyalty we were building. Two really great weeks with Easton, with no trauma, no secrets, no lies, nothing big being revealed other than he was a neat freak. And that wasn't so big as much as it was worrisome. I wasn't a slob but I wasn't big on living in a showplace. I'd grown up with that and as soon as I had my own place, I went for a lived-in look. Comfortable, inviting even, if I'd ever had any intention of inviting anyone into my space.

Even with the reminders, all the good I'd had, I still wasn't prepared. It wasn't what Dutch said, it was how he'd said it. Which made me realize he cared about me. All these years I'd had a version of what Zane gave his men, I'd just been too blinded by the need to guard myself against everyone that I'd missed it.

"Dutch," I whispered.

"Been waiting a long time for this. Pleased as fuck you found it. More pleased you found it with a good man I didn't have to investigate and find he wasn't good enough for my girl, then send Badger out to disappear him."

Dutch would totally do that. And Badger would happily disappear someone if that someone wasn't good for me.

Yeah, I'd missed it.

But I sure as hell wasn't missing anything now.

My eyes were wide open. And that came with my mouth now running away with itself.

"Am I allowed to come visit you?"

"I'd be pissed if you didn't."

Translation: he'd be hurt.

Hell, yeah, I wasn't missing a single thing.

"Once things settle down, Easton and I will come out."

"Heard your father's being released soon and Pidge is taking him home."

"You heard right."

Tomorrow was the day and I wasn't sure how I felt about that. Easton and I had visited every day after work. Every day my mother was sitting vigil at my father's side. Every day I saw a side of my dad I'd never seen. He stared at my mother like he couldn't believe she was real. And she looked at him with regret and yearning. I wanted to see more of that but my father was chomping at the bit to get out of the hospital, and bitched about it insistently.

I also wanted Charlie to spend more time with Easton now that Easton had warmed up to him. It was strange, in the sense I never thought I'd have my mom and dad in the same room as my man. Seeing as I thought my mom was dead, that would've been an impossibility. But in a plot twist I didn't see coming, I had that now and I wasn't ready to give it up.

I couldn't say all was right in the crazy world of the Bauer-Michaels family but Anna and Charlie were putting in the work to repair what had been broken with all of us. This included admitting that they'd been deeply in love (something I knew) and had been in a relationship for many years without me knowing. Around the time Anna caught wind Zenith was looking for her, Anna and Charlie had decided it was time to tell me about the relationship in preparation for us becoming a family. That broke my heart. But Easton, being Easton, giving me everything I needed held me while I cried over two people I loved losing so much. I cried for all that I could've had, all that I lost, and all I would never have. Thankfully Easton was generous with his soft, gentle wisdom reminding me I had it now and I had a choice—look back or look forward.

I chose the future.

"Got some business to discuss," he went on.

"Hit me."

I heard him chuckle and through that he muttered, "Those people have ruined you."

Translation: Those people fixed what was broken inside you and I'm all kinds of happy.

Okay, the all kinds of happy wasn't a direct translation, but that was my interpretation.

"Are you going to tell me what you need to tell me or hand me shit?"

"I'm gonna tell you, darlin'. We got nothing on Patricia. She managed to keep herself clean."

"Kira didn't find anything either."

"If Kira didn't find it, I know she'd punt it to Garrett. If neither found anything there's nothing to be found. Can't send a team out without proof."

He was correct. Black might work in the morally gray but the morality part of that didn't waver. If there wasn't proof, no action would be taken.

"So she walks," I noted. "What about Wentworth? Bishop have any luck getting him to talk?"

"When hasn't Bishop gotten the intel we needed?"

That would be never. The difference between Kira and Bishop was he gathered his intel up close and personal.

"Never," I answered. "What'd he get?"

"Black's handling this."

I didn't like that. I wanted to know the full scope of

what Maddon had done and what other connections he had.

"Maddon is mine."

"Maddon is dead. It's over. Wentworth is supplying everything we need to get Badger and the team ready. He's doing that hoping at the end he'll remain breathing even if it means he does that with an extended stay in Bogota in the less than luxurious accommodations he's not used to but currently occupying. We've funneled his money into our accounts. He has nothing but a pipedream Bishop is feeling friendly when he's done."

Bishop never felt friendly.

"Fine," I snapped, knowing I wouldn't get more out of him. "But I want you to know I'm not happy you're cutting me out of all the fun. Easton selfishly took Maddon from me and now you're taking the rest. Just because I have girly parts doesn't mean I can't handle business."

There was a beat of silence that stretched into seconds.

Then my old boss busted a gut with his roaring laughter.

"Good thing that mediator gig is done for you, Dove. That attitude you've found isn't conducive to swinging deals."

Whatever.

"You should give Stella a call. Maybe she's ready to settle down."

"That woman has the disposition of a Rottweiler. A snarling, slobbering one just waiting to take a bite out of you. And she's not the type of woman a man can settle down."

Um...*what?*

Dutch sounded like he wanted to be the man who tried to settle her down.

Unfortunately, he was right. My friend-slash-enemy would take a bite out of anyone who tried such a thing.

She was missing out.

Totally.

"I'll let you get back to work, Nebraska. Just one favor."

There was no hesitation when I answered, "Anything."

"Give Zane hell."

Since I was already doing that, the favor was moot.

"Done."

Dutch disconnected and I got back to work.

But not before I found my man in a gym down in the basement and gave him a sweaty kiss—him being shirtless and sweaty led to the door being locked and the kissing moved to other more pleasurable parts of my body, before I gave him a mid-afternoon blowjob.

One could not say there weren't a lot of perks working at HQ with your man. And afternoon orgasms were only part of that.

A MONTH *later*

I was in the kitchen with Easton. That was to say, I was keeping him company while he made supper. He was a far better cook than I was. He also insisted he did most of the cooking and this wasn't because he was a better cook. It was one of the many ways he took care of me. Who was I to complain if my guy wanted to feed me, and while in pursuit of that endeavor he looked hot wearing an apron? He had many. They all had graphics on the front that varied from silly to raunchy but they all were hilarious.

Easton was pulling the chicken parm that the smell of had my mouth watering when my phone rang.

As an unspoken rule, neither of us answered our calls or texts after dinner. That was our time. If work needed one of us, they knew to hang up and call back and the phone would be checked. That had only happened once in the last month and it was Zane calling Easton in to back up Jasmin on a case she'd been working on. That was the only night I'd gone to bed without Easton next to me. He'd come home in the middle of night. I'd woken up long enough to ascertain he didn't need medical attention then fell back asleep. Meaning he was there when I woke up. One night without, but not a single morning.

Since dinner hadn't been consumed I checked my phone.

Stella.

That could mean anything, and some of that not good.

"I have to take this," I told Easton and tapped the screen. "Everything okay?"

At my greeting Easton gave me his attention.

"You tell me. I heard you're out and all loved up, living in domestic bliss."

She sounded absolutely disgusted. I felt my lips curve up into a smile.

"Word gets around."

"It does when your badass man and the Viper King spread that shit far, making sure no one forgets you're under their protection and if anyone breathes wrong in your direction they'll be picking their balls out of their teeth."

That was oddly detailed and I wondered if that had been the exact message Zane had sent. Knowing him, it was. He could get creative with his promises. And I say that because Zane doesn't threaten, and neither did Easton.

I kept my gaze on Easton when I told her, "It's good to hear my man has my back."

"So it's true. You're shacked up with Easton Spears."

She didn't sound disgusted now, just curious.

A few months ago, I never would've confirmed my location or something so personal.

But I was a new me and I was shacked up with Easton —sort of. It wasn't official that I was living with him. He hadn't asked, but when Anna had sorted my condo and packed my stuff she'd mailed some boxes to Maryland and stored the rest, including my furniture in one of my father's big garages. Those boxes, minus the clothes I needed out of them, were stacked in Easton's basement. He hadn't invited me to unpack them, so there they stayed.

But still, I gave her an affirmative answer even if I didn't know if it was true.

"I am."

"When I get back to the States you owe me a drink."

"You know you can no longer get me drunk and torture intel out of me. The Prince of Pussy was the last of that."

Easton's eyes narrowed.

It was cute.

A look I didn't see on him often. Hot—always. Sexy— all the time. Badass—it was his nature so it poured out of him. Cute—only on a rare occasion, usually in the morning after he'd given me soft and gentle and sweet.

"So dramatic," she huffed. "I didn't torture you."

"It wasn't you hugging the porcelain the next morning."

"Just wait until you've got mini-Eastons planted in your belly and you're worshiping on the throne of the porcelain goddess, pondering the error of your ways letting his inherent badass sexiness inject you with his badass swimmers."

Ew.

But there you go. Easton's badassness couldn't be denied, neither could his sexiness.

"If the time comes I've been impregnated by Easton's super sperm, I'll make sure to let you know how that's going."

"If? You mean *when*."

That was not from Stella.

"If I tell you your man has a sexy voice, would you shoot me?"

"No, I'd slice your throat."

"Good to hear my Dove's still in there, even if she's buried under happiness and shit."

With that, Stella disconnected.

My Dove.

Translation: I'm happy for you, sis.

It would seem my frenemy wasn't so much an enemy as she was a friend. Not that I had any notions Lore wasn't Lore and she'd take care of herself above all else.

I put my phone down on the counter but didn't have time to do much else before Easton was in my space.

"Did you hear me?"

"Hear what?"

"Not if. When," he repeated

My heart rate ticked up.

I didn't know what to say so I said nothing, hoping my heart would stop pumping over time, making my head fuzzy, so that I could think of what to say.

"If you don't want kids, we'll talk—"

"I want kids," I blurted out.

His hand came up and cupped my jaw. His thumb glided over the apple of my cheek. The gentleness of it did nothing to slow my now erratic breathing.

"Then why'd your face go pale?"

Was he serious?

"Maybe because you just told me you wanted to have babies with me and that freaks me out."

"Why does it freak you?"

Again, was he serious?

"Um." I didn't get any further because I couldn't string a sentence together that was long enough to explain why him telling me he wanted babies with me would freak me the hell out.

"You love me?"

I felt my body jerk and my neck snap back. The movements were painful.

Terror leaked in.

Not fear that I loved him but bone-deep fear he didn't love me back. Rationally, I knew he loved me. He'd never said it but he showed it. But there was nothing rational about my lungs burning and my heart thumping. There was nothing rational about worrying about those boxes in the basement. Every once in a while—not often, but sometimes—the irrational, scared part of me I'd yet to eradicate reared its ugly head.

"Why?" I stammered.

"Because I want you to say it so I can tell you how crazy in love I am with you. I want you to say it so I can feel it and lock it down deep so I'll never forget the first time you gave me the words. I know you love me. But still I want the words, baby."

If it was possible for a heart to explode with happiness and still keep pounding in a chest—that was what was happening to me.

Right there in Easton's kitchen I felt like I'd died from happiness and had been resurrected by love.

Which only seemed fitting. It was because of him I laid Dove to rest, only keeping the parts of her I wanted. And with that, the real me was born.

Nebraska.

Easton's Nebraska.

Zane's Nebraska.

The Nebraska who belonged to a huge, obnoxious family that loved so hard it was scary to comprehend the enormity of their love.

"I love you," I whispered.

"I love you, baby." Easton did not whisper.

And now I knew why he wanted the words. They were soft and warm and blazed a trail to my soul.

"Unpack."

He was talking about the boxes.

Of course he'd bring those up now.

He took care of me.

"Babies—" he started.

"When we're ready I want that," I cut in, perhaps too eagerly.

Easton's smile refuted that thought. Not too eager.

"Now, about Greece..." He let that hang.

So I gave it to him straight.

"Greece is still on the table with a slightly modified plan. Instead of a cute one-bedroom cottage, I want a house big enough for a family. I want a place for us to take our family and disconnect from the outside world. When we're not using it, the rest of the family can. It'll be a family retreat for us and our extended family."

"Not sure those broke dicks can pony up to help pay for a seaside retreat."

He was full of shit. I knew from personal experience what Zane paid. It was more than generous and not a single person on the team was broke. If I had to guess they were wealthy.

"Then it's a good thing I'm loaded."

"Yeah, baby, good thing."

Easton stepped back, tagged my hand, and started pulling me out of the kitchen.

"Where are we going?"

"You love me?"

"Yes."

"Then we're celebrating. And as hot as fucking you on the kitchen counter is, and you riding me on the couch is on my top-ten spots to watch you fuck me, neither of those places say celebration. I want a bed, our bed, the place where I hold you when you go to sleep and wake up next to you, to be the first place you tell me you love me while I'm inside of you. After dinner, you can fuck me on the couch and scream it. Tomorrow, maybe the kitchen, though likely it'll be the shower; the way your breath hitches when I bang you against the wall drives me crazy. I reckon hearing that hitch and you telling me you love me will make me lose my mind."

Easton losing his mind meant good things for me.

"I love you," I told him.

Easton quickened his pace.

"Quiet."

"I love you."

We were in the middle of the living room when he abruptly stopped.

"I love you."

That did it.

With a growl that sent excitement drenching my panties, Easton spun me to face him.

His hands went to my cheeks. He yanked me forward. My hands went to his chest to stop my fall and in all that Easton had given me, he gave me better.

"I fucking love you."

His lips hit mine and he sealed his words with the best kiss of my life.

A kiss that reached my soul.

THIRTY-TWO

Smith Everette

"YOU THERE?" Zane asked through the sound system of the Escalade.

"Yep. Just pulled up."

"She there?"

The "she" being Aria Taylor. The latest social media personality to hit it big. After watching hours of her videos I understood why. Not only was the woman gorgeous in overalls, hair pulled into a ponytail hanging out the back of a baseball cap, face free of makeup, making swinging a hammer or using a drill look damn sexy, but she ratcheted up the sex appeal by *knowing* how to use the hammer she was swinging, the drill she was whirling, and whichever type of saw she was using in her videos. Hell, the fact she knew the difference between a coping saw and miter saw was enough for her male followers to get a hard-on. That coupled with her sweet, sexy, girl-next-door pretty, it didn't take a marketing expert to understand why she'd gained the popularity she had.

But she was a fuckuva lot prettier in person carrying a bag of trash to the garbage bins at the side of her house.

"Yep."

"Call me after you talk to her."

"Copy."

I disconnected the call and watched Aria toss the bag into the can and make her way back into the garage for no other reason than I liked the way she moved. It didn't hurt her ass looked phenomenal in a pair of supremely faded pair of Levi's. The fact those jeans were faded due to use and not trendy fashion was dead-ass cool.

Unfortunately, I wasn't there to stare at the woman's ass.

Her neighborhood was nice, as it would be, situated near the water just over the Bay Bridge on the north side of Route 50. Closer to the water—either side of the peninsula the Chesapeake or the Chester River, middle income would turn to upper. Waterfront would turn to wealthy. Her house was the nicest on her block. Not surprising with her occupation. What was surprising however, was she'd done all the work herself, only calling in day laborers when the job required more. It was impressive and not because she was a woman. The closer I got to her front door the more the craftsmanship became evident, her impressive skill level becoming clearer. The woman knew what she was doing.

I was admiring the shiplap planking of her wraparound porch when the door suddenly opened. Startled brown eyes locked on me from behind the storm door. And when I say locked, what I really mean was they held me hostage.

Until the fear registered.

"I'm Smith Everette from—"

"Right." She cut me off and opened the flimsy glass door. "I wasn't expecting you for another five minutes. I was going out to get my mail. Come in."

"I can wait."

"No. Please come in, and thank you for making the trek all the way over here. I know bridge traffic is a pain in the ass. I would've come to you but I need to leave in an hour to go up to Philly and I couldn't take the day off of work."

She paused, shook her head, and started again. "Not that I think my time is more valuable than yours. It's just that I can't break these plans. Rehearsal, then dinner with the bridal party, wedding is the next day, and Sunday's a whole farewell brunch thing. I would've come to you on Monday but my dad's a little...*a lot* protective and wouldn't stop nagging until I called Zane. Then he called Zane and made this huge deal out of the situation and here we are, you wasting your day sitting in construction traffic—"

"Aria?"

"Yeah?"

"Making sure you're safe isn't a waste of anyone's day. Especially not mine."

Her grin was lopsided when her lips bowed up.

Totally fucking cute.

"Great. You're one of those overprotective types, aren't you?"

I wasn't—not usually.

But standing in Aria's living room with her in those

faded jeans, warm brown eyes, sun-kissed brownish blonde hair, lopsided grin, teasing me after her explanation about why I was in her living room, meant I turned into one.

"Yep."

She rolled her eyes to her kickass vaulted wood ceiling that was done in a badass herringbone pattern. Then rolled them back, her grin turned into a smile and she swept her hand in the direction of the back of her house.

"Well, in that case, let's go sit in the kitchen where I can offer you some coffee, or a beer, or water since I deduced from that I won't be able to convince you that Captain Taylor is seriously overreacting."

Captain Taylor was her father, a friend of Zane's from the Navy who had called in a favor. The remark could've been interpreted as snarky or bitchy but the way her expression turned soft and the way her eyes danced when she mentioned her father, made the comment teasing.

"You've assumed correctly," I told her.

Her glossy lips pinched but one side remained hitched up.

I followed her into the kitchen and looked around.

"Did you do all this, too?"

She didn't break stride when she said, "Yeah. The kitchen was outdated. But the cabinets were custom made, even if the made part of that was in the seventies. So all they needed was sanding, stain, and some distressing so the door fronts that were beat-up wouldn't stick out. The countertops were a bust but those are easy enough to replace and nowhere near the cost of replacing cabinets. The appliances were so old they'd come back into style if I'd been going for vintage. But I wanted sleek and modern so they had to go."

Whatever look she was going for, it was shit hot.

Dark-stained cabinets with a black glaze that highlighted the distressing she'd done. The granite was black with crazy cool gold veining. Gold cabinet handles and drawer pulls tied everything together.

I rounded the bank of cabinets that delineated the kitchen from an eating area with a four-top table dominating the space and stood opposite her

"It's badass, Aria. You did a great job."

She stopped looking at her cabinets and tipped her eyes to look at me from under her lashes.

"Thanks."

That was shy *and* cute.

And fuck me, I felt that straight in my dick. The only reason I shoved that aside was the same reason I was ignoring how good her ass looked in those jeans, and her smile, and her pretty eyes and gorgeous face.

Her father was a close personal friend of my boss.

The shy slid away, flirtatiousness sparked in her eyes, and I knew she was going to say something smartass that was going to make it harder to ignore how much I totally dug this chick.

I'd been in her presence all of three minutes.

Fuck me.

Time to get to work.

ALSO BY RILEY EDWARDS

Jonny's Redemption

Red Team - Susan Stoker Universe

Nightstalker

Protecting Olivia

Redeeming Violet

Recovering Ivy

Rescuing Erin

The Gold Team - Susan Stoker Universe

Brooks

Thaddeus

Kyle

Maximus

Declan

Blue Team - Susan Stoker Universe

Owen

Gabe

Myles

Kevin

Cooper

Garrett

Silver Team

Theo

Easton

Smith

The 707 Freedom Series

Free

Freeing Jasper

Finally Free

Freedom

The Next Generation (707 spinoff)

Saving Meadow

Chasing Honor

Finding Mercy

Claiming Tuesday

Adoring Delaney

Keeping Quinn

Taking Liberty

Triple Canopy

Damaged

Flawed

Imperfect

Tarnished

Tainted

Conquered

Shattered

Fractured

The Collective

Unbroken

Trust

Standalones

Romancing Rayne

Falling for the Delta Co-written with Susan Stoker

AUDIO

Are you an Audio Fan?

Check out Riley's titles in Audio on Audible and iTunes

Gemini Group

Narrated by: Joe Arden and Erin Mallon

Red Team

Narrated by: Jason Clarke and Carly Robins

Gold Team

Narrated by: Lee Samuels and Maxine Mitchell

The 707 Series

Narrated by: Troy Duran and C. J. Bloom

The Next Generation

Narrated by: Troy Duran and Devon Grace

Triple Canopy

Narrated by: Mackenzie Cartwright and Connor Crais

More audio coming soon

BE A REBEL

Riley Edwards is a USA Today and WSJ bestselling author, wife, and military mom. Riley was born and raised in Los Angeles but now resides on the east coast with her fantastic husband and children.

Riley writes heart-stopping romance with sexy alpha heroes and even stronger heroines. Riley's favorite genres to write are romantic suspense and military romance.

Don't forget to sign up for Riley's newsletter and never miss another release, sale, or exclusive bonus material.

Rebels Newsletter

Facebook Fan Group

www.rileyedwardsromance.com

facebook.com/Novelist.Riley.Edwards

instagram.com/rileyedwardsromance

bookbub.com/authors/riley-edwards

amazon.com/author/rileyedwards

golden care

Northwestern

mutual life

new york

mutual of Omaha

nationwide

Made in United States
North Haven, CT
14 July 2024